Façade

By Freya Lyndon

Copyright © Freya Lyndon, 2024
ISBN: 9798323406692

For Mumma,

I miss you.

PRESENT DAY

It's unfathomable how one simple encounter can change your life forever. I think people tend to believe rather naively that life has a designated course, like a train trundling down a track – safe, secure, sheltered.

Then, without a flicker of warning, CRASH...

Have you ever watched your life crash before your eyes? The end is inevitable, you know that the train is going to crash and create a cloud of ash that will swallow you and everything around you whole, but no matter how hard you try, you can't do anything to stop it?

Because I do, I know exactly how that feels.

"Lyla, we're almost ready." Tom's voice breaks me from my daydream. The sun beams down upon us, a blessing to signify this special day. The bunting which we spent all morning hanging up glistens within the trees. We've been preparing for this for a long time- after all, a day like this only happens once in a girl's lifetime. The twins Madison and Mila are running around the garden barely able to contain their excitement, hopping from foot to foot, their identical dark braids swish in the late summer breeze.

"Is she here yet?" Mila asks, her blue eyes inquisitive.

"She should be here any minute now." I reply looking down at my phone and studying the text message she had sent me about an hour before.

I'll be home soon, is all it says.

Just at that moment, Lacey enters through the back door. Her pretty face collapses into a state of ecstatic shock as I watch her take in the decorations adorning the garden.

"HAPPY EIGHTEENTH BIRTHDAY LACEY!" We all chorus.

"Wow, thanks so much!" A smile spreads slowly across her dainty features. She looks more and more like him every single day. It's inevitable I suppose, for a daughter to look like her father, but it's like looking into a twisted mirror of my past – she's the memory of everything that happened. She's the memory of him and all the depravity and destruction that followed. A memory which I don't desire to recall.

She bounds towards me and pulls me into a hug, the scent of her soft sandalwood perfume surrounds me like a cloud. She's a lot more grown up and sophisticated than I seemed to be at her age and off to

PRESENT DAY

It's unfathomable how one simple encounter can change your life forever. I think people tend to believe rather naively that life has a designated course, like a train trundling down a track – safe, secure, sheltered.

Then, without a flicker of warning, CRASH...

Have you ever watched your life crash before your eyes? The end is inevitable, you know that the train is going to crash and create a cloud of ash that will swallow you and everything around you whole, but no matter how hard you try, you can't do anything to stop it?

Because I do, I know exactly how that feels.

"Lyla, we're almost ready." Tom's voice breaks me from my daydream. The sun beams down upon us, a blessing to signify this special day. The bunting which we spent all morning hanging up glistens within the trees. We've been preparing for this for a long time- after all, a day like this only happens once in a girl's lifetime. The twins Madison and Mila are running around the garden barely able to contain their excitement, hopping from foot to foot, their identical dark braids swish in the late summer breeze.

"Is she here yet?" Mila asks, her blue eyes inquisitive.

"She should be here any minute now." I reply looking down at my phone and studying the text message she had sent me about an hour before.

I'll be home soon, is all it says.

Just at that moment, Lacey enters through the back door. Her pretty face collapses into a state of ecstatic shock as I watch her take in the decorations adorning the garden.

"HAPPY EIGHTEENTH BIRTHDAY LACEY!" We all chorus.

"Wow, thanks so much!" A smile spreads slowly across her dainty features. She looks more and more like him every single day. It's inevitable I suppose, for a daughter to look like her father, but it's like looking into a twisted mirror of my past – she's the memory of everything that happened. She's the memory of him and all the depravity and destruction that followed. A memory which I don't desire to recall.

She bounds towards me and pulls me into a hug, the scent of her soft sandalwood perfume surrounds me like a cloud. She's a lot more grown up and sophisticated than I seemed to be at her age and off to university in September, and I can't help feeling I'll lose a part of me when she goes because for such a long time, Lacey was all I've had.

"I thought you'd forgotten all about me when you said nothing this morning." She laughs as she moves over to hug Tom.

"Of course not, we could never forget you."

"Well, thank you so much for all of this Mum and Tom and Madison and Mila of course." The twins grin wildly at the recognition they receive, even though they had spent the entire time messing up all the decorations and reeking as much havoc as humanly possible for two overzealous seven-year-olds.

"We have cake too, but I can't say we made it. Mine and your mother's cooking skills don't quite extend that far." Tom chuckles heartily. "Why don't you go and show her Mila? You too Madison?" The twins bound towards the glass screen kitchen doors gesturing for Lacey to follow suit. She catches my gaze before she is whisked into the house and it feels as though he is here, living through her. She inherited his opalescent eyes; she holds within her the one thing that I used to love about him so dearly and now that she's eighteen it's finally the day I promised. It's the day that I must reveal the truth to her, I must look into my mind and extract the dark tale from within its box where it had been residing since the events had occurred all those years ago.

Tom seems to be thinking the same thing, as he crosses the lawn and pulls me behind the large willow tree in the corner of the garden so that we're completely out of earshot of the others.

"It's time Lyla. She's eighteen now, I think you need to tell her." His brown eyes search for mine, but I can't bear to look up at him. I don't ever wish to retrieve those painful memories that I spent so long burying under the sand.

"It's her birthday, though. Maybe I should wait a few days and then tell her? I don't want to ruin this day for her. Afterall we've spent so long getting everything ready, would be a real shame to put a dampener like that on the day." I realise dampener is insufficient describe the trauma I was about to gift to Lacey.

What a birthday present!

"You've been waiting for the past ten years, Lyla. You always said when she turns eighteen that you'll tell her the truth. She's an adult now; she deserves to find out from you rather than from something or someone else. Think, what if she finds the truth on the internet? There are still articles out there about it, I know that there are." Tom's words shock me into sense. Lacey has to discover the truth from me, or else it may destroy her because finding out a secret like the one I'm about to tell her is not something a person can simply accept; it's something that lives with someone every single day. It lives with me every single day.

"Tom, I don't know if I can do it." The truth flows out of me. "I don't want her to hate me."

"She could never hate you, Lyla. Never." He hugs me strong and sturdy, a rock in a turbulent sea or a lone palm tree stood strong against an oncoming tsunami. Tom steadies me and quietens my mind, he helps me through the nightmares and the trauma from my past. I couldn't be more grateful for his presence in my life.

"You aren't to blame Lyla; it wasn't your fault. You need to stop punishing yourself and believe that you truly are a good person. Everyone can see it but you." He could tell me this over and over for hours on end, he could tattoo it onto the sky above or scratch it into the earth beneath my feet and still I would never believe him even if I walked for the rest of my life seeing only those words above and below me. I will forever carry internal blame for what transpired in my hometown, a truth which I must now reveal to Lacey, as the tale of her parentage is interwoven within evil and crime.

When I don't respond but simply stay there, limp in Tom's arms, he breaks from the hug and places his arms on my shoulders as if he's about to shake sense into me.

"You can't be scared of it anymore. As much as I don't want you to go through the pain of reliving your past, you have to tell her to be able to truly move on from it. You've been trapped for too long Lyla, is it too selfish to want you all to myself and not thinking about him?" Tom smiles now, bright, and slightly crooked. I've always liked his crooked smile and all his imperfections because sometimes I think searching for perfection was my downfall.

You've been trapped for too long. These words resonate within me above all else because they're true, the only way I can truly let go is by recounting to Lacey the whole story from the innocent beginning to the guilty end.

"Okay, you're right. It's now or never." I huff a sigh and set my mind upon the purpose. "Can you distract the twins whilst I talk to her? I don't know how long it will take."

"Of course. You have as long as you need." We mirror each other's smiles and I know that we are on the same page. We are always on the same page about almost everything.

The wind whistles through my mousy hair as I cross the lawn towards the kitchen, where I can see Lacey rapt in conversation with Madison and Mila who are giggling uncontrollably. The sun follows me as I walk, dipping lower and lower, just about to kiss the horizon. I always imagined the moment of reckoning to be a blustering grey day with torrents of rain and flashes of lightning illuminating the sky, this idyllic sunset wasn't at all like the storm I'd imagined.

"Lacey." I call as I enter the farmhouse style kitchen. Pots and pans, ladles, and cutlery litter the sideboards. I have always liked the mess; I find it oddly homely. Lacey turns and smiles sweetly.

"What's up?" She asks.

"Madison, Mila, why don't you go and hang out with your dad outside? He's asking to see you." At once, the twins jump up and head back outside their identical figures bouncing along.

When the twins are fully out of earshot, I pull up the nearest wooden chair and sit down, my head in my hands. The all too familiar wave of panic has begun to build up inside of me, I know that once I start the story it will all become easier, I know that once I begin, the words will flow out of me like a river flowing into the ocean.

Of course, I must start at the beginning, not the beginning of my story but the beginning of ours - one dismal morning when I was just fourteen with a rose-tinted view on the world and had no idea just how my world would crash and burn at my feet.

"What's up, Mum?" Lacey repeats, looking concerned. I can see the cogs turn in her mind as she figures it out. "Eighteen…I'm eighteen today, so you're going to tell me, aren't you? You're going to tell me the truth about my dad, right?" Instinctively, she sits directly across from me and takes my hand within hers. Lacey is a lot stronger than me; she always has been.

"Yes. I've been putting this off for so long now, but it's time. You deserve to know the truth, the whole truth. I must warn you though Lacey, that this isn't a sweet and romantic tale. This is a story of raw truth, of lies, of crime, of devastation, of the destruction of so many lives." Lacey's expression is unreadable, she appears to be processing my warning, unsure of how to respond.

"I can take it." She settles upon, and I know that if anyone can take the truth it is her. "Why have you waited so long to tell me? We had all those years just the two of us where I could've understood why I didn't have a dad." But, telling her as a child I believe would have ruined her. Some truths are just easier to stay buried.

"You'll understand when I tell you. I hope you'll forgive me for keeping it from you for so long, I did what I believed would be best for you." *And what was best for me,* the traitorous thought flits across my mind because truthfully the longer I could have kept her from potentially hating my guts, I believed it to be for the better.

"Okay." She says, "Go on."

"Right, well everything started one morning in October when I was fourteen. It was a morning just like any other, not one I expected to remember for years to come. But it is where our story starts." I take another deep breath and set my eyes onto hers, and begin...

14 YEARS OLD

"Lyla Kingsley, are you sleeping in class again?" I snapped to attention and gave Mrs Green, who was looming above me, a sheepish look. Since that day the previous July, when all our lives had come crashing down, sleeping in class had sort of become my thing.

"So, Lyla. Now that I have your attention, I was wondering if you could tell me what the leading cause of the Great Depression was?" Mrs Green asked me with that kind of sly look on her face which meant she thought I had no clue of the answer. Mrs Green was the splitting image of a foghorn, her booming voice would fill the classroom with a relentless drone which was much to the contempt of the pupils, well, all except one.

Clara Yale was looking at me dead on with a smug expression, as if she were some omnipotent being and I was well ... me. Clara was the worst kind of person, good at everything she did, and damn well aware of it too. Her sickly-sweet optimism made everyone want to hurl. She was the type of person whose snarky remarks made your skin crawl.

She was...

"I know the answer and it's obvious that Lyla doesn't, so let me answer Miss, please or we'll be here forever." I shot daggers at Clara, at her perfect black shiny hair, at her perfect green eyes, at her perfect life. Her mum wasn't lying practically unresponsive in a hospital bed like mine – how could one person be blessed with everything?

Just before I could answer Mrs Green's question or tackle Clara to the floor which had seemed very appealing to me at the time, the bell rang, saving me from the embarrassing torture I was about to face.

****

The lunch hall was abuzz with people fluttering around, everyone from our small village and the next two villages were all sent to the same school, so it was always ridiculously overcrowded. My eyes scaled the bustling hall attempting to find an empty seat…

"Hey Lyla, how are you doing?" I heard Nate's voice behind me. He normally ignored me at school, as per the unspoken rule of having a sibling at school. Nate was my opposite, tall with the same bright blue eyes as our mother. Nate captured the attention of the room wherever he went. He was infamous at our school, the person that every girl would whisper about in the hallways much to my disgust. I don't even think people knew that he had a little sister. Ever since Mum's accident though, he had been checking-up on me every single day.

"Yeah, I'm fine thank you." I paused and heaved a heavy sigh. I was lying of course, in reality I was a crumbling mess on the inside. In reality, I hadn't been fine for a long time.

I spotted concern on his face, so I added, "You know you don't have to keep checking up on me Nate, I really am fine." I forced a weak smile to prove my point.

Despite how pathetic it was, it seemed to persuade him that I was indeed fine, that my world wasn't falling apart shard by serrated shard.

"Okay then Lyla, I'll see you around." He rushed off to his lunch table which overflowed with throngs of people, many of whom were more like his fans than his friends. I had never seen someone who could command as much attention as Nate did, he called it a gift, I called it people's stupidity.

I spotted my friends in the very far corner of the cafeteria, Marina's fiery auburn hair was difficult to miss, and we often used to joke that you could see it from space. Marina sighed as I crossed the sea of people and sat down at the table, hinting to me that something was wrong.

"Ignore her, she's just annoyed that she still hasn't heard from Gabe." Quinn informed me. Quinn was always blunt and blatantly rude at times, but she always got away with it, purely because she was so beautiful. Her hair was a silky waterfall blonde, and her eyes were like two priceless sapphires. We looked like two completely different species.

Quinn and I had been friends forever and growing up we were more like sisters. These days though, we were more friends out of habit than anything else. You know, those kinds of people who you couldn't imagine being absent from your life, no matter how obnoxious or blunt they sometimes were.

 "I'm pretty sure that he is back with Jen Latten, that's what Lana told Amelie who told Lily who told me in history class this morning." Tiffany interjected. Tiffany was the biggest gossip at our school, probably the biggest gossip I've ever met. She was sweet as icing sugar, but you just couldn't tell her any of your secrets unless you wanted all of Jade Town and maybe even the entire country to know them. Believe me, I learnt that the hard way. I had been feeling down about my mum's condition one morning in French class and without thinking I let it slip to Tiffany and from then on, I had practically the entire school, asking me how I was doing 24 hours of the day. It was all ridiculously suffocating.

Marina rolled her eyes, "I guess it's hopeless then, I just thought that maybe... it was stupid to think he actually cared about me at all, I know that. I only met up with him once after all."

Quinn nodded her head which made her silky blonde hair bounce up and down. I kicked her forcefully in the shin under the table.

"OUCH... I mean it was worth a try though right Marina." Quinn managed through gritted teeth, glaring in my direction.

"Did you know that apparently the new boy is..." Tiffany began, completely changing the subject. That's when out of the corner of my eye I saw him...

He was standing at the edge of the cafeteria surveying the bustling scene.

Blue. His eyes were a deep blue like they held the deepest depths of every ocean known to man. His hair was a glowing blond as if God himself had bestowed upon him a halo of enigmatic light. He wasn't particularly tall or broad, but he created a presence of massiveness within the room. All eyes were suddenly on him, everyone was infatuated by the beautiful stranger.

And he knew it.

A slow and easy smile emanated from his lips as he glanced from person to person in the cafeteria. I think that my heart stopped beating entirely for a minute as he caught my eye and his gaze lingered there. His gaze was intense, it struck right to my heart, ricocheting right through my ribcage.

Tiffany must've noticed because she grabbed my arm, breaking the spell that he had cast over me.

"Lyla, are you listening to me?" She asked. To be honest, I'd completely tuned out of the whole conversation.

"Sorry Tiff, what were you saying?". I muttered and dragged my eyes from the stranger and back to my table, giving her a pleading look to prove I was sorry.

"I was saying," She huffed, obviously put out by my lack of interest in whatever she had to say. She could have been talking about the most interesting thing I had ever heard, my favourite novel perhaps, or some celebrity we all loved but it wouldn't have made even a slight difference. I couldn't stop thinking about the stranger, mostly who he was, whether he was our age and why he was here.

Furtively, I kept glancing over at him and his perch at a table in the opposite corner of the cafeteria. A large gaggle of people had swarmed around him, almost blocking him from view, almost. I could see him deep in conversation with Roman Huxley, who wasn't a wise choice of companion- Roman was easily one of the worst and most sickeningly obnoxious people besides Clara that I'd ever met.

Roman, however, had a massive presence within the school and Jade Town, as his father Dean Huxley was the mayor and owned a successful publishing company. Before the arrival of the new boy, the Huxleys were all anybody ever spoke about. Dean, his ex-model wife Jeanie, and their only son Roman were like royalty in Jade Town. I however, had never been a fan of the Huxleys as I always found them to look down upon the rest of the residents of Jade Town. So, it's easy to say that I had an idea straight away of the type of crowd the new stranger would fall into, one that I wanted nothing to do with.

"The new boy's apparently the descendant of some duke who disgraced the Queen and his family all moved here to live a quiet life so that they weren't recognised for who they are." Tiffany was trying to explain this clearly entirely fabricated story to me, but I was so distracted that her voice sounded muffled like it was coming from far away. There had been many theories circulating about the elusive new kid ever since the announcement of his arrival a week before. If I knew Tiffany, chances are that she was responsible for about seventy five percent of those rumours. It was quite a spectacle to have a new student at school, a new kid in Jade Town, because no one ever came and went to Jade Town. People just existed there and lived their lives out in the same spot, and everybody knew everyone.

"I doubt that's true," said Quinn, staring down at her neon pink nails. She seemed to be the only person who seemed unfazed by what had just occurred. Quinn's lack of interest was probably down to the fact that as she often liked to inform us, she only liked older guys, and the stranger didn't look any older than about fourteen or fifteen. It was abundantly clear to just about everyone that the older guy in question was my older brother Nate. She had been deeply infatuated with him for as long as I could remember. Maybe that was the reason why she'd stuck around with me for all those years?

Just at that moment, the bell rang signalling the end of lunch and the start of fourth period. The bustling swarm of the cafeteria dispersed in different directions.

Geography. Human torture more like. Another lesson in which Clara Yale would relish outshining me in every way possible with her extensive worldly knowledge. She often liked to tell everyone she'd travelled far and wide during her life. The fact that she'd actually left Jade Town made her somewhat of an enigma for everyone, people didn't understand how she would go travelling every summer and the rest of us were stuck hanging around in the same gut-wrenchingly familiar places in the dull heat and under the grey sky. When I was younger, I used to go camping in Europe sometimes but since my mum's accident, there was no way we would ever have been able to afford to leave Jade Town for even a single day during the summer.

Heaving a heavy sigh for about the one hundredth time that day, I took my seat in the chaotic class that my young and increasingly agitated teacher Miss Samuels was attempting, with no avail, to make silent. I was ready for another monotonous hour of what I'm sure would be considered torturous and too harsh to endure even in the deepest depths of hell.

Then, the door bashed open violently and there he was. Stood illuminated by the flickering hall lights. Everyone seemed to sense his presence, he was magnetic, he emitted a force field so strong that everyone was caught up in it and reeled in. I knew that everyone must have noticed him because the loud room fell silent just like the cafeteria had done.

"Finally. Hello class, this is our newest student, who obviously doesn't understand the concept of being on time." Miss Samuels said with a sweet tone, dripping with agitation. She'd been trying everything to get the class silent for at least ten minutes and yet a stranger had the ability to reduce the class to silence with no effort at all.

"Why don't you introduce yourself then?" Miss Samuels pressed, her tone was suddenly rather cold, she was punishing him for his lucky genetics and ability to have power over everyone because public speaking is something which frightens the life out of most people, especially people who you've never met before. He, however, was totally unfazed of course.

"I'm Lawrie Hartwell," he said with a slight smile, the kind which had the power to melt your insides. Lawrie Hartwell – I had no idea at that moment just how important that name would become to me and so many other people. That's the thing though, so many minuscule things happen each and every day and yet something which seems so insignificant like a chance meeting can hold so much weight years later.

"Thank you, Lawrie for that introduction, it was very informative, and we all learnt so much about you." Miss Samuels said sarcastically, I never knew why she disliked him so much, but he had clearly annoyed her somehow because she was usually as mild as milk. Lawrie looked taken aback at her remark too and stood there glued to the spot at the front of the class rather awkwardly. I guessed that he wasn't used to people being annoyed with him and that he was probably usually hailed as some kind of greater being by everyone he met.

"You can go and sit over there in that spare seat next to Clara Yale. She can catch you up on everything we've done so far this year before our exam next week."

Of course, he would be sat next to Clara Yale. Clara clearly didn't even attempt to mask her joy as her pretty features twisted into an expression of smugness. It seemed that another excuse for her to prove that she was far more superior than everyone else had just fallen straight into her lap. Everybody liked Clara with her flowing black locks, petite frame, and great big glassy green eyes so it was crystal clear that if Lawrie were going to like anyone in this class it wouldn't be me.

Lawrie crossed the class towards where Clara was sitting, smiling, and fixing her hair. She looked ready to pounce on him as soon as he sat down. I may have imagined it but as Lawrie crossed the room and glanced my way, I swear that I saw him smile.

All that commotion almost made me forget about my mum. Almost. The thought was always nibbling at the back of my mind, eating away at me piece by agonising piece. My mind was a packed commuter train, bustling with activity day and night. No matter how hard I tried, I couldn't clear the train, nor could I pinpoint one passenger. That's the thing with people, no matter how much you try, you will never know the inner workings of someone's mind; you will never know their truth. Everyone uses a façade; some people are just harbouring deeper, darker thoughts than others.

****

The rest of the month dragged past in a similar way, I was distracted and constantly worried that my mum's condition would worsen. In Geography, I would look over praying that there was nothing going on between Lawrie and Clara. I don't know exactly why I did it, it wasn't like I stood any kind of chance with Lawrie, I was too terrified to even say hello to him. Despite this, ever since that moment in the cafeteria he had me hooked along with most other girls in my year. He possessed an air of mystery about him- no one knew where he came from and why he came to Jade Town. The mystery surrounding Lawrie just made him even more enticing.

The first time I had a proper encounter with Lawrie was in early spring of that year. In a flash, the willowy dead plants of winter had sprung into a kaleidoscope of beautiful colours. Days began to get longer; we were blessed with more hours of blissful sunshine. You could almost taste the salty sea in the fresh spring air. Everything had turned away from winter and towards summer.

I, however, was firmly in a state of eternal winter. I was walking down the hallway, my mind consumed by thoughts of Mum. She'd become a fragile shadow of herself, the accident had taken everything away from her. She was completely unrecognisable; her happy carefree self was just a distant memory. I was completely hollow I felt as though all the life had been sucked out of me. I walked with an impenetrable dark rain cloud above my head, and I didn't think anything could lift my spirits.

CRASH.... I collided with another student with a thud. The books I was carrying slipped out of my hands, paper spilled out across the floor in all directions.

Great! Heaving a sigh, I knelt down and attempted to pick up the papers which were rapidly escaping my grasp and being kicked around by other students in the hall. That was when I noticed the student who I'd crashed into me was still looming over me.

"Do you need help with that?" He asked. In truth, I wasn't really interested in having a conversation with anyone at that moment let alone someone who had just made my day a fraction worse. I looked up to tell him that I was perfectly capable of picking up my own books- even though this was a total lie because I clearly wasn't capable of doing anything in my current state of mind.

Looking up, I registered the student's golden blond hair and enchanting opalescent eyes. Features of this distinction could only belong to one person...

Lawrie.

Immediately, I blushed a completely unflattering shade of crimson. *Of course.* My day could always get worse.

"I...uhm...I'm ...uhm." I spluttered.

What was my malfunction? I probably looked like a gawking idiot, an idiot who couldn't even formulate a proper sentence. I'd been pining after this boy since he'd arrived, and I single-handedly ruined any chance that I might've had in about 0.5 seconds.

If Lawrie noticed my utter incompetence of stringing a sentence together, he didn't say anything. Instead, he knelt down to help me collect up the papers. As he reached to grab one, his finger brushed against mine, it was barely a form of contact, but I felt a jolt of electricity soar up my spine. I had to say something, anything, I couldn't just sit there on the floor looking like an idiot...

"Are you and Clara Yale dating?" *Anything but that.*

The words tumbled out before I could stop them. I picked up the last of the papers and stood up. *Maybe I could make a quick run for it before he noticed?* Then I could move somewhere far away like the golden coasts of the Maldives or the Seychelles and spend the rest of my days as an island recluse with only a squawking parrot named Pierre for company. Yes, solitary confinement felt like the best plan after I'd just embarrassed myself so greatly.

Lawrie laughed slowly and easily and stood up to face me. It was too late for a getaway now, not that I wanted to run away from Lawrie that was. I don't think anyone could run away from Lawrie; he had that strong force field surrounding him; the type which no one was immune to - especially me.

"No, Clara isn't really my type." he said utterly unfazed like he got asked this kind of thing all the time - to be honest he probably did.

"She's a little bit intense, isn't she?"

I laughed. At least Lawrie could see straight through Clara just like I could. Clara was the epitome of intense, she always appeared to have this endless bouncing energy every day when everybody else was just struggling to get by.

"Why? Are you jealous or something, Lyla?" I was absolutely, completely, totally, and utterly jealous. Jealous of anybody who got to spend time with him, anyone who knew him.

Hang on, he knew my name? I didn't even realise that he knew I existed.

"Wait, how do you know my name, Lawrie?" I once again felt that buzz of warm electricity within me. I watched as Lawrie pointed down to the books I was carrying - the books which had my name plastered on the front in bold letters.

Oh of course. The buzz of electricity was quickly replaced with a burning hot wave of shame.

"Oh... yeah, right of course." I muttered whilst avoiding eye contact. "Anyway, thanks for the help, Lawrie, I've got a class now, so I better get going." I paused for a minute and then turned on my heels towards my English class, my face red hot with shame.

Just before I turned the corner, I heard Lawrie's voice over my shoulder. "Hey Lyla, wait up!"

I turned around in response and watched him jog down the bustling hallway towards where I was standing.

"You dropped this." He was holding my tattered, dog-eared copy of *The Great Gatsby* which I'd read about a hundred times, it had been a birthday present from my mum the year before and I think I almost believed that if I kept reading it, it would bring her back out of the depths of her mind and back to how she was before.

"Thanks." I smiled as he handed the book over to me, I had barely let it out of my sight in the past few months, I hadn't gone anywhere without it.

"It's a shame your taste in books is so bad, I was kind of starting to warm to you." I looked up into his face suddenly ready for an altercation, I didn't know him at all but suddenly I started to dislike him a fraction more than I had before.

"That's probably because you've never actually bothered to read it." I said, feeling the most confident I had since we had bumped into each other a few minutes before. I didn't care if it was just a book, to me it was so much more than that at the time, it was my most prized possession because I had no idea if I would ever receive a gift from her again.

"Who says I haven't read it?" Lawrie said back in retort looking slightly taken aback.

"You don't fool me, waltzing in and pretending you are some kind of literary enthusiast as well as captain of the football team and a decent human being. No one is all three of those things, I know that much." Lawrie had quickly associated himself with the self-proclaimed 'in' crowd at school and he was likely only one step away from becoming captain of the school's football team. As a result, I couldn't believe that he was secretly an avid reader of twentieth century novels and a decent human being all rolled into one. Afterall, it was real life and not some kind of over-budgeted low-grade romance movie.

"You're a cynic, aren't you Lyla? For your information, I did start to read this book last summer, actually, and I just didn't understand why *Gatsby* spent so long pursuing *Daisy* when it was clear she didn't care about him." Lawrie said in a voice that suggested he knew exactly what he was talking about.

"She represents nostalgia, he looks upon the past with a rose-tinted view and believes he can recreate the past by winning *Daisy*. That's why he built this whole life of success. She's a metaphor not just a spoilt brat." Lawrie gave me a look in response which told me he didn't quite believe me and actually thought I was rather insane by suggesting such a prospect.

Before I could argue back to him though, the bell sounded signalling the start of the next lesson and the buzzing hive of the hallway started to disperse in different directions.

Lawrie smiled, said goodbye, and turned to walk back up the corridor towards the main hall of the school. He only made it a couple steps before he hesitated, turned around and said, "Now *Frankenstein*, that is a good read, the original version that is." And then as an afterthought, "I'm never going to be captain of the football team you know Lyla, I'm horrible at it, I'm never going to take Huxley's spot, so you've nothing to worry about there. Perhaps I am a real-life human after all?" He laughed out loud, and it was the best sound I had ever heard.

I couldn't help but crack a smile as I watched his figure retreat down the hallway which was suddenly practically empty. Once he was out of sight, I turned and rushed down the hallway in the opposite direction towards my English class, which I was undoubtedly late for. This was something my sultry teacher Mr Gleeson always took personally, as if by being thirty seconds late a student had cursed his bloodline.

Down the hallway, I spotted Marina hanging aimlessly by the lockers and gave her an enthusiastic wave.

"Wow, someone's cheerful today." She said with a slight chuckle as she moved from her perch by the grey lockers and approached me. Her auburn curls were pulled into plaits which made her look like an Aztec princess, and her brown eyes were framed with smoky black like a skunk. She'd started experimenting with makeup long before any of the rest of our friends did and I still don't think she quite had the hang of it back then.

"Is there any reason why you're suddenly smiling so much?" She pressed, her eyes sparkled, inquisitive.

At that moment, it occurred to me that for the first time in what seemed like forever, probably the first time since last July, I hadn't thought about my mum. Even if it had been for about five minutes, Lawrie had managed to distract me, and I was eternally grateful.

"No reason. Can't I just be happy for once?" I shrugged as we walked into the back of Mr Gleeson's class, both simultaneously heaving a sigh of relief that he hadn't turned up yet. Instead, the class around us was in a state of utter disarray. People throwing paper aeroplanes and climbing up onto the desks was a common sight in our school. I think it was because there was nowhere really to go in our village so every kid who grew up there just felt completely trapped, I know that's how I felt. Jade Town sometimes felt like the only place in the world.

"So, this has nothing to do with the fact that I saw you talking to Lawrie Hartwell just now?" Marina pressed playfully, I knew she didn't mean anything by it, and was likely just glad to see me smiling and operating like a regular human being for once.

"No, nothing to do with that. He just has a terrible taste in books, it's a disappointment really." I whispered as Mr Gleeson sauntered into the class, glaring as he saw the state of the classroom. He shouted at us all that day and kept us back, making us clean every desk until they were spotless, but I was smiling the whole time.

****

Lawrie left the school a day or so after that. As soon as he'd arrived in Jade Town, he had packed up and left again in a cloud of smoke, in a way just as mysterious as when he had arrived. Nobody believed that they would hear from him again, I never thought I would see him again, that he would just be chalked down as some childhood crush. But that's not true, it wasn't the last time I would cross paths with Lawrie Hartwell.

I'm getting ahead of myself. All you really need to know, at this moment, is that that seemingly minuscule interaction started off the tale of Lawrie and me.

The innocent beginning.

15 YEARS OLD

I always used to hate hospitals. I hated everything from the dull white-wash walls to the intoxicating chemical smell which hangs limply in the air. I was sitting on a hard plastic chair in the waiting room, waiting for visiting hours to begin. Time seemed to have completely stood still, the clock on the wall moved at the pace of a snail. I just wanted to see her, I needed to see her.

This was the first time that I had come here by myself. Normally I was accompanied by Nate or my dad, but Nate had a big football game and Dad was working overtime trying to make up for Mum's current lack of income, so I was here alone. I missed the company, Nate and Dad made me feel secure- like Mum's condition was only temporary and that she would be back to her normal self soon. Being there completely alone however, exposed me to the truth, exposed me to the toxic side of life. I think it is easy to forget the realities of a situation when you aren't there in the thick of it, but there I was, right in the thick of it.

Nowhere to run, nowhere to hide.

Mum had been trapped in this prison for a few months. After the accident, her health had deteriorated right in front of my eyes. It was like my mum was a burning candle and suddenly her warm glowing light extinguished leaving nothing but a dull, hollow lump of wax. It scared me more than anything, the thought that one day she might not be here. I know that I shouldn't have been so morbid, but it was hard not to let the façade slip. All of us knew that she wasn't going to get better, she wasn't going to wake up, we were just too frightened to admit it.

"Okay Lyla, visiting time has started." Ivy, the small dark-haired receptionist informed me. I'd been here so often that we were now on a first-name basis. She wasn't particularly friendly or talkative, but it was nice to have someone else in the waiting room with me so that I didn't feel so hopelessly alone.

"Thanks, Ivy." I called as I made my way past her desk and out into the hospital corridor which was equally as headache-inducing with its pale white walls and hanging stench of bleach. It was overwhelming to me that every patient I passed had a story, a life outside of the hospital, a life outside of their illness. Remember, every person you pass on the street has a life you know nothing about, everyone experiences joy and suffering. Everyone has fears and passions, you are never alone in your feelings.

Despite how early it was, the hospital was a hive of activity. I approached a section of the hospital and pushed open the heavy-duty blue doors which looked totally out of place against the synthetic white hue of the rest of the building.

"Excuse me Miss, do you have an appointment?" the exhausted looking receptionist asked me. She was tapping away on her computer barely paying any attention to me. Her bedraggled brown locks were pulled into a messy ponytail, and she was clutching a flask of straight black coffee.

"Uhm... visiting hours just started, I'm Lyla Kingsley here to visit my mum, Renee Kingsley, she's a patient here." I responded with a timid tone, the receptionist frightened me, she was buzzed up on coffee so who knows what she could have done. Then again, she didn't look like she was up for a fight, she looked as though she needed to sleep for a thousand years. Didn't we all? Recently, I had been so worried that I'd developed a major case of insomnia.

The receptionist looked up at me and for a minute I thought she was going to argue but instead she just waved me through.

"That's fine, she's in room 104."

I offered a smile, my expression trying to convey, *'I haven't been sleeping either I know how it feels to be a walking zombie'*. The receptionist just frowned and looked down at her computer. I guessed that we weren't going to be friends anytime soon, which was fine by me.

Room 104 was small and tucked away in the corner. My mother would've described it as cosy if she'd been awake, but I didn't see how a hospital room could ever be considered cosy. That was Renee Kingsley though, she saw the silver lining in just about everything. I used to wish that I could steal some of her optimism so that I wouldn't worry as much as I do, for I have always been plagued with worry about everything, whether it was out of my control or not, it's always been my biggest downfall.

My mum's bed was right in the corner of the room by a large window which strangely let barely any light into the room. The view from the window though was incredible, you could see the whole of Jade Town and the sloping green hills which framed it. Mum would've loved it if she could have actually seen it, that was.

She was still there, motionless, in the bed like she had been for the past eighteen months. Ever since that disastrous night which took everything away from me. She had only gone out to get candles for my birthday cake. Laughing that she couldn't believe she had forgotten the most important part of a birthday, she set off into the sticky July air. We all had no idea that she would end up like this. I wish with every part of me that she hadn't gone, that I'd told her I didn't need candles that year, because maybe then she wouldn't have been lying there.

"Hi Mum." I smiled down at her face which was entangled with tubes and ventilators ardently trying to sustain her life. Doctor Bahiel had told us all that hearing familiar voices was likely to improve her condition quicker so we had been visiting her as much as we could and offloading our lives onto her. I quickly delved into the tale of my recent exploits, which mostly just consisted of Tiffany, Quinn, Marina, and I hanging out with Alessia Chang at her parent's café which was the only hangout spot for the children of Jade Town. I told her about Nate's football game and how Dad was struggling to get by without her. I told her about how much we missed her smile and her laugh, how much I missed her.

I was just engrossed in a story about Tiffany's cousin Daphne who had gone to university for a term and then dropped out, when I heard the door open behind me. Immediately, I snapped to attention and let go of Mum's hand which I had been clutching as I spoke to her. It was wet with tears that I wasn't even aware that I'd been shedding.

"Sorry, I don't mean to intrude. Doctor Bahiel just asked me to check Renee's vitals." A rather strikingly familiar voice said behind me. Overcome by confusion, I sat there for a moment looking out of the hospital window and out onto the emerald slopes surrounding Jade Town.

I have definitely heard that voice before. I thought, but I couldn't place where I'd heard it. It was a foggy memory right at the back of my brain like that voice had some meaning to me somewhere, but I 'd somehow forgotten about it for a long time.

I turned around, having convinced myself that the voice probably belonged to one of the doctors, even though it sounded like it belonged to someone no older than a teenager. My eyes registered with shock as I saw Lawrie Hartwell standing in the doorway of the dimly lit room. He looked different than he had nearly a year before, he was considerably taller, his shoulders were broader, and his golden hair was shorter so that it no longer hung into his eyes. His eyes were the same though, piercing flecks of the purest blue substance known to man.

Despite Lawrie's change in appearance, I looked completely the same as I did a year before. My hair was still long and mousy and always a tattered mess, my appearance was still just as bedraggled. Any kind of makeover hadn't really crossed my mind amongst everything that was going on. Plus, I had never imagined I would ever actually see him again- but there he was, back in Jade Town like he had never left in the first place.

"Hey, it's you." I spluttered as I got up from my seat beside Mum and crossed the room towards him. He did the same, and we met awkwardly in the centre of the room. I had no idea if he would even recognise me seeing as he barely even knew me in the first place, he had been in Jade Town for such a short amount of time it was highly unlikely that he would remember me from one of our miniscule conversations.

"Hey Lyla." He said calm as an August breeze, he remembered me somehow. It was so strange, I barely knew him, but I had never been so happy to see someone again in all my life. Nobody, despite a couple of his friends, even knew that he was leaving in the first place. I guessed he had left once he stopped turning up to geography class consecutively for a month. Of course, hundreds of rumours had circulated surrounding his departure but as far as I knew nobody actually knew why he had left.

"I just need to check her vitals." Lawrie said motioning to the hospital bed, as I was clearly blocking his path.

"Oh ... yeah... of course." I muttered as I moved to the side and watched as he crossed the room to where my mum lay in the bed, picked up the clipboard at the end of her bed and started scrawling something onto the paper. He looked like a medical professional and not a fifteen-year-old boy. My brain remained cloudy with confusion the whole time he stood there looking at the monitors and taking notes. *Why was Lawrie back in Jade Town and why was he here, checking on my mum?*

I opened my mouth to ask those things, just as he put the clipboard back and turned to face me, his cool blue eyes on mine.

"I'm just about to go on my break if you wanted to join me?" He offered and I was too curious to turn him down. So, I muttered a weak goodbye to mum, nodded wordlessly, and followed him out of the room and down the harshly lit corridor which offered a headache inducing contrast to the low light of room 104.

I followed him to a room with a sign that screamed 'Hospital Break room. 'STAFF ONLY'. I tensed up with panic fully expecting to be thrown out of the room for trespassing. Fortunately, the break room was completely empty- for now at least. Lawrie pushed open the door and held it out to me.

The breakroom was the only room in the whole hospital where you weren't immediately overcome by the stench of chemicals in the air. It contained a long table with chairs protruding from each side and a sideboard containing a range of cooking implements. Up on the wall, a shift timetable stared down at me from a whiteboard, filled with names I didn't recognise. It seemed like a little haven, a little space of normality amongst the chaos of the hospital.

Lawrie had barely sat down on one of the plastic chairs when I bombarded him with questions: "What are you doing here, Lawrie? How long have you been back in Jade Town? How come you're working here?" He looked taken aback and I knew that I'd overdone it with the questions. I guess acting like an MI5 agent interrogating the ringleader of an infamous drug cartel wasn't exactly the best way to make a new friend.

After a couple of agonising seconds of silence, Lawrie answered:

"I'm volunteering here, I want to be a surgeon one day and my dad said that this would be a good step for me. He works here at the hospital."

I suppose that made sense, but it didn't answer what I really wanted to know, which was why he was back in Jade Town and why he left in the first place.

"When did you come back to Jade Town?" I asked him as I glimpsed down at his arms which were laid out onto the metal table in front of him, they had an end of summer glow like he had spent last summer in some far away exotic location.

"About a week ago." He replied without elaboration whilst running one of his hands over his face. I could tell that getting any information out of him would be as hard as getting blood out of a stone. On reflection, I think that getting blood out of a stone probably would probably actually have been an easier feat.

"So how come you came back here then and where did you go before?" I pressed, the mystery around him may have been alluring the year before but at that point I just wanted answers. For some reason unbeknownst to me, I was suddenly angry at him for being there and seeing my mum in the state that she was in, I hated people knowing the vulnerabilities and cracks in my life and Lawrie had just seen my biggest vulnerability first-hand.

"I had to come back. My brother and I were living with my aunt after we left here but it was only temporary, so we came back." Although I longed to know more, like his reason for leaving, I knew that I wasn't going to be able to get any answers any time soon, so I simply nodded and changed tact.

"She's, my mum." I said quietly. "That's why I'm at the hospital, I'm visiting her."

Lawrie's eyes had been fixed studying the intricacies of the tabletop, but they flickered to meet mine in that moment and his eyes appeared to be illuminated by understanding sadness for a second before they returned to their natural state. He didn't respond, instead he sat there studying me as if I had suddenly become fascinating to him. A huge wave of panic started to wash over me, so I opened my mouth rapidly to try and dispel the strange stagnant air that had suddenly hung between us.

"Can you not mention this to anyone, Lawrie?" I added hastily before I could think better of it. I had no idea if he even still knew anyone in Jade Town or if he was returning back to school with us, but I felt incredibly self-conscious and even though I'd told Tiffany the previous year and she had spread the news around the whole school, I still felt as though it was a secret, a secret that I ardently desired to keep.

Lawrie nodded slowly; a dark look cast over his perfect features. "Oh of course Lyla, that's what you think of me is it? That I'm just someone who goes around spreading confidential information about people. First of all, it's my job, and I'm not allowed, nor would I ever talk about any of the patients to anyone outside of the hospital." I mean I wasn't sure what Lawrie was like at all, I had only had a handful of conversations with him after all. We weren't really at the stage of knowing anything about each other. He looked almost hurt by the remark but based on my track record of telling people personal information I found it rather difficult to trust anyone.

"No, of course I don't think you are like that, it's just really personal and I don't think you would understand it." I knew immediately that I'd said the wrong thing. Rapidly, Lawrie got up from his chair and headed towards the door. *Great Lyla you have blown your chances already-way to go,* I thought. I thought he was about to leave me, sitting there in the hospital staff room, all alone.

To my surprise, he fiddled around with the door ensuring it was shut and glanced down checking the corridor was empty and then went to sit back down on the same plastic chair. He paused for a minute, staring down at the table again before he heaved a sigh. His gaze left the table and flitted towards me, his eyes landing directly on mine, and I swear that my heart momentarily stopped beating.

"I understand more than you know Lyla, I've been here before." Lawrie huffed. *He had been here before. What did he mean by that? That he's been to the hospital before- was this some kind of joke?* I thought. He wasn't laughing though, his eyes still lingered on mine, and he looked completely and utterly serious.

"What do you mean you've been here before? Are you talking about the hospital?" I asked inquisitively. The atmosphere had suddenly become electrified, any awkwardness that had been present had completely dispersed. It was like something inside us entwined at that moment- we were connected.

"No, I mean with your mum… with my mum." Sadness was audible in his voice; I knew that this was a touchy subject for him like it was for me. I could tell this was something that he didn't usually share with people, yet he had chosen to share it with me.

 "Your mum was sick too? I'm sorry I know how hard it can be." It was weird to see someone else going through the same thing as me. For some reason, Mum's condition had made me feel isolated and different from everyone else. I knew that Nate was going through the same thing as me, but he was older, and he seemed so strong in comparison to me.

"Just over a year ago she was driving home, and someone skipped a red light and crashed right into her at the junction, the car swerved and hit a wall, bursting into flames. She didn't make it out."

Oh.

Suddenly my situation seemed less dismal, at least my mum was still there; at least I could've still seen her and knew that she heard me. Lawrie couldn't do that, and he didn't even have the time to prepare for what happened. She was there one minute happy and healthy and the next she was stone cold and being lowered into the ground. I couldn't imagine how that must have felt. I couldn't even find the words, what are you supposed to say when someone tells you something like that? I knew that the basic *I'm so sorry* wouldn't cut it, but I genuinely couldn't think of anything else.

"Oh... I'm so sorry Lawrie that must've been...." I placed my hand on his shoulder in an attempt at a comforting gesture. He flinched, his rapid heartbeat bleeding through his skin and onto mine. I wasn't an expert at the inner workings of the human body, but I could tell that wasn't a good sign. The last thing I wanted to do was to make him angry. It was clearly a touchy subject for him, and I had just shown him about as much compassion as a potted plant could- a plastic potted plant that is.

"Let me guess Lyla, you've gotten tired of people telling you how sorry they are for you and how they will be there to talk whenever you need it?" He sighed and something of a strained laugh emanated from his lips.

"It's almost as bad as, *there's nothing you could've done* or *I'm sure she'd be so proud of you.* I'm so damn tired of people trying to understand how I feel or believing that they can genuinely help me, when deep down they will never understand what it feels like. Everyone making all these empty promises all the God-damn time when you know they couldn't actually give a shit about you. Everyone's just feeling sorry for the kid who lost his mum and wants to look like they're helping you."

His tone wasn't exactly harsh, but his words shot me right in the heart. I mean it was true that I'd gotten a little exhausted of people trying to understand my situation when they clearly couldn't, but I still appreciated that people said something to me at all.

I must've looked like he had physically shot me because he placed his hand over mine which was still resting awkwardly on his shoulder.

Suddenly, my entire arm felt like it had an electric current pulsating through it.

When he spoke, his tone was soft and barely audible.

"That's kind of why we came to Jade Town in the first place and it's the reason I want to be a surgeon, actually. I know there was no hope of saving my mum, but surgeons have the hand of God, I've always thought it was incredible the idea that someone else's life is entirely in your hands."

I was still reeling and absorbing the information that he had told me about his mum and how someone could be knocked down in their prime, there one minute and gone the next. It was a very difficult concept to comprehend at fifteen, it would be a difficult concept to comprehend at any age. Grief and loss are still just as hollowing at any age, the wound of losing a love may never heal but time can dull the pain at least.

At least Lawrie had answers though, I had no idea what had happened, at least he could process it and attempt to move forward. I was stuck, in the mirth of grief, grieving the past I once had whilst the person I was grieving for was still in the present.

He looked at me then, and I knew I had to tell him my story. He never pressured me to, but, for the first time since it happened, I wanted to tell someone. I had to tell him what happened to my mum. I didn't know how much he knew from working at the hospital, I didn't know if people gossiped about it, but I told him everything. He was surprisingly easy to talk to and knowing that he had gone through something similar brought me such comfort.

"It was July, my fourteenth birthday. I'd complained that she'd forgotten to buy candles for my cake. I made such a fuss, so she said she'd go out and get me some. She was mad at me when she left because I'd been so ungrateful, she said she'd be back soon and then we could properly celebrate…" I paused for a minute, my eyes stinging with tears at the memory of that evening before I began to speak again.

"So, the hours passed by, and we thought that maybe she'd just got stuck in traffic or something, because why would you imagine the worst? That was until my dad got a phone call late that night which told us that she was in the hospital. She had been found face down by the side of the road with her keys clutched in her palm, just next to her car. She's alive and still breathing but she can't tell us what happened, she can't tell us anything." The tears were now cascading down my cheeks, stinging as they slid down.

"No one really knows what happened, they almost didn't find her. The paramedics told us that there was a massive car accident just up the road. Someone's car had caught fire, and it was only because the paramedics were there trying to save the person in the car that they found my mum. There have been so many theories over the past year- that she was robbed or attacked, that her body just suddenly gave up…" I trailed off and put my head in my hands to stop the tears from falling.

"You're so brave Lyla." He said when I'd finished. "I hope you always remember that you're brave, and you're important."

****

Lawrie and I talked all day, until the sun started to slip beneath the clouds creating a pattern of warm colours in the sky. In his own words he was a volunteer and not staff, so he could afford to take the rest of the day off. It was nice having someone to talk to, someone who understood exactly how I felt. We talked about everything, from our favourite authors to our nicknames.

"So, hang on, your name isn't actually Lyla?" Lawrie and I were sitting huddled up at the bus stop outside the hospital. We had to leave the break room because people kept coming in and giving me dirty looks as if I were violating their privacy by being in their precious break room. It was the middle of January, and the air carried a deathly chill. It had snowed the day before and the remnants of it had turned into a thick grey sludge which clung to the pavements.

"Nope, my name is Delilah. Lyla was just a nickname that Quinn came up with when we were kids and it's kind of stuck." It felt weird to say it, I'd gotten so used to being called Lyla that my real name just seemed so formal. It was like I was talking about a stranger.

"What about you, is Lawrie your real name? It seems like a nickname to me." It was so weird how comfortable I'd gotten around him in only a couple of hours. Some people you just click with, Lawrie was one of those people to me.

"It's completely embarrassing. My name is Lawrence, but I hate it, so I have always got everyone to call me Lawrie. My brother and I both have names that have never fit us- my father said we had to have proper gentlemanly names. My little brother is called Arthur, but we just go by Lawrie and Rory."

Everyone learnt the name Lawrence Hartwell though. At that point, I had no idea that eight years later it would be the name on everyone's lips. The name which people spoke about in whispers wherever I went. I didn't know that everybody would know him, everybody would be talking about him. I had no idea that everybody would be talking about me too...

"I have a question for you Lyla." Lawrie asked as we trundled back down the winding road towards the centre of Jade Town.

"Shoot." The air had become blisteringly cold, and my body was shivering violently from head to toe in protest.

"Did you read *Frankenstein*? I tried *The Great Gatsby* again when I was staying at my aunts and although I still don't quite see your argument, I must admit it does have a certain charm about it, this idea of nostalgia you were talking about." My heart warmed hearing him talk.

"I did actually, I read it last summer and you have a point it is a good classic. I'm guessing you're interested in the whole playing God complex." I retorted as I watched the last rays of the sun dip below the horizon.

"Got it in one, you're a smart one, aren't you Lyla? You know I was hoping I would run into you when I came back here, I wanted to see the girl who had the power to change my mind because I'll tell you that doesn't happen very often." We both laughed then at his obvious stubbornness and slowed to a stop as we reached my front gate.

"Well, this is me." I gestured up at my house which stood above us in the darkness. "I'm glad I ran into you too. It was good to have someone to talk to who understands you know, and I'm glad you changed your mind. I would've just kept annoying you until you did anyway." A genuine smile spread its way across my face which was mirrored on his.

"I'll see you around Lyla."

"Yeah, I'll see you around." I walked up the path towards my house and looked back as I reached my front door just in time to see Lawrie retreat up the road, illuminated by the flickering streetlamps, a light against the growing darkness.

I smiled the whole evening long.

****

The rest of the year flew by. Mum wasn't getting any better, and it seemed as though every moment I shared with her was gone in a fizzle and a flash. I struggled in school because of my lack of focus. Test after test paper came back with an 'F' scrawled in red ink on the front. Everything seemed dreary and dark but there was at least one slither of light, I had an incredible support network- my dad, Nate, my friends, and Lawrie.

 Since that day at the hospital in January, we had become fast and firm friends. It was nice for me to have someone who didn't just pretend to understand what I was going through. Lawrie understood me, and he was there for me throughout it all. He was there at the hospital making sure I was okay. He had returned to school, and he was a friend to me there too which was much to the contempt of Roman Huxley and his crowd of followers who regarded me as unworthy of their time. Lawrie, however, was strong and always stood up for what he wanted and believed in, he never let anyone push him around and I liked him all the more for it.

Everything seemed fine during those months, as if despite the darkness within my life things would turn out okay. With every part of me, I wish that were true. I wish that this was some sweet story about how I met the love of my life and how he became the person who I relied on to hold my heart and guide me through life's challenges, but as I have already told you this story is far from it.

16 YEARS OLD

Alone for the first time that day, I stared at the mound of earth at my feet, the place where a plaque would soon sit- a plaque detailing the life of my mother. All the light inside of her, all the life inside of her had extinguished.

Somehow, unfathomably, the whole of her life would soon be condensed down into a few words on stone. And the span of her life, represented through a singular hyphen between two dates.

 Lots of people had shown up that day, I think my mother would've been astounded about just how many people cared about her. The day had been so hectic that it had been nice to find some quiet for a while. I wasn't even sure how long I had been standing there staring intently at the displaced earth as if I could will her back to me with my mind. I tried everything to bring her back, because I couldn't fathom the possibility that I would never be with her again. I couldn't bear the fact that she left us just when I needed her the most.

It was late Autumn; the amber leaves had just started to fall in flurries from the trees. It was crazy how much could change in a couple of months, and I was just starting to realise that nothing in life was really permanent. The idea that life never plays out how you imagine it to, how time with people is precious and limited.

My dad had to make a tough decision a month before, Mum had been mostly unresponsive for more than two years and the doctors finally admitted that they didn't think she would get any better. So, we chose to let her go to let her discover the mystery of what lay beyond mortality. Even though I had been expecting it for quite some time, the reality took months and maybe even years to really set in. Mum may not have physically been with us for years, but her presence was still there which comforted me a great deal, and suddenly there I was standing above her eternal resting place. Her grave was surrounded by two broad, obstinate oak trees, I liked to think that they would protect her and keep her safe for as long as they stood there.

"It was a beautiful service." I startled out of my daydream. I had been so distracted that I hadn't even heard him come up behind me. I wiped my hand across my cheek which was sodden with tears. I hadn't even noticed that I was crying, it had happened to me a lot recently all I felt was a dull, aching numbness in the pit of my stomach. Apparently, grief can affect people in different ways and all that I had felt since that fateful day four weeks prior was painful nothingness.

I turned around to face him. Lawrie was standing with his hands shoved into the pockets of his long charcoal trench coat. His hair was tousled and windswept and his eyes were fixed on me. "Yeah, it was," I replied and wrapped my arms around myself. In the rush of the day, I had forgotten to bring a coat, something which I was severely regretting as I stood there shivering like a lunatic.

Lawrie closed the distance between us in two steps and placed his hand on my shoulder. If I wasn't shivering before I definitely was then.

"Lyla you're shivering, here take my coat." Lawrie took his coat off in one swoop and placed it around my shoulders. The coat completely swamped my tiny frame. It smelt like mint and sandalwood, just like Lawrie, just like home.

"Thanks Lawrie and thanks for everything… you know for being here today and everything."

No. Don't cry again Lyla.

I pushed back against the press of hot tears which once again clouded up my eyes even though I believed I'd cried out all the water inside of me over the course of the day and I was well on my way to becoming a shrivelled peach. A lone tear escaped and cascaded down my cheek.

"I... don't think that I could've..." I started; too choked up to finish the sentence.

"I know Lyla, I understand." Lawrie pulled me into a hug, he made me feel safe and secure. He made me feel as though everything would be alright again, for once I didn't feel like my world was falling apart. My world had fallen apart though, the day that my mum ascended to those pearly white gates. Since then, my family had split into different directions like we had all been travelling down along a road when we suddenly hit a pothole sending us swerving off in different directions.

Nate had surrounded himself with as many people as possible, his gregariousness skyrocketed whilst I hid away from everyone and everything. The only person I wanted to be around was Lawrie. In just a short time, I felt like Lawrie knew me and understood me better than anyone I had ever met, after all he understood the pain that I was feeling better than anyone else could've done. It was a strange pairing, no one would have ever expected us to be friends because on the surface we were polar opposites, but for some unbeknownst reason it just worked.

I broke from the hug, suddenly aware of a group of people approaching which consisted of my incredibly spoiled cousins Tristan and Paris and my crazy aunt Julie. Julie was my mum's older sister and she 'hit it big' as my mother used to say by marrying a top investment banker who had more money than he had sense. The product of their union was their two rather stuck-up children. Tristan who was the biggest misogynist that I have ever met and Paris who was frankly so smug and condescending that she made Clara Yale look like Gandhi. When I was about thirteen, Julie's husband had upped and left her for a model who was only a few years older than I was. Ever since then Julie had gone slightly insane. Then again if you were solely in charge of the horror kids (as I liked to call them) I'm sure that you would probably have gone crazy too but despite their flaws, they were family, and I needed all the people there for me that I could get.

Each of them greeted Lawrie and me like they had known both of us for years. He had become very popular amongst my family- he was very popular around everyone that he had ever met. The effect that Lawrie had on people was so fascinating to me. Everybody seemed to trust him as soon as they met him. I used to say that scientists should study the effect that he created on people as if he was an enticing mystery with great depths to discover. Now looking back, I realise how stupid that sounds, but I was young and completely infatuated with him.

"I'm sorry Lyla, Renee was always such a great person. She always stuck to her morals, even when I told her not to." Julie placed an arm around my shoulders as she spoke. Although vague, I knew exactly what Julie was talking about. My mum and dad had Nate and I when they were very young, Mum always dreamed of being on stage, she had the most incredible gift, but she gave it all up for us. Even though she often told us she liked it that way, I always knew that I had thrown a spanner into her plans and aunt Julie recognised that too, but where had marrying for sense rather than love gotten her?

"Yeah, Aunt Renee was always so kind to us." Paris offered, she was a year younger than me and had likely only seen my mum as many times as you could count on one hand, but I appreciated her comment all the same.

"I'm sorry for your loss, Lyla." Tristan said and the three of them walked off to find Nate and my dad who were already in the car waiting for Lawrie and me.

I stood there for a few more moments simply staring at the earth and the soft pink lilies that I had laid down. I could feel Lawrie behind me, waiting. He didn't have to speak because his presence simply comforted me enough.

Finally, I dragged my eyes away from the grave and turned to face Lawrie and the church which stood at the bottom of the grounds.

"Are you ready to go?" He asked me.

"Yeah, I'm ready." We trundled down the path towards the car park, which was virtually empty at that stage, only the cars belonging to my dad, aunt Julie and the priest still stood there. As we walked, Lawrie entwined my hand with his own, spreading warmth throughout my body.

"I'm here for you Lyla, do you know that? I'll always be here for you, I promise."

****

The year dragged past. Every day, the dull ache of losing Mum lessened. It took a while, but by late spring I could finally breathe again. She was at peace, and I finally found peace with the fact that she was gone. Once you find acceptance and realise that things don't have to make sense, it is easier to let something go. I don't think my family ever properly recovered though.

Sometimes, we still seemed like strangers to one another. I hadn't known it at the time, but Mum was the glue that held our family together. Nate had gone off to university at the other end of the country just after the funeral. He might as well have been halfway across the world; I didn't hear from him much. We were never close to begin with, but after everything that had happened the past couple of years, any tie that we had to each other had completely severed. Dad had evidently been struggling to cope, he was working like crazy to try and provide for us. Every night, he would come home from work utterly exhausted. He looked like a zombie.

As for me, I constantly worked on my grades, and it paid off. My grades started improving and I was no longer struggling to keep up with everyone else like I was a first-time runner trying to face off against a bunch of Olympians. My friends had supported me throughout the difficulties with my mum and if it were not for them, I wouldn't have coped.

 "I can't agree with you on that one." My friends and I were holed in Quinn's plush pink terrace room one night in late June, discussing our opinions on a new band Marina had discovered. It felt completely normal being with them, it was like I was transported back to before Mum was sick.

"I just think that they're so different from anything I've ever heard before." Marina said nonchalantly. She was idly braiding her fiery auburn hair into one long plait down her back. Tiffany, who was painting her nails a screaming neon pink, looked up. "See that's where you're completely wrong Marina, they sound exactly like every band I've ever heard. There's nothing new around these days, everyone is just trying to copy what's been done before. Our parents were so lucky, you know, to grow up during a time where music was actually expressive and not simply a money-making formula designed to pray on people's desire to fit in with society." Tiffany, I should probably mention, had a lot of strong opinions on many subjects especially focussing on individuality, she was a free spirit born in the wrong decade.

Quinn nodded in agreement and focused her attention on me. "So, Lyla, what exactly is the deal with you and Lawrie? You two always seem to be together now and you're telling me you're still just friends?" Quinn asked breezily, completely changing the subject.

Lawrie and I were only friends. Even though sometimes, well actually all the time, I wished that we could be something more. I just wanted him to look at me the same way that I'd been looking at him ever since we had met. I was smart enough to know that realistically nothing was going to happen, my life wasn't one of those romance films that

Marina was completely obsessed with. My life was real, and in reality, Lawrie had no interest in being anything more than platonic with me.

"Yeah, we're just friends." I sighed audibly enough that the others noticed and turned their attention towards me.

"Someone's totally annoyed about that." Tiffany heckled.

"Yeah, but wouldn't you be annoyed Tiff, if like the hottest guy you've ever seen only wanted to sit up braiding hair with you." Marina laughed slowly and easily. I laughed too in spite of everything that had happened, I finally felt pure joy by being sprawled out laughing with my friends.

"We don't braid each other's hair just so you know." I called back in retort. "But sometimes we do trade friendship bracelets and stuff though." The others paused for a moment and stared at me, three gaping fish, before we all cracked the hell up.

"I mean sure he's cute but he's not perfect." Quinn choked out in-between laughing.

"Yeah, because he's not Nate." Tiffany, Marina, and I all said in unison. Hearing his name felt strange to me now, somehow along the way we had managed to become like strangers which was something that I knew I had to fix. Family after all are everything because underneath it all, family is all that we have.

"Yeah, Quinn I'm still not sure that you have a chance there, plus I have no idea why you like my brother anyway he's a total idiot." I was about to give her examples of the countless times in my life that my brother had been a complete idiot when I felt my phone buzz in my pocket. Owning a mobile had become a recent phenomenon, a way to connect with people instantaneously no matter where you were. I'd been working in Jade Town corner shop on the weekends and had saved up all my wages for it.

I fished it out and stared at the screen expecting the message to be Dad informing me that he was going to be late home again. Which is why I was so surprised to see Lawrie's name at the bottom of a text which read- *'Are you free right now?'* To tell the truth, I wasn't, and I probably should have just texted him that I was busy with my friends, but I just couldn't.

Lawrie had reeled me in a long time ago and I was totally at the mercy of him, ready to drop anything and everything to see him. I often think back to this seemingly innocent moment as a turning point. If I hadn't chosen to meet Lawrie that night, then everything may have been completely different.

'I'm totally free.' I keyed back and cringed at how desperate I must've sounded.

Then a few moments later, I typed up *'Why, what's up Lawrie?'*. My phone was silent for a while, and I thought that Lawrie may have given up on me, possibly decided I wasn't worthy of his time when the screen flashed violently with another message:

'I need to get out of the house. Can you meet me outside mine?'.

I thought about it for a moment, toying against myself in my mind. On one hand I was happy for the first time in a long time and building bridges with my friends but on the other, well there was Lawrie, a riptide in an otherwise predictable sea.

"Who're you texting right now?" Tiffany asked me inquisitively whilst attempting to peek over my shoulder. I thought for a minute about telling them, it's not like they would have minded. If anything, they probably would have encouraged me to go but for some reason I felt as though I couldn't tell them. I felt as though it was illicit and forbidden like I was about to commit a bank robbery or something, not meet up with a friend.

"It's my dad, he needs me home. The power has gone out or something and he needs me to help." I pressed the power button on my phone and shoved it into the pocket of my jeans. It was a completely weak excuse, but they seemed to buy it or if they didn't, they didn't let it show.

That's how fifteen minutes later I ended up standing outside of Lawrie's gigantic Victorian house. I had been out here a couple of times but had never been inside. I had never met any of Lawrie's family even though he seemed to be best friends with everyone in my family. All I knew was that he lived with his dad and little brother Rory. The house looked too big for only three people; I couldn't imagine that a house like that could ever really feel like home. Each member of the family may as well have been on opposite ends of the planet. It suited the Hartwell's though because they were never a close family, even before everything that happened.

The night was cool and overcast. It looked ominous and threatening like the sky was about to break out into a violent thunderstorm at any point. I glanced down to check my phone- it was just past midnight. If my dad knew that I was out here instead of sleeping over at Quinn's, he would probably have killed me but at that moment I couldn't bring myself to care. For the first time in my life, I felt a streak of quintessential teenage rebellion. I had spent the past couple of years growing up way too fast and caring about my mum, that for once I wanted to feel like a teenager again.

I was just about to message Lawrie to ask where he was when I heard a bunch of raised voices emanating from the house. Lawrie had told me to meet him outside and not to knock on his door. I thought at first it was because he didn't want his dad to find out or something but hearing the shouting from inside the house it made me feel as though it was something else entirely. I was standing too far away to be able to understand what they were saying so I edged a little closer up the path to the house.

"WHY DIDN'T YOU TELL ME? HOW COULD YOU DO THAT TO HER, TO US? YOU MONSTER!" I heard Lawrie's familiar voice screaming. I felt illicit as if I were doing something forbidden by eavesdropping on the conversation. It felt entirely private but based on the tone of their voices I was pretty sure that the rest of the street heard the altercation too.

"YOU'RE JUST A STUPID KID, YOU DON'T KNOW ANYTHING." A booming voice I didn't recognise responded.

The argument went on for a little while and I stood there, frozen. It was a constant retort between Lawrie's sweet familiar voice and that gruff voice I didn't recognise, both were rallying against each other like some aggressive tennis match. I have never liked tennis, and I hated the idea of it even more whilst shivering outside the Hartwell's mansion.

Suddenly, there was a large crash which drowned out the yelling and I covered my hand over my mouth to stop myself from screaming. The sharp metallic tang of blood hit my senses; I had bitten down on my lip, hard.

I guess I knew why Lawrie didn't want me to meet his family.

After a few moments of eerie silence, the front door swung open, and the dark lawn was cast under a half-light. Panic began beating its drum inside my chest ready to go to war, my organs constricted and tensed. I didn't like being there at all. I should have turned on my heels and ran as fast as I could with my hair trailing behind me like running water, but at sixteen years old I had no idea what I was getting myself into. Instead, I crept back into the holly bush behind me which I knew was a mistake as soon as I felt the prickles brush against my skin. I felt like I had a million needles stuck into my body.

"Lyla?" I heard a familiar voice call from the top of the garden path. I had no idea how I was supposed to explain to Lawrie how I ended up camped in a holly bush in his garden. I didn't think that our friendship had reached such a level that a conversation like that could have been considered normal. I stood there for a minute unsure if I should just emerge from the holly bush and scare the life out of him or if I should text him that I'm on my way to buy me some time and find a way to crawl back to the front gate.

In the end, I settled for the first option and slowly I emerged from the bushes. Lawrie had been pacing around looking for me, so I turned around and headed towards him. He saw me as I approached, my hair was completely bedraggled. After all, I had literally just been dragged through a bush. Lawrie looked completely taken aback that I'd just appeared out of the depths of the night, but he didn't say anything. Instead, he just stood there rooted on the spot.

It wasn't until I was a couple feet in front of him that I noticed it- a livid purple bruise, carved along his left cheek. The bruise looked angry and violent like it was ready for a fight itself. I hadn't quite put two and two together until that moment. The shouting, the crash, the silence. *Oh God oh God oh God.* I didn't know exactly what I'd heard occurring in that house, but I knew from the state of Lawrie's face that it was bad, astronomically bad.

"Oh my God. Shit. Lawrie are you okay?" I felt myself blurt as I approached him. I had a sudden urge to trace the line of the bruise with my finger, but I immediately thought better of it. Lawrie was just my friend, a concept which for some reason I couldn't quite seem to understand.

"Yes Lyla, I'm fine." He said irritably. If I was smart, I probably shouldn't have pushed it, but clearly, I wasn't.

"You don't look fine; I heard an argument. I didn't mean to overhear anything, but I couldn't help it. Was that your dad? What happened?" Lawrie gave me a look which told me that he didn't want to be having this conversation with me then or possibly ever.

"I said I'm fine Lyla. Can we just go?" It didn't seem as if he was going to open up to me anytime soon, so I just nodded and offered him a weak smile.

"Yes, but I've no idea where we're going, Lawrie." It occurred to me at that moment that I hadn't really thought this plan through. I'd agreed to meet Lawrie in the middle of the night, and I had no idea where we were going. It was starting to sound like the plot of some horror film.

"I know a place. It's not far from here." Lawrie replied. He seemed freakishly calm based on what had just occurred a few minutes earlier.

"Okay then," I said, and I trailed after him as he strode down the path towards the dimly lit street.

We walked in complete silence; the only sound was the faint buzz of the flickering streetlights and a dog's hollow cry from far away. I had no idea what to say to him, so I just kept my mouth shut. The silence hung sharply between us. We trudged up the path towards the obstinate looking hill which loomed over Jade Town. Some locals used to spread a story that behind the hill was the end of the Earth, others used to say that behind it was Australia. One truth came out of those stories, which was that the people of Jade Town didn't tend to ever leave the village so for all they knew Australia could well have been on the other side of the hill.

Eventually, we reached the summit of the hill. I had been up here a couple of times, and the view was truly divine, especially at night. A glistening array of lights sparkled below us like a blanket weaved from strands of pure liquid gold. I felt like the king of the world when I sat up there looking down upon tiny ants fluttering about their lives.

"Come on." Lawrie said to me as he turned off towards the rows of trees to our left. I followed him and we weaved between the stuck-out branches from a collection of trees. He stopped abruptly under a particularly large tree, and I had to break so fast that I almost tripped over him completely.

"Up here's the place. Come on Lyla." I huffed out a nervous breath. He wanted me to climb a massive tree in the pitch black. The last time I'd climbed a tree back when I was about nine, I'd fallen, and I broke my arm in two places. So, I was rather reluctant to repeat the experience especially in the middle of the night.

"I'm good, thanks. I think I might just hang here; I've got a nice view; I wouldn't want to spoil it."

Lawrie, who had already scaled halfway up the tree, looked down and smirked at me.

"Why, are you scared or something, Lyla?" He said it in such a smug, condescending way that I felt my blood boil. Lawrie knew just how to push my buttons and patronising me was a sure-fire way to get me riled up. I always liked to believe that I was strong, as capable as the next person, I certainly didn't want to be perceived as weak.

"No, I'm not scared, Lawrie, so please shut up." I scolded but I was smiling. Lawrie continued climbing until he reached the top of the tree, and he sat in amongst the branches.

"Come on then Lyla." He called down to me. Then, "It's not hard, don't worry, plus I'm here to help you." I didn't know how Lawrie could actually help me from where he was sitting but in spite of that I trusted him. So, I clambered up the tree and to my surprise it was easier than I thought. The tree was broad and safe. I reached the top and sat next to Lawrie, there was barely a foot between us.

"Told you I could do it." I said, reflecting his smugness from earlier.

"I like to come up here and think." He said with his eyes fixed on the wide-open space of glittering radiance below.

"Well, it really is a pretty place. You've been living here for like a year and somehow, you've discovered better thinking places than I have. Mine is by Jade Town lake but I think everyone has the same idea as me, so it's always a little too crowded for my liking."

It was weird to think that two years before I'd never even heard of Lawrie Hartwell. At that point, it felt as if I'd known him forever. So much had happened in those two years, and I had no idea just how much was about to happen. I had no idea that just a year later our small village would-be front-page news.

"He was trying to hurt my brother." Lawrie revealed suddenly. He had opened up in front of me as if I had somehow cracked the code to

Pandora's Box. I knew that it probably wouldn't last long, so I had to take my chance to ask him what was going on.

"Who, Lawrie? Do you mean your dad?" I asked him. His eyes were firmly fixed on the sprawl of lights below.

"He was trying to hurt him." Lawrie repeated like a stuck record.

"Why was he trying to hurt him?" I pressed. "You know that you can talk to me about anything Lawrie, I'll always listen to you I promise." Lawrie sighed and stretched his hand out, so his pinkie finger brushed mine. I wasn't quite sure if it were intentional or not.

"He's a monster. He gets in these wild drunk rages, and he just attacks us; he treats us as if we're just punching bags that he can beat the shit out of, and Rory can't defend himself yet." Lawrie revealed to me. Hearing this information put me in a state of shock. There was a stark difference between thinking something exists and actually hearing that it does. Even my suspicions about Lawrie's family hadn't been nearly as extreme as he described them to be. None of the rumours that had circulated about the Hartwell's had been anything like that.

"Oh my God Lawrie, that's awful. I'm so sorry." I spluttered out.

He turned to look at me then for the first time since we had left his house. His face displayed something akin to physical pain as though his dad had just physically struck him. The livid purple bruise on his cheek gleaned in the pale moon light. I remember thinking how honourable it was that Lawrie took a hit to protect his brother and I wondered how often this had happened. I thought back to a couple of instances where Lawrie had come to school with an injury that he blamed on a bike incident or a fall at the hospital. It occurred to me that the signs had been there all along, such as Lawrie's obsession with wearing long sleeved shirts even in the midst of summer. But I had been too wrapped up thinking about my own life and my mum to even notice them.

Then, as quickly as he had opened up, he shut me out again.

"It's okay." Lawrie said to me surprisingly and alarmingly nonchalant as if we'd been talking about the weather and not his abusive father. Unlike Lawrie, I couldn't let this go easily.

"No, It's not okay. Something really needs to be done about this. Have you tried calling the police or social services?" It wasn't quite the night of teenage rebellion that I had been expecting but it was better because Lawrie had felt confident enough to confide in me something so horrific. Despite the depravity of the news, it showed that he trusted me, and I trusted him with my whole entire heart.

Lawrie sighed as if I were simply being an inconvenience.

"Look Lyla, it really is fine. I'm dealing with it. You know, it doesn't happen that often and I doubt that the police would even care let alone do anything. It's easy to try and suggest advice when you're on the outside, but you don't know what it's like being in the thick of it." He completely backtracked on what he had said to me just a couple of minutes before.

Whatever window I had of him opening up to me was most certainly closed at that point. I was sure he'd shut himself off from me now and If I knew one thing about Lawrie Hartwell it was that he was mightily stubborn. Once he got an idea into his head, you would need nothing short of a miracle for him to change his mind. It was one of his best and his worst qualities. I probably should've pushed him; I should've helped to resolve the situation then and there but I was tired and in no mood to fight with Lawrie so I did the worst thing that I could have done...

nothing.

"Okay, whatever you say but if it gets worse, please just think about contacting the police. You and Rory shouldn't be living with a monster like that." I knew straight away that I had hit a nerve because Lawrie physically tensed up in front of me.

"Yeah, Lyla, like you know what the hell is good for me and my brother. I didn't know that you were an expert on child protection." I hated Lawrie when he was like that. No matter what you said, he would just get angrier and angrier and more and more confrontational. His anger was a part of him, like a monster which laid dormant with one eye open ready to pounce. He had a short fuse and sometimes it terrified me.

"I'm sorry. I didn't mean to make you mad; I was just trying to help. I'm being stupid, I'll stop." I fiddled with my hair, I suddenly felt awkward as if Lawrie and I barely knew each other, like I had no right to know what he'd just told me.

After a couple moments of painful silence, Lawrie offered me a smile which made my insides break down and turn to mush.

"No, Lyla, thank you really. I know that you're trying to help, and I appreciate that, but it really is okay, as I said I can deal with it, and I'm dealing with it for Rory and me both. You're so kind and helpful and are always wanting to do what's best for people and that's why I lo..." He stopped himself at the last moment before it all came tumbling out. I nodded to show him that I understood exactly what he was trying to say. His eyes lingered on mine for a moment too long before he broke eye contact and leaned back confidently and fell right out of the tree.

He hit the ground with a thud and there was an eerie silence. I peered down at him on the ground, he didn't move. "Oh my God. Lawrie are you okay?" I shouted down. My heart kicked up inside my chest and my breathing shallowed. I had never had a panic attack before, but I was sure that I was on the verge of having one. My whole body went rigid in response to the shock, and everything seemed out of focus somehow more and less intense all at once. Millions of thoughts raced through my mind: *What if he's seriously hurt? What am I going to tell my dad? Will his dad literally kill me?*

That was when I heard laughing reach me from the ground below. It started off quiet, but the sound grew and grew. Lawrie sprung up from the ground and looked up at me mid laugh. A wave of relief flooded over me, and I started to laugh too. "It's not funny Lawrie, that's the precise reason why I'm scared of trees." It was quite a fall. I'm surprised that he didn't break anything, but it was also the funniest thing that had happened to me for a while.

"Really, trees? I don't think that is a literal fear, Lyla."

"Yes, it is, it's called Dendrophobia. Look it up." My dad had made me learn that because apparently, he thought that naming the fear would help me to combat it. I often had to remind him that I wasn't actually scared of trees themselves but rather falling out of them. I had a fear of falling- falling apart, falling over, falling in love. Somehow, I didn't think that Lawrie was going to understand that either.

"Wow. It has a proper name and everything now I am impressed. Is there like a club that you can join to combat your fear? Trees anonymous or something?" He sniggered.

"Trees anonymous would suggest that the person had some kind of addiction to trees not a fear, so shut up." I laughed and swung my legs in front of me. That was something which I regretted straight away as I felt myself wobble on the top of the tree.

"Easy tiger, looks like we better get you down from there before you fall out too." Lawrie chuckled, noticing me wobbling precariously on the branch. "That will really damage your recovery with trees anonymous."

"I am not a tree addict!" I protested and crossed my arms. I didn't want to let Lawrie win, we were childish like that sometimes, we were both competitive as hell and we didn't like to give in easily.

"You can't make me come down there." I called down to him and looked down at his golden mass of hair. It was a total mistake because I felt my head whir as I realised how far up, I actually was for the first time. Lawrie may not have broken anything, but I knew that if I fell, my arm would definitely end up in a cast like it did that time when I was nine, and perhaps both of my legs too.

"That's fine with me. I'll just go, you can stay up here all night. I might come back in the morning for you, but I have a shift at the hospital, so it isn't likely. Hopefully you can find your way down Lyla." He began to retreat down the hill at the pace of a snail. I knew that he wouldn't actually leave me there but the fear of being stuck up on that tree all night got the better of me.

"Okay, okay you win. Now please help me down from this tree before I fall to my death or something." Lawrie paused for a moment where he was and then turned round to face me. I could feel the smile on his face rather than see it. Lawrie loved to win at just about everything.

"Well, I could help you down, but then again I could also just leave you up there." He pretended to consider it for a moment. He was torturing me, and he knew it. In response I let out the most ear-splitting scream that I could muster. It worked because Lawrie caved and climbed up the base of the tree to offer me his hand.

"Fine lady, I'll help you, just stop screaming, will you? You'll wake up the whole of Jade Town." I smiled in triumph and shuffled down the tree so that I could be near enough to take Lawrie's outstretched palm.

When I was near enough, Lawrie grabbed my hand and helped me down. A jolt of electricity buzzed up and down my spine due to the contact. My stomach became a home to a cornucopia of butterflies. It was completely indescribable how Lawrie made me feel. Whenever we were together, it was as if we were the last two people on Earth. Nothing else mattered to me aside from the fact that he was here with me.

It was at that moment that I realised he was still clutching onto my hand and his steely blue eyes were fixed on me like... well, like I was the only other person on Earth. We stood there without dropping our gaze for what felt like an eternity. Stood there in the milky twilight, it was as if we were just properly seeing each other for the first time. As if before that moment, we hadn't truly been looking at each other, we were just coexisting. Breathing the same air but travelling in entirely different circles.

Eventually Lawrie spoke and his voice was so quiet. "All I could think about tonight when everything was happening with my dad, was you Lyla. All I've been able to think about for the last two God-damn years has been you. I can't get you off my mind Lyla, no matter how hard I try to."

"Lawrie, I..." Words escaped me, I wanted to tell him that he was all I'd been able to think about. I wanted to tell him how much he meant to me, but my feeble frame couldn't utter a word to him.

"Shit. I don't want to cross a line here because you mean so much to me, and I don't know what I'd do without you now. But you are so incredibly beautiful I don't think you even realise it. Everything you do, everything that you are is just beautiful and I've been trying to ignore it for the longest time. I've been trying to be there for you throughout everything that has happened this year thinking that if I keep trying one day, I'll finally be able to ignore it. I can't seem to ignore it anymore though." His cheeks flamed; we were most certainly crossing a line. We were traversing a road we couldn't come back from, but I didn't care.

"I've gone too far, haven't I?" Lawrie stepped back and let out a strained laugh, running a hand over his face. "I've ruined everything, I'm so stupid. I'm sorry Lyla I shouldn't have gone there; I should have just left this as a nice night between friends. Now I fear nothing's ever going to be the same between us. Please, forget I said anything if you can. I guess I just thought maybe you felt the same but…"

"No, I'm glad you said it." I finally had the courage to say. He walked closer to me and took his hand in mine, the warmth felt like home. He felt like home to me.

"You really mean that?" He smiled; his blue eyes sparkled even in the low light.

"Yes Lawrie, I really mean it."

I nodded, and that's when he leaned in to kiss me. Every nerve ending in my body glowed, everything around us blurred. Being in his arms felt right, I felt as if I could finally cope with everything that had happened the past two years and everything that was going to happen from that moment onwards. I knew he wasn't going to fix all my problems, but for a moment it felt as though he could shelter me from every storm.

As we broke apart and looked down at the town sleeping beneath our feet, the heavens opened. Thick icy drops cascaded all around us, blurring our vision of the golden village below. We both laughed despite it all, despite our sodden clothing, despite our waterlogged shoes. The rain brings something magical to a situation like that, it was as if God was sending an omen, as if we were being warned of what was to come, of what our pairing would mean for Jade Town.

Whether you believe in divine intervention or omens, the rain that night signified something, which is likely why I remember it so clearly. Perhaps it signified a clean slate, washing away the pain of the past. That night, I felt content. That night I felt safe. That night, that one kiss set Lawrie and I onto the path we had perhaps already started on two years before. That night set Lawrie and I onto a path of mutual destruction.

17 YEARS OLD

"What's the stark difference between a prokaryote and a eukaryote?" Our rather giant-like and terrifying teacher Mr Roberts bellowed at our class. Biology had dragged on and on that afternoon. It got to a point where I couldn't imagine what my life was like before I was sat in that exact chair in Biology class. It was truly hell to be sat in Biology, but it was a good option to take. My dad had kept reminding me that it kept my options open. I had no idea what I wanted to do with my life after I left the state of purgatory that the country liked to call 'School' so I just took subjects that would look good. Plus, there was one upside...

Lawrie sat at the other end of the class scrawling something onto a piece of paper. We had been practically inseparable since our little midnight rendezvous last year. I was worried at first that it may have been awkward between us, as if we had crossed the threshold into something new and subsequently broken any friendship we may have had. Nothing however had been awkward, we just seemed to slot into place as if it were always meant to happen. We had been dating for close to a year and it was easy and right, I had even managed to get used to the rather not-so subtle abuse Clara had subjected me to as I'd taken the one thing she wanted and couldn't have.

Speaking of the devil, Clara Yale was sitting directly next to me. Her sleek raven hair was tied up into a perfect messy bun. I have never been able to understand the girls who could make a messy bun into a fashion statement without it looking like a dead rodent perched on their head. Clara Yale was of course just blessed with perfect hair as well as perfect everything else. She had everything she could have ever wanted except one tiny thing- she didn't get the guy. Clara had evidently been pining over Lawrie and practically throwing herself at him the past couple of years so when news broke that Lawrie had resisted Clara's charms and dared to choose me, she wasn't very pleased to say the least. Not just displeased, she was furious, and she had been trying to make my life a living hell since then. I guess she was hoping that one day I would have had enough and sworn off men for the rest of my life and moved to a convent somewhere. Unfortunately for her, that day never came.

Clara's torrent of abuse directed towards me had started off rather mild. She would shoot me horrid glances and give me the occasional shove in the hallway, but I could deal with that stuff and laugh it off. When she found that it wasn't working, she had upped the ante and had started to deliberately sabotage me in class. She put graffiti on my desk and blamed it on me; she had deliberately written a really bad essay and labelled it with my name; she had told our English Literature teacher that I was bullying her in class. I was shocked at the lengths that this girl would go to because I ended up dating the guy that she liked, and most of all I was shocked how completely juvenile she was. We were both turning eighteen that summer and she was acting as if we were still six years old. That same six-year-old who had all the shiny toys but wanted desperately to have the one tatty one I was holding.

Clara amongst others seemed to be under the impression that Lawrie had an entirely perfect life, that everything came easily and naturally to him. The idea that he came from a nice family and would go on to become a world-class surgeon with a wealth of income and a perfect family. This was perhaps the mask he was presenting to the world, but I had begun to peek underneath it, I recognised the hurt and emptiness inside. I knew the Lawrie who had lost his mother, I knew the Lawrie who was scared to see his father every single day. Lawrie and I understood each other more than we understood anyone else, we were individuals of a shared experience, something Clara would never be able to understand.

That day, sat in biology class, Clara had been surprisingly quiet- well except for her answering all of Mr Robert's questions in a tone which could curdle milk:

"It's obvious, isn't it? A prokaryote is a single celled organism, and a Eukaryote is a multicellular organism." Clara called in response to Mr Roberts. Mr Roberts sighed and rubbed a hand over his sweaty, lined forehead.

"Yes, well done Clara. Now I think you've answered enough for today. You should let someone else have a go so I can see if anyone else has learnt anything." The class erupted with laughter in response. When in a class with Clara Yale, there was no real point in being there. You were about as useful as a chocolate fireguard. That was something which our class had become increasingly aware of so any chance to ridicule Clara Yale (even if it were only miniscule) was greatly appreciated by almost everyone there.

My eyes were fixed firmly on the clock which didn't appear to be moving. When I was a kid, I always wanted to be able to freeze time and knowing my luck I bet I had suddenly been blessed with that ability at the worst time possible.

A hand tapped me on the shoulder, and I looked around to see that it was Roman Huxley. Roman was even more of a rather arrogant excuse for a human being at eighteen years old than he was as a child. He was the most athletic kid at school and rather intelligent and that combination led him to believe that he was a greater human than everybody else. He used to get everyone to call him 'The King' which I always thought was totally absurd and egotistical and I never understood why people actually did. I knew that Lawrie and he were friends, although I had no idea why you would want to hang around with someone who called themselves 'The King' it all sounded rather infantile to me, and I was sure that I'd heard Lawrie vent his frustrations about Roman on countless occasions. The sad part is that Roman could have been a good guy. He was pretty smart, but he acted as if his head was made from air, plus he was disgustingly misogynistic. He believed that every girl fell at his feet and that he was entitled to everyone which often made me want to scream and punch his smug face. He was a worse version of my snotty cousin Tristan, which was really saying something.

"Lover boy over there wanted me to give you this." Roman sneered. He passed me a folded piece of lined paper. So, that was what Lawrie was scrawling.

"Thanks, Roman." I turned back around actually astonished that Roman hadn't taken the opportunity to make a disgusting remark like he always did.

"You know if you ever get bored of giving it to him. I'm always here Lyla to satisfy each of your needs." *Ah, of course.* How could I ever have expected Roman Huxley to be even a slightly decent human being? I rolled my eyes and turned to face him, my face burning with frustration. I wasn't really spurring for a fight, but I couldn't just let it go exactly.

"Well Roman, maybe if you actually focused on becoming a decent human being then you wouldn't have to be begging for a girl to go out with you." That shut him up completely, he just gaped at me, and I turned back around in triumph. People never really stood up to him, I don't think his parents ever told him 'No'.

Now, Roman works at the tiny little convenience store back in Jade Town, he is a recovering alcoholic, and he will tell anyone who listened about how he was destined to be a football player but retained an injury after he left school, an injury that he has no proof of, and legend has it he is still begging women to go out with him, but he has less of an appeal these days. This of course must have been devastating for Roman's overbearing parents as I knew for a fact that Dean Huxley had always attempted to push Roman into taking over his publishing company and becoming the next mayor of Jade Town.

I feel that it is important to tell you a bit more about the Huxleys as the information will prove important later on in my story. Dean Huxley grew up in Jade Town in the same year as my father and they were old friends turned rivals a little like my situation with Clara. After school, Dean became something of a success undoubtedly pushed into it by his own parents who my dad had told me were always overly concerned about his future. Dean met and married Jeanie who was somewhat of an enigma for the residents of Jade Town- she was an American model who traded her life and successful career to move to Jade Town with Dean. Undoubtedly, people questioned why she would leave her success and move to the middle of nowhere, but it later transpired that she had fallen pregnant, and Dean and Jeanie married quickly before the birth of their son Roman. On the outside it looked like the Huxley's had the perfect life, two parents and their darling son but of course it is easy to put up a façade and present your life in a certain way. As you will discover in time, the Huxleys like many of the residents in Jade Town were hiding deep secrets beneath their façade...

I opened the crumpled-up note and beamed down at the contents. Three words were scrawled onto the paper in his smudged handwriting, just a collection of letters perhaps, just three singular words but which created so much weight when put together. Three singular words which had the ability to make me smile broadly as I glanced down at them.

I was so distracted, smiling like a lunatic at the note that I didn't realise that Clara's glassy green eyes were peering over my shoulder surreptitiously at the note. Oh No. Clara had been surprisingly sweet to me recently, as sweet as a sociopath maybe, but still. The last thing that I needed was to give her more ammunition in her little war against me. I quickly crumpled up the note and placed it into my coat pocket. I hadn't been quick enough though.

"So, he's sending you notes now huh? How adorable." She asked mildly. I'd known Clara Yale since we were little kids, so I knew that underneath her cool façade she was probably thinking about ripping my head off with her own two bare hands. Although I hate to admit it, Clara and I were once best friends when we were kids, she was my first ever friend really. I spent countless hours playing around in her parent's enormous, luscious green garden or playing dress up in her bedroom. Clara had the biggest house in the whole village- It was a gorgeous pale pink colour and I always dreamed of owning a house just like hers one day.

Our friendship ended the day that Quinn Vermont arrived in town. We were about nine years old; it was just after my tree accident, so I had my arm in a bright magenta cast. I felt so self-conscious about it and Clara would often tease me about it, but I remember that Quinn came over to me during class and doodled all over it to make me feel better. We were friends ever since that moment. Clara, however, took an immediate dislike to Quinn and then in return she took a dislike to me, and I never went around to her house again.

Ever since then, she had somehow decided that I was her number one enemy even though I had no real idea why she hated me so much, and that was before I started dating the guy that she liked. At seventeen, she was so unbelievably spoiled and cruel. Now though, I just feel sorry for her. I feel so unbelievably sorry for what happened to her...

Usually, I would've tried to appease Clara in some way, downplay what was between Lawrie and I so that she would feel better about herself. But, for once, I had had enough. At that moment, I was fed up with Clara always getting what she wanted, I was fed up with her being able to trample over people like dirt on her shoe. So, I said-

"Yes Clara. Lawrie and I are dating, and we have been for a while. I don't know why you have got it into your head that you are going to scare me off and suddenly Lawrie will fall into your arms. Because Clara, Lawrie can see straight through you, just like I can. So, why don't you just give it up and leave me alone?"

Clara was stunned into silence, I normally wasn't someone who would stand up for herself or put others in their place, but I had had enough. Her pretty features contorted into an expression of disgust. If I hadn't done so before, I really got under her skin at that moment. Perhaps I never should have said it, perhaps If I hadn't then the callous events of the year wouldn't have occurred...

Seconds later, Clara yanked out a section of her raven hair and let out a high pitch scream. The whole class turned around to gape at us. I felt everyone's eyes burning holes into me.

"Sir, Lyla jut went insane, I told her that she couldn't look at my notes because well she should have been listening instead of sending dumb little notes across the class and she just went for me, she pulled out this section of my hair. Look." She held up the clump of hair that she was clutching so that Mr Roberts could see. I had to control myself from actually starting on her and slapping her right around her smug face. Gosh, Clara literally acted like a three-year-old having a tantrum because I stole her most precious toy.

Mr Roberts actually sighed out loud and rolled his eyes. "Come on girls, I thought I was teaching sixth formers and not pre-schoolers. I don't get paid nearly enough to be dealing with this idiocy." In response, Clara shot him a death glare. God, you don't understand how annoying that girl could be. Her parents mollycoddled her from birth. She was an only child and her parent's little angel bestowed upon them from the heavens.

"Surely Sir, your job is to sort out bullying within your class. I think you should remove Lyla; she is the one causing the disruption. It will be best for everyone else if she just leaves. Then I can get on and actually do my work. She is completely out of control, frankly I think she should be expelled from this school because she is a danger to other students."

Mr Robert's was right, I felt as though we were transported back to being six years old again when both of us would argue over Barbie dolls and who got the last piece of dessert. Surprise, surprise, Clara always won those arguments.

Sure, Clara was a brat of the highest degree, but she really didn't deserve what happened to her; nobody deserves the fate that befell Clara Yale. Sat in Biology class that afternoon I was completely oblivious to the events that were about to follow in the coming days. I had no idea that life in Jade Town would be completely different and unrecognisable, and that nothing in this idyllic little village would ever be able to be normal again.

"Alright then Miss Yale, if it will stop this absurd distraction, then Miss Kingsley please leave the classroom and you can go to the headteacher's office and explain just why you've disrupted her morning." Mr Roberts clearly couldn't be bothered to deal with the issue and in all honesty, I couldn't be bothered to argue. Clara had messed up my life enough that I knew arguing with her would be pointless. I sighed and collected up my stuff. I could feel the eyes of every class member burning through my skin into my skull. I could feel Clara's smug expression.

The room was deadly silent as I walked to the door aside from Roman Huxley's sniggering. As soon as the door whipped shut behind me the whole class erupted into fits of laughter.

****

Later that night, I was sprawled on the couch in our tiny living room ranting my frustrations to Lawrie, my snow-coloured cat Orchid purring at our feet.

"My God, she's so annoying. I haven't even done anything to her and yet she acts like I'm the devil. I swear she's made it her life's mission to destroy me or something."

Our couch was close to breaking point. Honestly, I think I was only one thread away from sitting on the floor. Still, my mum had bought it second-hand at a charity auction back when I was about seven and ever since she left us, we had all been very reluctant to get rid of any metaphorical piece of her.

"Yeah, I mean don't get me wrong, what she did was cruel, but I don't think anybody actually believed it and frankly we've got more on our minds than the current status of your infantile feud with Clara Yale." Lawrie was wearing a frayed faded blue hoodie I remember which made his eyes look very, very blue.

"We don't have a feud! That's the problem. It's completely a one-sided feud on her part, she completely humiliated me in front of everyone just because I dared to stand up to her for once. I would be happy to just live my life without ever talking to her again. I swear to God, my life would just be so much easier if she just didn't exist anymore." I sighed with frustration, throwing my head back.

Lawrie nodded and inched closer towards me.

"Can we stop talking about this now? Don't worry about Clara, Lyla. Karma will probably get her in the end. She'll get what she deserves, I'm sure of that." He reassured me.

"You think so? I can't imagine anything ever going wrong for Clara, everything always seems to go her way."

"I'm positive Lyla. Remember I'm on your side, always. I would do anything for you Lyla, do you know that? I will do anything for you Lyla." Lawrie smiled his characteristic smile and leaned in close. He kissed me there on the couch until the frustrations of the day melted away.

****

A few days later, I woke up to the sound of my phone buzzing uncontrollably on my nightstand. Dull rays of sun were streaming into my tiny room, casting shadows on the electric blue walls. I leaned over and forced my eyes open. It was barely morning. I had been obsessed with the sea when I was younger and I'd begged my parents to let me paint my room ocean blue, eventually they'd agreed.

My clock informed me that it was just after 6AM. There was at least a dozen missed calls and messages on my phone, and one from Nate right at the top of the screen which simply said '**TURN ON THE NEWS**' in block capitals. I knew that it must've been important because Nate was away at university millions of miles away and he rarely messaged me anymore, he was probably too busy having fun to check in on his little sister.

I rushed downstairs to turn on our TV and found that my dad was already sitting there with a cup of coffee in one hand so strong that I could smell it from the top of the stairs. He must've heard me come up behind him because he turned around and patted down the frayed seat next to him on the couch.

"Lyla babe, you might want to sit down and see this." I followed his advice and sat down next to him.

As soon as I fixed my eyes on the screen, I jumped out of my skin in horror. I felt completely nauseous, as if someone had lent inside me and twisted my internal organs, hard, or had punched me directly in the stomach and caused extreme internal bleeding. The news reporter drove on in the same monotonous tone seemingly unconcerned that he had just turned my and every resident in Jade Town's life upside down…

"Jade Town resident, seventeen-year-old Clara Yale has been reported as missing. She was last seen around 72 hours ago on Wednesday evening leaving her home at about 9:00PM. She is around 5 foot 6 and she has long straight

black hair and green eyes- If you have any information, you believe could assist the investigation, please contact the Lyntonshire police..."

I felt like I was going to throw up all over the floor or faint and never get up again, I felt like I wanted to cry my eyes out until it burned. After all, she'd been my first ever friend. I can't even really describe how horrifying it was to see that she was missing. Clara never went anywhere without telling her parents first, she was an angel of a child really. If Clara's parents had no idea where she had been for three days then it was clear that something horrible had happened to her, something completely despicably evil...

All at once, the reality of Clara's situation overwhelmed me in tsunami waves so great that they could wash away the whole of Jade Town in a matter of moments. I began to sob uncontrollably.

"Hey Lyla, girl, it's okay." My dad pulled me into a hug, the scent of his familiar musty aftershave closed in around me, he was the only person in the world who made me feel completely safe and secure. Being in his arms transported me back to being a little carefree child. At that time, we only had each other. Nate was away and mum wasn't there anymore, He needed me just as much as I needed him. We sat there on the couch for hours, we didn't utter a word to each other the whole time, letting the news wash over us.

I knew that Lawrie was working at the hospital that morning so more than likely wouldn't have heard the news. I decided to go and intercept him to tell him before he got home that afternoon. I grabbed the keys and got into the car that my aunt Julie had gifted to me for my seventeenth birthday (it was much to the contempt of my dad who thought that he should be the one giving me important items like my first car). She'd initially bought it for Tristan, but at the last minute he decided that he wanted a silver model instead of a black one, so the car was a little masculine for me, but I was just grateful that I had one. I still wasn't a competent driver but luckily, I lived in one of the quietest neighbourhoods imaginable.

We really were a close-knit community; everybody had known me since the day I was born. It was rare that we ever got a new resident in the village, Jade Town was like a sinkhole. People were born there, and they lived in the exact same house until they died there and passed it onto the next generation. Before my father, my grandfather had lived in our house and his father before him and so on, our house had been owned by the Kingsley's most likely since it had been built. I always used to think that it was kind of morbid but that was just the way of life over there. That was why everybody was so intrigued when the Hartwell's rolled into town for the first time three years earlier.

I looked down at the clock in my car as I pulled up outside the hospital- 12.30pm. Lawrie's shift would have just finished. The coast was completely clear though, besides from old Mrs Wilma who was being helped across the street by a bright eyed, fresh faced looking nurse. I hadn't been back to the hospital since the previous year. I hated coming here, it was a reminder of everything that had happened and everything that I'd lost. Normally, I would directly change my route in and out of town so that I could avoid passing by it, but I felt that I needed Lawrie here with me, but one thing was clear- Lawrie wasn't here.

The minutes ticked by, and it became increasingly obvious that Lawrie wasn't at the hospital so after about half an hour of waiting, I put the car into reverse and headed up the long winding road towards his house. I got about halfway up the road when I saw him outside the village's café. He stood there laughing animatedly and another girl was by his side.

Immediately, I felt sick to my stomach. Although I had no reason to doubt Lawrie's loyalty, I'd been completely broken down by the news of today and seeing him with someone else really hurt me, so I did something totally irrational, something that I never normally would have done. I parked the car up the street, got out and headed in the direction of Lawrie and his mystery girl.

I didn't recognise her at all, she wasn't a resident of Jade Town. She was tall, with blonde hair and ice blue eyes. The worst part was that by the way she was smiling and laughing, she honestly looked like a warm and friendly person, it made her a lot harder to hate. The way that she was laughing so effortlessly with Lawrie, my Lawrie made my skin crawl.

They saw me turn the corner as soon as I did. I have never been stealthy, and I think I was too busy staring at her to realise that they had noticed me. Lawrie's bright blue eyes widened, overwhelmed, like a deer caught in the headlights. *Good* I thought *Let him squirm a bit.* My heart began to beat frantically inside my chest, the rush of adrenaline that had coursed through me and caused me to approach them had completely faded, like a lighter which lit for a second before running out of juice. I considered running back to my car and hiding out under my duvet all day long eating ice cream and attempting to forget that any of this had ever happened but that really would have made me look pathetic and I wanted to look good in front of Lawrie's mystery girl.

"Hi, what're you doing here?"

Confusion was evident in Lawrie's voice, I picked up a hint of frustration too. I felt as though he were scolding me for being there, for seeing him with whoever this girl was. The girl in question tucked her blonde locks behind her ears and smiled. Gosh they looked perfect together, like a storybook couple who would live happily ever after together with two annoyingly perfect children and a friendly golden retriever. I didn't like this one bit.

When Lawrie saw that I wasn't going to answer, he changed tact-

"This is Ally Tinsley, she's an old friend of mine from my hometown." Lawrie provided likely in response to my bemused expression.

Oh, of course they were old friends, likely the kind of friends who had a history, one that no one else could compete with.

"Oh hi. I thought you were working this morning, I came by the hospital, but you weren't there. I guess I found you." I said rather defensively, crossing my arms across my chest. I wanted to make him feel guilty, I wanted to hurt him.

Lawrie didn't answer me, instead Ally set her cool blue eyes on me.

"Oh, hi so sorry, It's my fault. My parents and I came into town this weekend as we wanted to see where the Hartwell's ended up. We heard that they were in the middle of nowhere and I mean this is pretty close to it right?" Ally laughed; she had one of those seriously annoyingly cute girly laughs. I had no reason to hate Ally, after all every friend of Lawrie's should've been a friend of mine, right? I just hated the way that he had neglected to tell me about her completely and the fact that she was there in my town.

"Okay, so you're the reason Lawrie lied about being at work, I see." I said back in retort without even thinking. I had to remind myself to be the bigger person, I'd hated Clara and where had that gotten her. I couldn't expend any more of my energy disliking someone.

Immediately, Lawrie blanched. His eyes clouded over with what I interpreted as anger.

He's angry at me I thought.

He lied to me about where he was, yet he has the audacity to be angry at me.

"Why, are you keeping me a secret, Carson? Is this your girlfriend or something?" Ally laughed again, and I realised I hadn't introduced myself to her, for all she knew I could've just been any girl that Lawrie knew.

If he's even told her about me, that is.

The traitorous thought fluttered through my mind. I didn't know why she called him 'Carson' or why the name made him look so flustered, I guessed it was some kind of private joke between them- one I'd never be able to get in on.

"Sorry I'm being rude. Hi Ally, it's so nice to meet you. I'm Lyla." I went to outstretch my hand and then immediately thought better of it, so I stood there swaying slightly on the spot as I watched the cogs turn in Ally's mind. My name clearly conjured up something for her.

A second later, her face illuminated with recognition.

"Oh wow, so you're the famous Lyla? Lawrie's told me so much about you."

I stole a glance at Lawrie who had been uncharacteristically quiet since I'd turned up, he looked embarrassed like Ally had revealed he had some tropical disease or an obsession for country music.

At least Lawrie had told her about me, and Ally didn't seem to me someone who would pursue a guy with a girlfriend. I wondered; however, just how much Lawrie had told Ally about me. This girl had something almost ethereal about her, everything about her seemed perfect. I was sure that I didn't want someone like that to know about my life the past few years, to know just how vulnerable I was. To know how I lost my mother and how I had wished to never see Clara again and now...

It hit me like an off the scale seismic wave at that moment. It felt as if it was all happening to someone else entirely, like I was watching a movie about a girl who looked and sounded like me but had a considerably more fucked up life than my own. Suddenly, I remember, my whole body became weak and floppy, I could barely even stand. Clara was missing and nobody had any idea where she was or if she would even turn up again. I don't really remember a lot of that afternoon- it is all a haze in my memory. Maybe I blacked out, I'm not sure.

All I remember next was being sat on the familiar sagging couch in my living room with Lawrie by my side.

"Hey Lyla, it's okay, don't worry about it." Lawrie was as calm as the early morning still of Jade Town Lake. I thought at the time that he was just holding it together for me. He was holding a cup of sweet tea which he placed into my hands. "Here, drink this, it will help you with the shock."

I looked up into Lawrie's sharp blue eyes. "Do you think she's okay, Lawrie?... Do you think they'll find her?"

Lawrie's brow suddenly furrowed, and I thought I saw that same fog of anger that I saw earlier, cloud over his cobalt eyes.

Just as quickly as it had appeared, the fog cleared and his eyes were the same as ever, once again still as the surface of Jade Town Lake in the spring.

"Lyla, unless I'm mistaken, I thought you hated the girl. All you did was complain about her. You said you'd be happy to never see her again." That shut me up, somehow, I knew that Lawrie was never going to understand how I was feeling and how guilt was gnawing at my ribs, even though her disappearance had nothing to do with me.

Instead, I sat up and took his hands in mine. "Ally seems nice, how do you know her?" I said, I realised, more out of jealousy than anything else- I needed to know what this girl's deal was, why had Lawrie never told me about her?

"Ally and I go way back." He explained. "Her dad worked at the same law firm as my father, we practically grew up as brother and sister."

So, Lawrie's dad used to be a lawyer. It was interesting to hear him talk like that because Lawrie never spoke about his father, or the reason why they moved to Jade Town. All I knew, aged seventeen, was that Lawrie's mum had died in a car accident and his family then moved to

Jade Town. I also knew that he and his brother left to live with his aunt for a year, before moving back to Jade Town.

What I didn't know at seventeen, was the story he had told me was only the very tip of the iceberg- something incredibly dark was lurking beneath it. Something which you won't quite be able to comprehend if I were to tell you now, something you will only understand when you have heard the full story...

****

The next morning, I was woken up by a rap on my bedroom door and my dad's voice- "Lyla, there's someone here to see you. You might want to get dressed and come downstairs."

Confused at who could possibly be here to see me, I pulled on yesterday's jeans and a crumpled t-shirt, ran a brush through my tattered hair and headed down the stairs.

I did a double take as I took in the figure standing in my living room...

Ally Tinsley, Lawrie's childhood best friend, stood rocking on her heels, as if she were uncomfortable to be here. Her blonde hair was scraped into a ponytail on the crown of her head, making her look a lot older and more sophisticated than she had the day before.

"Do you have a place where we can hang out and talk in this town?" She asked, without elaboration. My mind was whirring, but no thoughts filled it, I had no idea why she wanted to talk or hang out with me or why she looked so uncomfortable at the prospect of being here.

Still, it would be nice to have another friend, at least one who could tell me what I didn't know about Lawrie. He said himself that they grew up as brother and sister, she must surely know everything there was to know about him.

I walked towards her with a smile plastered on my face.

"Sure, Topaz Café is a good spot. It's owned by my friend Alessia's parents." I offered.

"Perfect, show me the way." And we set off through Jade Town, past the row of chocolate box houses and towards the high street. Ally didn't really speak to me until we had entered the pink-walled café and settled in a red leather booth at the corner, furthest away from the large windows that I had seen her hanging out with Lawrie outside the day before.

"Hey Lyla, I'm sorry that we didn't get to talk more earlier, and I know that you probably aren't going to trust me on this because what is my word over his right?" Ally said suddenly, as she took a sip of her vanilla bean milkshake which had just been delivered to the table, her face a mirror of anxiety.

What could she possibly have to tell me? What did she mean I wouldn't trust her word over his?

"What are you trying to tell me, Ally?" I said in a tone which came out much harsher than I meant for it to - I couldn't help it, this girl made me mad for some reason, undoubtedly, I was simply being consumed by the little green jealousy monster.

Ally sighed and raked a hand through her blonde wavy ponytail. "Look I've known the Carson's... I mean Hartwell's for as long as I can remember. Our mothers were school friends, and they did almost everything together including moving into the same street, Lawrie and I were neighbours growing up."

It was a cute sentiment, but I failed to understand why she felt the need to tell me this and why she looked so frightened. I also recognised how it didn't match up at all to the story that Lawrie told me about how they met through their dads being lawyers. Just as I was about to cut my losses, make my excuses, and walk out, she continued.

"Well, I bet you wondered why Lawrie moved all the way down here to basically the middle of nowhere. In truth I don't even know the full story- my mum won't tell me all the details. She honestly treats me like I'm six and not nearly eighteen. She doesn't even let me have a mobile phone because she thinks it'll corrupt my soul or something ridiculous like that. All I do know is that there's something dodgy with that family, something dark going on there. I just want you to be careful Lyla because you seem like a nice girl, and I don't want you to get mixed up in something like that."

I had no idea what she was talking about. Sure, the Hartwell's arrival in Jade Town had been shrouded in mystery, but I always knew that Lawrie didn't like to talk about his abusive father, so we never really did. I didn't know it at the time, but Ally was giving vital clues, but unless you are actively looking for them, I think that clues will always pass you by.

"What do you mean?" I asked inquisitively.

"Something happened the summer before Lawrie left for here, it wasn't just his mum's accident. His father was mixed up in something, I know that he lost his job, and they packed up and left pretty quickly after that. Lawrie only told me the day before they left that he was leaving, he wouldn't tell me where he was going though or why. I had no idea where they even were until my parent's drove us here yesterday. I remember his little brother Rory was crying his eyes out and clutching onto me, he didn't want to leave." I'd always been apprehensive about Lawrie's father ever since the night I heard him shouting at Lawrie, when I directly saw the damage that he had caused. Now the mystery of whatever had happened last summer made me even more so, but what had his father done?

I sat with Ally for about an hour, she was genuinely one of the nicest people I've met. When she left, she gave me a big hug and wrote her number on one of the Christmas napkins which were scattered on every table even though it was well into April by then- "Take care Lyla, keep in touch." I never did keep in touch with her. I wonder how Ally's doing these days. I wonder how she felt when she heard about how the world came tumbling down all around me for everyone to see.

Before she left, a thought overcame me. I hated doubting Lawrie, but I had to ask her- "Ally." I said slowly.

"Yeah, what's up?" she asked calmly.

"I was just wondering, is your dad a lawyer?" I fiddled with my right earring as the nerves set in.

"No, he's a carpenter. Why do you ask?"

"Oh, no reason." I called as I backed out of the café my mind alight with wonder about why Lawrie had lied to my face.

****

As the months dragged past, I didn't see much of Lawrie because I was busy studying for my end of year exams, the exams which would decide my fate and whether I would ever be able to get out of Jade Town or, if I would have to continue working at the little corner shop at the end of the street with Daphne, Tiffany's university drop out cousin. She had recently gotten pregnant and had to provide for her future child all by herself as her strongly religious parents wanted nothing to do with her anymore. I felt so unbelievably sorry for Daphne, I couldn't imagine what being abandoned by those who are meant to care for you must feel like.

 Daphne was extremely evasive about her child's father; I clearly remember pushing the point one dull evening when we were both stacking shelves in the deserted corner shop. She had simply waved away my question and responded with-

"He's younger, and I don't think his family would at all approve of me or our child, so I refused to let him have a part in her life." After a moment, she added- "I think that suits him though, he isn't really a relationship kind of person, and I never expected him to be. But I just can't give her away you know."

"So, it's a girl then?" I remember exclaiming and Daphne nodded her tanned head making her dark hair float effortlessly in the air and I hugged her jumping up and down with glee.

****

By the start of exam season, I had finally decided what I wanted to do. I wanted to go to medical school, and I wanted to help people. I was so grateful to every person who helped my mum during all those dark years, that I knew there was no other path for me. I hadn't told yet Lawrie about my plan and how I'd already applied to medical school because I was aware that when I did it would feel so real. I had no idea what would happen to Lawrie and me when that year finished. He was set to go to London and despite my childhood desire to leave Jade Town, I knew that I couldn't leave- I couldn't leave my dad, he was still struggling, and he needed me around whether he wanted to admit it or not. So, I'd applied to schools closer to Jade Town, all of which were miles and miles away from London.

I'd been avoiding Lawrie ever since I found out that he'd lied to me about how his family knew Ally. It was a tiny thing, but it suddenly made me aware that I wasn't entirely sure I could trust him. Luckily for me, Lawrie had been busy pulling shifts at the hospital, so I had an excuse to avoid him.

Clara was still missing even all those months later. Searches around Jade Town and its neighbouring villages for any signs that could lead to Clara's whereabouts proved entirely fruitless. Every day, hope was dwindling that she would be found alive, people didn't want to admit the fact that she could've been harmed because Jade Town and the villages of Greenstone and Knox were the only patches of civilization for miles. We all knew the residents of Greenstone and Knox as well as those of Jade Town. I went to school with the kids from there and people would often cross between the villages. This meant that if someone had hurt Clara, we knew who it was, it was someone who we saw day in day out and that made the prospect even more frightening that someone I knew could've been caught up in something that malicious.

"Alright time up, Pens down." The heavy-set exam invigilator called at the end of the final biology exam and a collective sigh of relief filled the school hall- that was it, I was finally finished, and I never had to return to school. I couldn't help glancing at the empty seat right at the back of the hall which was meant to house Clara Yale. I could envisage her, clear as smoke, sitting there scrawling away a look of smug knowledge on her face, her raven fog hair flowing around her shoulders as she wrote. She would have finished long before everyone else, would have aced that exam and every other one she took.

I was so distracted with the thought that I nearly tripped over someone as I left the hall, someone was sitting on the step just outside the hall with their head in their hands. I looked down and muttered an apology just as they looked up at me, blue eyes tainted with a combination of frustration and sorrow.

"Lawrie, what's up?" I asked as I stepped out of the way and sat down next to him on the cold concrete step. "All the exams are finished; we're finally free." I smiled, the sweet realisation dawning on me for the first time.

"I didn't write anything... in the exam." He muttered almost inaudibly. I thought I hadn't heard him correctly, Lawrie always aced exams, he was nearly always top of the class, and he always seemed prepared for every eventuality possible.

"What do you mean you didn't write anything?" I leant in to hear him more clearly. Maybe I'd just misheard him after all.

"I've been so distracted with everything going on Lyla. I've been working at the hospital from noon to night and I couldn't study at home with my dad, he's been in one of the worst moods I've ever seen him in. So, I didn't, I didn't study, and I opened the first page of the exam, and I didn't know anything. The only thing I knew how to answer was my own fucking name, I just sat there staring at it and then the exam ended." He said without any real emotion in his voice; you would expect this kind of thing to be crushing for him, he had most likely just ruined his chance of going to medical school in London, something he had dreamed of for as long as I'd known him, and yet he was talking about it with as much emotion as if describing how to operate a toaster.

"Oh, it'll be okay, I'm sure of it. You did well in your other exams, though, right?" I was struggling to find the words. If anyone I knew was going to mess up their exams I never in a million years would have expected it to be the ever-studious Lawrie Hartwell.

"Nope. Like I just said, I couldn't study. Were you not listening to me at all, Lyla?" He was suddenly bristling with anger, not at himself but at me. The little monster inside was projecting itself onto the only other soul on the cool stone step. I was equally filled with frustration.

"Why are you taking it out on me? I'm just trying to help you, Lawrie but if you'd prefer to just sit here in misery, then be my guest, I'll go." I got up to leave but he tugged on my arm and pushed me back down onto the step beside him.

"No, I'm sorry Lyla, I shouldn't be taking it out on you. I just don't know why you have been avoiding me so much recently. Every time I try to be near you, you just bolt away as if I'm some kind of monster. Don't lie to me, I've noticed how you look at me differently now. It's just I'm going to be stuck in Jade Town next year and probably forever and I have no idea what you're doing next year. Where did you even apply to? He all but spat out the last words, his tone domineering. I remember feeling frightened, for the first time since I'd known him, Lawrie scared me.

It was true, I had been avoiding Lawrie since I'd spoken with Ally at Topaz Café, but equally he had been so wrapped up in himself that he had never asked me what I wanted to do after exams were over. We were drifting apart gradually, pulling away from each other without being sure as to why.

"I'm not leaving Jade Town next year, I never was. I have to be here for my dad because I can't leave him. I'm the only person he has left now, and I need him with me." I sighed before continuing, I didn't want Lawrie thinking I was simply following in his footsteps by going to medical school, that I couldn't think for myself. I didn't want him to think I had no willpower, that I was so devoted to him that I would follow him wherever he went, although I more than likely would have done.

"I want to go to medical school. I applied to a few around here. One of them is right next to the hospital a few miles out of Jade Town. I didn't do it because it was something you wanted to do; I genuinely just want to help people like they helped..." I trailed off suddenly, a lump in my throat, thinking about her. Even a year later, it didn't seem real to me, the idea that she was gone. She still felt so familiar to me, as if my life changed drastically after she left but, in some respects, it stayed the same.

"Your mum." Lawrie answered for me.

 I nodded.

"Well, it looks like we'll both be in Jade Town next year then." Lawrie looked completely unbothered that he had screwed up his aspirations for next year and had no backup plan. He smiled and my apprehension melted away, I believed he understood my future plans. After all, he understood me more than anyone else ever did.

"It looks that way." I smiled at him and rested my head on his shoulder.

If only I'd known then what was going to occur in Jade Town the following year, or the years following that. I would have packed up my bags and moved far, far away.

Clara Yale's disappearance is only the start of the tale. Our dreary, idyllic little English village was about to be rocked by something incredibly dark, something which made the name of our village known to people across the country.

18 YEARS OLD

"Faith Baxter was last seen 72 hours ago leaving her home in Jade Town, Lyntonshire. This news has once again cast Jade Town into the spotlight as less than year before, another Jade Town teenager, seventeen-year-old Clara Yale went missing and has still not been found. If anyone has any information about the whereabouts of either Faith Baxter or Clara Yale, we are encouraging them to contact the Lyntonshire police immediately."

On a particularly sweat-inducing July afternoon a few days after my eighteenth birthday, and around three months to the day that Clara Yale disappeared, I sat in front of the TV in our living room and heard those devastating words. It was highly unlikely and out of character, but Clara's singular disappearance could have been chalked up as a runaway or something completely non-malicious but two girls disappearing within a few months of each other, that was rather a harrowing prospect.

Jade Town was abuzz with chatter about Faith's disappearance. Faith was a year younger than me and was in her last year of school when she disappeared one night. She was on her way back from her swimming coach job at the dinghy leisure centre just outside of Jade Town and she never came home. Speculation of all kinds spread through the village, and you couldn't help noticing the similarities between Clara's case and Faith's case- both girls were seventeen when they disappeared; both disappeared at night, and it was completely out of character for both, in a place where crime rarely occurred. It was undeniable that the cases were connected somehow, someone had taken them, but people didn't know why, or where they were. This put the residents of Jade Town on edge.

In late September, during our monthly village meeting, in which the whole of Jade Town attended to vote on how our village should be governed, Jade Town mayor Dean Huxley proposed the idea of imposing a curfew.

"There's no point in that." Tiffany whispered to me as we sat at the back of the Edwardian age town hall which didn't look like it had been cleaned since it had been built. That particular village meeting had dragged on for well over two hours.

"It might stop people being..." I started but then trailed off, unable to comprehend what I should say. We didn't know for certain that Clara and Faith's disappearances were connected, and I hated thinking about the prospect that they were, I hated feeling unsafe within my own town. For about the four hundredth time, I silently wished that I'd gone off to medical school far away instead of sticking around in Jade Town.

"I would say about eighty percent of Jade Town residents are over the age of sixty, so why should they try and punish those of us who are actually trying to live out our teenage years. Dean Huxley is so out of touch with the youth and having fun that he wouldn't notice fun if it were dancing in front of his face." Tiffany said in a too loud voice so that lots of people turned around and shot us dirty looks. I mouthed a silent apology to them all.

Tiffany did have a point, the majority of Jade Town residents were over the age of sixty which was what made the idea that young girls were disappearing even more petrifying, *there aren't that many to choose from* I thought.

"I think this issue is a little bigger than your social life Tiffany." I whispered angrily to her, she simply looked at me, turned her head, and didn't speak to me for the rest of the meeting which lasted another long-drawn-out hour. I noticed that Roman sitting a few seats across from us began to snigger.

I usually found the monthly village meetings extremely dull especially at that point seeing as neither Nate, Quinn, Marina, or Lawrie were there. Quinn and Marina had both left for university. Luckily though, neither of them was that far away that I could go and visit them whenever I desired to. Lawrie was back retaking his last year of school, trying to pass his exams. He hadn't wanted to go back initially but I managed to convince him. He had given up volunteering at the hospital but had secured a part time job at Topaz Café in the centre of Jade Town and between going to school and working at the Café, he didn't have the time for things like village meetings. Between our busy schedules, I found it difficult to find time to spend with him.

He'd been making up for the lack of time spent together by showering me with gifts which I had to admit I was suspicious of how lavish they were. I wasn't sure how his wages at Topaz Café were allowing him to buy these gifts, but I was too overwhelmed with everything that was going on in Jade Town to question him on the subject. Plus, I thoroughly disliked questioning Lawrie on almost any subject because he always became so defensive, treating every question of mine as a personal attack.

"Come on Tiff, I'm sorry for snapping at you." I muttered to Tiffany as we left the village hall, pulling our coats tight around ourselves due to the blistering cold. The night was dark and cloudless, Jade Town was illuminated only by the sharp white light of the moon. It was the perfect night to sit in the tree Lawrie and I had sat in on the hill when we were sixteen which had become a favourite place of ours, but I knew that it was too risky. Afterall, if the events in Jade Town were connected, I fitted perfectly into the category of the previous victims. So, Instead I trudged down towards my house with Tiffany who had quickly forgiven me for our earlier argument.

"Do you think it could happen to us?" She asked me, her olive features were screwed up, a look of terror plastered across her face. Tiffany was never usually scared of anything; it is what made me like her so much because I was terrified of almost everything and I always felt like I could rely on her to fill me with courage. This, however, was beyond all superficial calm- something evil was going on and we both knew it.

"I don't know." I sighed and I noticed how we both quickened our speed towards our respective houses. Tiffany lived three doors down from me, so we didn't have far to travel alone. "I wish I could just know it would all be fine you know; I can't stand the idea of losing anyone else in this place."

"At least you've got Lawrie though Lyla. I'm sure he'll protect you." She said as she walked up the crooked path towards her grey-stone thatched house. I had no idea just how true that statement would prove to be, but I wish with my whole heart that I'd never needed protecting.

****

I was just about to turn out my light and go to sleep in an attempt to gain peace from the fear ensuing all around me when I heard a *clunk* against my window. I paused for a moment, unable to decide whether I'd imagined it or not. No, the *clunk* sounded again a few seconds later. Tentatively, I peeled back my curtains and squinted down at the sight in front of me.

Lawrie was standing looking up at my bedroom window looking like a mess, a dishevelled mess at that. He looked frightened; a small golden animal caught in headlights. He had been so quiet the past few days and hadn't responded to my messages, so I was shocked to find him standing below my window in the autumn chill.

Quietly, I pulled on my dressing gown and padded down the stairs to see why he had randomly showed up looking like he was on the run from the mafia.

The cool air bit at my arms and legs as I closed the front door behind me silently so that I didn't wake my dad up, he had only just started sleeping properly after everything that had happened with Mum, so I greatly didn't want to disturb him.

Face to face, Lawrie looked even worse than he had from my view from my bedroom window. His straw-coloured hair was unkempt, his jeans were muddy and underneath his eyes were wells so dark that you could swim in them. This sight perplexed me extremely, Lawrie had always put a great deal of effort into his appearance, he always looked smart and presentable. The figure in front of me however, looked nothing like that.

As I approached, Lawrie raked a hand over his face nervously.

"What are you doing here?" I asked, holding my dressing gown closer into my chest in an attempt to dispel the biting cold. "What's going on?" I pressed when he didn't answer me but rather stood there wordlessly in the foggy darkness.

"I need your help," He responded after a while, he looked tensely from left to right as he spoke like he was looking for people who could possibly be spying on our conversation.

"Are you drunk? What the hell is going on?" Anger was rising inside my chest, I was mad at him for dragging me out here in the freezing darkness, I was mad at him for not responding to my messages and then just showing up and daring to ask me for help.

He shook his head violently and looked around again before stepping closer to me. So close that we were almost touching.

"I'm in some trouble, Lyla. You see there are these guys and I kind of owe them a lot of money because I took it from them, and I used it to buy the stuff I've been getting you and they have given me forty-eight hours to pay them back or….." He trailed off. I had to stop myself from laughing out loud, if it weren't for Lawrie's entirely serious disposition I would have laughed and congratulated him on telling such a good joke. Criminals after Lawrie in Jade Town- the idea was preposterous; Jade Town was likely the sleepiest place on earth. I couldn't fathom the idea that there were dangerous people around. Aside from the fact that there clearly was evil in Jade Town, someone had taken Clara and Faith- I was sure of it.

"What are you talking about Lawrie? You haven't responded to any of my messages or calls and then suddenly you show up out of the blue with some bullshit story about people being after you and how you need my help. What has gotten into you?" I snapped, my fuse had finally been lit. I was tired, worried about what was going on in Jade Town and in no mood for Lawrie to be messing me around.

I could feel him tense up in response, his jaw clenched, and he seized my arm in a grip that was so tight I was sure he would break something.

"I'm not lying Lyla. I shouldn't have taken the money, but it was there, it was so easy to take and then they came after me. They showed up at my door one night- there were four of them and they seemed to know all this information about me. They told me that I had to give them what I owed, or they would hurt me and the people I loved."

My brain whirred as I attempted to take in what he had told me. *There were people after Lawrie, He had stolen something?* It all seemed rather unbelievable, but Lawrie genuinely looked so petrified.

"How much do you owe them?" I quizzed him, wondering how on earth I was going to be able to help him find enough money to pay them off. My family were not drenched with cash, we barely had enough to get by and my wages at the Jade Town corner store were dismal at best.

"Eight thousand pounds." My mouth dropped to the floor, why had Lawrie stolen eight thousand pounds? I knew I should have been more suspicious about the lavish gifts; I should have confronted him about them and told him to stop.

"EIGHT THOUSAND POUNDS?!" I practically screeched. Lawrie's vice-like grip on my arm tightened and I winced. "Eight thousand pounds!" I repeated in a quieter voice. Eight thousand pounds wasn't a sum of money that we could possibly find in only forty-eight hours.

"How the hell do you think we can find eight thousand pounds in less than forty-eight hours Lawrie, are you out of your mind?" I noticed that a few of the neighbouring houses had switched lights on, obviously awoken by the commotion, I crept backwards towards the looming darkness of the house.

"They don't want the money in cash. They told me they want me to get them something else- a necklace." Lawrie whispered hurriedly, still glancing around.

"Who are these people? How do you know them Lawrie, and where are we supposed to find this necklace that they are after?" The night had grown steadily darker in the time that Lawrie and I had been outside my house which made Lawrie's bright eyes standout incredibly, they looked tense.

I could just about see his mouth move in the darkness, working out the best way to tell me about the men after him. My limbs were now numb from the piercing cold. However, the place on my arm which Lawrie was still gripping throbbed with pain, but my hands were too numb to reach up and remove it.

"I met them a while ago." He answered finally after clearly toying about telling me for a while. "They are from a little way away from Jade Town, nearer to Knox village and they were at Topaz Café one evening about two months ago when I was doing the late shift. Well, they asked me if I wanted to make some more money, my wages at Topaz café are pitiful at best so I agreed. It started off fine. I just had to pick up these packages of off-brand products that they were selling and deliver them to places, sometimes I would transport money between them too. They told me I would get my cut, but it came increasingly clear to me after a few weeks that it had been a lie. So, one day I was delivering money between them, and I took some of it. There was so much there that I didn't think they would notice but they obviously did and now they are after me."

"So where do we find this necklace?" I repeated calmly, I knew that I had to help him at all costs. He hadn't told me what the people who were after him looked like, but I had horrible visions of them being menacing and domineering, the kind of people who wouldn't let Lawrie off easily.

"It's in a jewellery store in Knox. It's called Opal Jewellers" and then as if sensing the question, I was pondering- "They want that particular necklace because it contains a rare sapphire, it is the only one of its kind in England and they have a client who wants it. They told me my debt would be repaid if I delivered it to them and I have tried everything Lyla, I really didn't want to have to ask you for help, but I don't believe I have any other choice."

Desiring a rare sapphire for a mystery client seemed a rather outlandish request for the kind of petty criminals who I imagined Lawrie had angered, he said they sold fake branded products, they didn't orchestrate jewellery store robberies. Still, if it was the only thing to clear Lawrie's name, I was completely onboard.

"So how do we get this necklace then?" I asked earnestly, Lawrie's anxious expression faded somewhat and was replaced with a kind of admiration for me.

"You really want to help me steal a necklace from a jewellery store?" He whispered.

"If it is the only thing-and I mean the *only* thing that will help you out of this mess then yes I'll help you." For some reason, I partially blamed myself for Lawrie's problem. I believed that by accepting his gifts I'd gotten him into this mess, so I had to help him out of it.

"Okay... so I kind of have a plan." Lawrie started but he paused and glanced up to the window to my dad's room where the curtain had just twitched ever so slightly, the fact that my dad could peer down and see Lawrie and I plotting underneath his window was too much of a frightening prospect, so Lawrie released me and turned back towards the gate at the end of my driveway.

"Thank you, Lyla, I knew I could count on you." He said as he hurried along the pitch-black street, I watched him go with a pit of dread forming in the bottom of my stomach because as I regained feeling in my limbs, I also realised with horror what I'd just agreed to. I'd agreed to help Lawrie to commit a crime, I'd let my feelings for him cloud any form of rational judgement.

With the pit increasing in size with every breath I dared to take, I headed back into the house and lay awake for most of the night wondering how on earth Lawrie believed we could steal a rare necklace and get away with it.

****

The next evening, I was sitting in the front seat of my car, my heart running marathons within me. I was doing something I never imagined of myself, I'd never thought that I would be involved in criminal activity, I didn't even dare to dwell on the prospect of what would happen if we were caught. My dreams would be shot to smoking smithereens, that was for certain. You are probably wondering why exactly I consented to helping Lawrie steal from a jewellery store and the answer is ultimately I felt like I had to. I remembered how he had gripped my arm so tight the previous night that I was sure he would shatter it, I remembered how frightened he had appeared, how he had told me he had no other option, and I was scared to push him away. With whatever was behind Clara and Faith's disappearances likely prowling around looking for their next victim, the next girl to abduct, I urgently needed all the protection I could get, and I believed that Lawrie would protect me. Although, there I was protecting him.

Knox village was only a fifteen-minute drive from Jade Town. I'd visited there so many times growing up that I knew the place like the back of my hand, I knew all of the little side roads and exits. It was a lot larger in proximity than Jade Town and most of the students at school had hailed from Knox village. Despite all this, sitting in the car that dark evening, I felt as if I was somewhere entirely different, like I'd never been there before.

Up in the distance, I could just about glimpse the illuminous sign of a 24-hour off-licence and next to it, just out of my vision, I knew was Opal Jewellers. Lawrie had told me to keep watch whilst he entered the store. I was too relieved at not being directly in the thick of criminal activity that I didn't really question how Lawrie was going to break into a jewellery store by himself. I later learnt that the jewellery store was owned by the uncle of Matt Wilkins who was a friend of Lawrie's at school. Somehow, without my knowledge, Lawrie had managed to procure a key from Matt which made breaking into the store rather worryingly easy. Still, I was sure that there would have been security measures in place and Matt's uncle lived above the store so he could have easily heard a commotion and come running down or worse call the police.

Which as a matter of fact is exactly what happened. I'd been sat surveying the empty black void all around me, when suddenly out of the silence came an ear-splitting siren which grew nearer and nearer until I could see screaming blue lights cut through the silky black night. Panic immediately rose up from the tips of my toes to the crown of my head - my body buzzed with panic. *We can't get caught. My whole life will be over*. As I sat there frozen with dread, the lights became clearer, and the wails of the sirens horrifyingly became louder.

After a few seconds which drew out like days, I felt able to move. My hands shaking, I reached down and grabbed my mobile ready to alert Lawrie of the police presence even though I was sure that if the police had been alerted, he must have already been caught by Matt Wilkins' uncle and by calling him I was sure that I would incriminate myself too. I wasn't thinking about myself though, and truthfully, I couldn't imagine anything past that calamitous night. I didn't see how Lawrie and I could ever just return to Jade Town like nothing had happened. The faces of my friends bounced around inside my mind, they would be horrified if they knew where I was and what I was doing. *What would she think if she were here?* I let my mind stray to the subject of my mum and I immediately felt wretched, all I had wanted to do was make her proud and I certainly wasn't at that moment- the thought made me sick to my stomach.

The blue lights and sirens shot past me in a whirl and with great difficulty I pushed the faces of those I loved from my mind. I only had one purpose now and that was to help Lawrie get away in whatever way I could. Fumbling with my phone, I clicked on his name and began to type a shrewd warning before I remembered that he didn't take his phone with him so he couldn't be tracked to the jewellery store and my heart lurched in my chest. There was nothing I could've done, I had to just pray with every cell inside of me that he would appear in the next few moments.

So, I waited and waited. My pulse rising and my breath shallowing with every second that passed...

Five minutes passed, and then ten, and then fifteen with no sign of life on the streets beside a pair of cats that were hissing at each other on the other side of the road, both attempting to assert their authority within the area. *You can have it, I thought, I never want to come back to Knox village ever again, for as long as I live.*

Close to twenty minutes had passed, when a sharp rap on the passenger side window made my soul swiftly leave my body. In the chaos of the night, I'd forgotten the fact that there was supposedly a kidnapper stalking the local area who was kidnapping girls of around my age who were alone at night. In vain, I attempted to hide myself without looking at who knocked on the window. My mind was alive with strife, I knew that I couldn't leave Lawrie, but I also knew that by being out at night in this deserted street I was an easy target for the abductor.

Another knock on the window sounded, more aggressively than the first and a voice rang through into my car.

"Open the door. Open the door." It was a voice I recognised immediately, a voice I knew above all others. Truthfully, I'd just about lost hope that Lawrie would appear when he knocked on the car window. A storm wave of relief washed over me as I opened the door and let him inside.

Lawrie was wheezing for breath; he had clearly been running for some distance. Through ragged breaths he managed to get out- "Let's... get out of... here... go."

In response, I slammed the car into reverse and peeled off back towards Jade Town at an ungodly speed that pushed my car to the limit. Luckily, the roads which were typically practically empty in daylight were completely deserted. Lawrie and I sat there wordlessly the whole journey; the only sound came from the spluttering cries of my car as it struggled to retain its speed.

We were back in the familiar picture-book village of Jade Town in a matter of minutes, somewhere which had once brought me comfort, but that night felt like the worst place on Earth. As I reached the centre of Jade Town and then my derelict house, I didn't even attempt to slow down. Instead, I blasted along through Jade Town and continued driving without a care for where I was going or where I would end up until the sun rose on the horizon putting an end to what I believed at the time to be the worst night of my life.

****

Lawrie and I hadn't talked about what had happened that night, he seemed extremely keen to forget it had ever happened and likewise so was I. I'd been trying to avoid him as much as humanly possible since that night which was increasingly difficult in our tiny village, especially when Quinn and Marina returned for the Christmas holidays and on their first night back had invited him to join us at Topaz café for a catch-up the next day.

Obviously, I couldn't tell them why I didn't want to be around Lawrie, so I reluctantly agreed, which is how I ended up sat in the same red booth I'd sat at with Ally the previous year, at Topaz café with Quinn, Marina, Tiffany, Tiffany's cousin Daphne and Lawrie on a chilly late December afternoon. Jade Town had been dusted in icing sugar snow and Topaz Café was decked out in glittering red and gold decorations; a grand real fir tree stood strong in the corner.

"I heard about Faith Baxter from my parents. It's so terrible. I can't believe that there's someone out there that evil enough to do something like that." Marina said as she finished the last of her vanilla milkshake. We had lasted a long time making polite conversation, but everyone knew that the topic of Faith and Clara and the potential abduction of them both was bound to come up- everyone in Jade Town was always just tiptoeing around the conversation.

"I know and if it's true which I believe it is, there's no way Clara and Faith would've just left here on their own. Really in such a small place, it's likely that it's someone we know." Quinn interjected, she had cut her hair short since being away which made her features look sharper, she looked more like a supermodel than ever before. "That's what they always say isn't it? That victims normally know their abductor or murderer?"

"You knew Faith, didn't you Lawrie? I never really knew her so it must be hard for you to believe that she's actually missing." Tiffany looked across at Lawrie who had been surprisingly quiet for his usual extroverted self the whole time we had been sat there. Lawrie was normally always the loudest and most overstated person in every social situation which was what made his quietness so bizarre.

"Yeah, I did." He replied slowly, "She was in a few of my classes this year, I didn't spend that much time with her, but she was always such a happy person. Of course, we don't know that there is a connection between Clara and Faith though- there's no proof of it is there?" I caught his eye for a second, but he immediately cast his gaze intently onto his finished glass in front of him. "I think everyone's jumping to conclusions when we don't have the slightest idea of what happened."

"The police don't seem to have found anything which is awful, I've been keeping up with the whole thing in all the papers. There was also this burglary at a jewellery store in Knox and the police can't find the culprit. I'm pretty sure it's Matt Wilkins' uncle who owns it too, It's just so terrible." Quinn said and I felt Lawrie tense up across the table. The burglary had been in the news recently as another unexplained crime which had occurred in an area which only saw crime around every four decades.

In a stroke of luck, Alessia Chang approached our table in her waitressing uniform at that moment with a tray balanced in her left palm, so any potential conversation about the jewellery store burglary in Knox was squashed.

"Everything good over here?" She asked with a pretty smile. "I just started my shift today; I had no idea you guys were coming in today, I would've asked for the day off, so I could've joined you."

Alessia's smile faltered slightly as she realised Lawrie was sitting with us. "Where have you been recently, Lawrie? You've missed a lot of shifts; I've been trying to get a hold of you- my dad's getting really mad about it." Lawrie had clearly been too preoccupied in criminal activity to turn up to work, the anger I was already feeling towards him for dragging me into helping him burgle the jewellery store a few weeks before, intensified.

"Sorry Alessia, I've just had a lot going on recently and I dropped my phone a little while ago, the stupid thing won't work. I've been trying to get it fixed for ages." Lawrie gave her one of his best smiles, the kind which could send anyone swooning and which clearly had the desired effect on Alessia as she smiled back broader than before.

"Yeah of course, I understand things can get really overwhelming sometimes. Just text me when you get it fixed so I know when you can come back to work." She looked across the café and sighed at how busy it had become. "I should go and serve the other tables, it's nice to see you all. We should all meet up sometime, I've been so distant from everyone recently, working here full time was never the dream I wanted but I have to save up to leave here somehow, right?" We all nodded in agreement and told Alessia that we should all definitely hang out sometime, something which of course never materialised.

A few moments later, Alessia had moved on to serve Mr and Mrs Elin, an elderly couple who ran the little cinema just outside of Jade Town that I always used to sneak into with Ava Aurelia- a childhood friend of mine, after dance class in the years gone by. Ava and I had grown up as next-door neighbours, we used to do everything together back in the days when Clara and I were friends. The three of us spent more time with each other than with our own families, we all attended dance class together where it was clear even at such a young age that Ava had real talent, the kind of talent you couldn't teach, and I always knew she was destined to be a performer. When I was nine, her parents moved away to Australia, and I'd never heard from her again.

It had been several minutes after Alessia left our table when Daphne sighed audibly and bent her head low, indicating that she had something to tell everyone. "I saw her that night." Daphne said so quietly it was almost inaudible.

"What are you talking about?" Quinn asked in a similar hushed tone, her pale blue eyes alight with curiosity.

"Yeah, who did you see?" Marina quizzed, as she tucked her auburn hair behind her ear attempting to listen closer.

Daphne sighed again, "Faith. I saw her the night she went missing." The whole table looked around at her in astonishment, even Lawrie who had seemed particularly disinterested in the conversations of the day suddenly came to life and asked:

"Where? Where did you see her?"

"It was outside the leisure centre. I'd been there taking Willow to swimming lessons; Faith was one of the trainee coaches there and we were talking as we left the leisure centre. You know, she was asking me what it's like to raise Willow all by myself, she said that her parents had been really young when she was born and that they gave her up, so she was raised by her grandparents. She told me I was really brave for keeping Willow and then she said she was meeting someone that night, she wouldn't tell me who it was but..." She broke off for a minute clearly in a tangle of emotions, she raked a hand through her sleek dark hair.

"Anyway," She continued, her voice wavering slightly as she spoke which told us that dredging up this memory was clearly hard for her. "I think I saw him. I waited around a little longer in the car park because I didn't want her to be all alone out there, especially after what had happened to Clara Yale and plus it was hammering it down with rain. This man showed up and she walked off with him. I didn't get a good look at his face though, because Willow was crying, I think she was scared of the rain. I looked down to comfort her and the next moment Faith and the man had walked out of sight. I can't face the fact that I may have been the last person to see her, and I didn't do anything about it." Daphne's lip trembled and her honey-coloured eyes glazed with tears that spilled down her cheeks.

"Hey, Daphne It's okay. There's no way you could have known." I said giving her a sympathetic smile and I was speaking the truth; how would a person ever expect the worst that Faith meeting a friend would lead her to going missing.

"I should have asked her who it was." Daphne sobbed from somewhere underneath Tiffany's arm who had pulled her into a hug. "I shouldn't have let her walk off with him."

"Lyla's right Daphne, there's no way you could have known. Did you not get any kind of idea of what this man looked like?" Marina asked.

"Not really... he looked tall, but he was... w... wearing a black cap which c...covered all his h... hair." Daphne sobbed as she struggled to break free from Tiffany's grip.

"Have you told the police about this?" Lawrie interjected; his face lit with an expression I couldn't quite read.

"No, I didn't know it had any relevance at the time and I didn't want to say it out loud because then it makes it real you know- that she's gone." This revelation surprised me a great deal more than the information Daphne had just bestowed upon us. It was extremely likely that Daphne had been the last person to see Faith and that the man she was with was her kidnapper, this seemed exactly like the kind of thing you ought to tell the police.

"You really should tell the police; it seems to be information that's too vital to keep to yourself." Quinn said forcefully as if reading my mind in that moment. In response, Daphne sobbed harder than before so that all that came out of her mouth was indistinguishable noises, but I kept hearing her repeating 'Faith' over and over again.

"Well at least we know one thing now, that the Jade Town ... the Jade Town Monster is a man." Tiffany said in a rather louder tone than was necessary, so that Mr and Mrs Benson sat by the door to the café and their twin toddlers who were usually screaming their heads off turned to look in our direction.

"The Jade Town Monster, huh?" Lawrie said with an air of contentment, "I like that, it's a good way to describe him."

From that day forward, the abductor was known across the village as the Jade Town Monster, the name just exacerbated the anxiety we were feeling about him because labelling him as a monster made his hold over the town seem even greater. The name gave him a sense of omnipotence because the word conjured up countless images of terror and Jade Town was well and truly at his mercy as no one knew if and when he would strike again.

The table left one by one as the day progressed until when Quinn made her exit because she had an assignment to finish, only Lawrie and I were left sitting across from each other at the table. Neither of us made any effort to leave, simply sitting there across from each other unable to meet each other's gaze. I'd barely spoken to him the whole time we had been there. Topaz Café was completely empty as it was close to closing time. The silence which hung around us spoke volumes.

After a few moments of painful silence, he spoke hurriedly "I understand Lyla. I know you've been avoiding me, but I managed to sort everything out and I shouldn't have dragged you into that mess, I know I shouldn't have but I didn't have anyone else to ask because I don't really trust anyone else Lyla- not in the way I trust you." I knew exactly how he felt because I was truly a guarded impenetrable fortress, I made it my mission to not let anyone in, to know the inside of my mind or my weaknesses.

When I didn't respond, Lawrie changed tact "Can we just forget about it all, please? It's all sorted now, and I'll never put you through anything like that again for as long as I live- I promise." Silence was my only answer, I was still so cut up inside thinking of my mother's face and her voice and how she would have told me to run far away from Lawrie because he had brought me nothing but trouble and uncertainty. Being with Lawrie was always an uncertain mess, I never knew what would happen or where he would take me, which of course was very exciting to me at eighteen years old.

"Look, let's just go to our place up on the hill- I have something for you, just give me one more chance please." I looked up at him then, and he was fixing me with one of his best smiles, the type that even I couldn't resist.

"Fine, you have one chance, Lawrie." I instructed him and we got up from the table and headed up the hill, the sun dripping below the horizon in our wake.

The walk was steeper than I'd remembered it being, I hadn't been up there in such a long time, especially not after dark. A ghost of memory of the time we came here for the first time aged sixteen flittered and flapped through my mind like a majestic bird- everything had seemed so enticing and possible back then, and it was hard to believe that the night I'd kissed Lawrie in the rain only occurred two years previously. I was sure a lifetime had passed since then.

Despite the recent depravity, upon reaching the summit of the hill, a cloud of calm surrounded me. Jade Town sparkled and glittered below our feet like a golden carpet encrusted with clear precious gemstones as the setting sun kissed the horizon. The emerald blades of grass surrounding me were sprinkled with white snow, for once I didn't mind the crushing cold.

"It's beautiful up here isn't it." I found myself exclaiming, the silence all around which I usually found suffocating seemed liberating as though by being away from Jade Town I had escaped all my problems and anxieties. The best part was looking down upon Jade Town, I could have been in any corner of the world peering down at any expanse of civilization below me.

"Yes, it truly is. Whenever I come up here and I look down at Jade Town, it always reminds me of you. It's this place, it has always made me think of you, even when I went away for a year. As soon as I came back here, all I could think about was you and when I would see you." Lawrie's soft voice startled me somewhat as I had been so absorbed in the glistening scene below, I had forgotten I had company with me.

Looking across at him, my heart warmed at the sight. The liquid gold village below us reflected into his eyes, making them shine brighter than I had ever seen them, every light was visible within them. We sat there gazing at each other taciturnly for a long time as cool ribbons of air danced around us.

"Tell me Lawrie, what happened after the night at the jewellery store?" I said after a while, finally ready to hear the answer I'd been avoiding for the past few weeks. Lawrie sighed, signalling that it was something he didn't want to talk about, but he told me regardless.

"I got the necklace, and I was just leaving when Matt's uncle called the police. I never saw him, but I think he must have heard a disturbance from upstairs and called the police straight away. I saw them pull up and I honestly thought I was going to be caught, I couldn't imagine what my dad would do to me if I got arrested. I was panicking like I never have before but there was an open window to the back of the store, so I ran for it and managed to get through it and then I ran and ran all around Knox before I came to find you. Anyway, I went straight to the guys and gave it to them, and they told me I'd cleared my debt with them but said to watch my back. They seemed surprised. I don't think they actually thought I could do it." Lawrie explained in a frantic hushed voice which mirrored the one he had used when he told me about the trouble he was in a few weeks before. Again, he kept looking around as if the guys were lurking in the shadows ready to pounce at any moment.

"Couldn't the police trace it back to you though? Isn't there CCTV by the jewellery store?" It was a very likely possibility. I'd been frightened each morning when the post man visited that it was the police knocking down my door and arresting me. I'd imagined this prospect so vividly that I could picture my father's horrified face as I was thrown in the back of a police car and driven away.

"Come on Lyla, I'm not stupid. The night before, I went to Knox and cut all the wires around the security cameras. I know how not to get caught; I'll assure you of that one." Although this may sound like a tough feat, I knew that Knox village only had about two security cameras in the entire vicinity. The residents of Knox all trusted each other complicitly, as well as the residents of neighbouring villages Jade Town and Greenstone.

"What about Matt Wilkins? Won't he tell his uncle that he gave you the key to the store?"

"Not exactly, seeing as Matt never knew I had the key in the first place." Lawrie laughed then, as if proud of his delinquency.

"What did you do, Lawrie?"

"Why are you asking when you already know the answer? I stole the key, Lyla. I was over at Matt's house and got him talking about the jewellery store, he told me he had a key. The idiot even showed me which key it was, one he always carried around on a chain I think for his own ego. Some way to prove he was better than all of us as he had the key to thousands of pounds worth of jewellery. So, one day I took it from him, really it was his own fault for blatantly carrying around that stupid key I say he had it coming."

"It's not Matt's fault." I said quietly, already regretting the words as they came out of my mouth.

Sure enough, Lawrie turned to me with anger painted across his face. "Why are you constantly trying to find things wrong with us? Why are you always looking for things to complain about Lyla? I 've been trying to do what is best for us, what is best for you. I've sacrificed so much for you, the only reason I had to steal in the first place was because of the gifts I got you."

I felt like I was losing the battle before it had even really begun. I was annoyed with Lawrie for what he had done, but one thing was true- I was a part of it. At that time, I wholeheartedly believed that his actions, albeit wrong, were for me.

"So, why did you want to bring me up here Lawrie?" I asked, hoping to dispel the negative feelings hanging between us. I hated when he got mad, I hated the way he'd look at me, and I hated the prospect that I might lose him. So, I always did all I could to make sure that would never happen.

"I have something for you. I know you told me to stop getting you things, but this is the last thing I promise you; I've been feeling so wretched about everything recently. I fucked up Lyla, I understand that. So, I got this made for you. The money I used was mine, I swear I'm telling you the truth."

After I gave him an alarming look, he added hurriedly "I used my wages from the café, I promise you that. I'm not involved in that business anymore and I don't plan to be, ever again." He reached into the pocket of his silky black trench coat and extracted something from it.

Holding it up to the weak light emitted from Jade Town below our feet, it sparkled effortlessly. A long snaked golden chain hung in his left hand, at the bottom of the chain a heart charm swung in the December breeze. It was truly magnificent, the kind of timeless emblem found in a royal museum.

I couldn't contain my excitement "Oh, It's wonderful." Lawrie flashed a grin as he passed it over to me. The golden snake chain twinkled in my palm.

"Look at the back." Lawrie instructed and I turned the glossy heart charm over to read the inscription cast in bold into it. The last thing I remember about that night was being overcome in a bubble of joy, the kind of joy that I didn't believe could ever burst.

19 YEARS OLD

It was late July, a few days after my nineteenth birthday and Jade Town was a pit of panic. Not because another girl had gone missing, rather on the contrary. As it passed the year mark since Clara Yale and Faith Baxter had gone missing under similarly suspicious circumstances, everyone was terrified that the Jade Town Monster would strike again. People no longer left their homes after 10PM and bolted their doors shut, something which our close-knit community had never done before. Back in the times before evil had descended upon Jade Town, residents used to walk freely between each other's houses because the village was built upon the very foundations of trust- something which had been irrevocably broken. I believed even then that the residents of Jade Town would never completely be able to trust each other again.

Certain individuals were optimistic that the Jade Town Monster had simply stopped prowling around Jade Town and perhaps moved further afield, while others were betting on when he would strike again and who would be the next unfortunate victim. Personally, I hoped with every fibre of my being and honestly believed that there would be no further disappearances in Jade Town. Nevertheless, Panic was always there, clawing away at me. Panic that I could become the next disappearance, that I could simply become a statistic, a chapter in a story of evil. I had Lawrie though, and I believed that he would somehow be able to protect me from the evil stalking Jade Town.

I'd been at medical school all day, a day just before the end of term, which had shaped up to be incredibly dreary and monotonous. More than anything, I wanted to go home and sleep for an eternity and not have to think about the future or exams that were once again looming over me. I kept thinking maybe I should have taken a path in life like Lawrie, after finally passing his exams in school, he had changed his mind about medical school and had got a job in an office in Greenstone. The work he did seemed tedious at best, but he always came back with bulging pay checks rather than a hollow empty pocket like I did.

To my surprise, when I entered the living room of my dad's house to put my bag down before traipsing up to bed, I found that it had been decorated. Decorated in streams of red and pink, petals and hearts and other imagery which would make even St Valentine sick to the stomach were scattered across the room. A large and expensive looking bottle of Champagne sat on the coffee table surrounded by two crystal champagne flutes that I knew didn't belong in my house. In my weary state, it took my eyes a long time to focus on the figure standing in the centre of the room. Gradually I took in his tattered golden hair and sapphire eyes which were fixed directly onto mine.

"Lawrie, what are you doing here? What's all this?" I asked inquisitively, there was a look on his face that I didn't recognise, the best way to describe it was longing- a look of pure longing entwined with his clearly nervous disposition. A seed of thought began to grow inside of me, I had an idea about what was about to happen, what he was about to ask me, and I was neither surprised nor filled with intense joy. The thought seed grew to a tree inside of me as he walked closer towards me, and I felt the emptiest I had ever felt in my entire life.

Then, the tree wilted and withered; dead.

"Lyla… Delilah." He paused and I knew what was coming next. As he knelt on one knee and fished around in his pocket for a black satin box, I willed with every part of me that he would stand back up again and reveal that it was all some elaborate joke like April fools had come in July that year.

Instead, the fears that I had no idea I'd even been harbouring up until that moment proved to be true. He looked up at me and I felt my throat clam up as my pulse quickened in response. I wanted more than anything to run far, far away but I had no idea why I was feeling like that.

"I love you more than I know I could ever love anyone ever again and I know that I want to spend my life with you Lyla. I want to spend every day that I have with you." My body began to shake involuntarily. My heart was empty.

Empty.

"So, will you do me the honour of becoming my wife?"

The words didn't even penetrate through me, they were stuck just outside of my body, hanging in thin air. I was unable to absorb his words because I couldn't let myself contemplate it.

I stood completely frozen on the spot. This was meant to be the pinnacle of romance, a moment in life when everything was supposed to fall into place- the dust would settle, and you would see your life for what it is and what it could be. An eternity with the person down on one knee in front of you. As a child, I always used to secretly imagine this moment, the enchantment of it, how I would feel in the moment when someone bared their soul to me like that. A moment when someone would let me hold their heart in the palm of my hand.

As I stood there in front of Lawrie, I felt nothing. Nothing but a little sprig of doubt which seeped through into my brain. I knew only one thing at that moment for certain- I didn't want to marry Lawrie. I couldn't picture our entire lives together. I couldn't see us walking down the aisle or raising a family and growing old together. Nothing about this felt like it was supposed to, everything felt wrong.

Lawrie was looking up at me with those beautiful blue eyes aglow with expectation.

He thinks I'm going to say yes. He hasn't even considered the fact that I might say no.

My organs were a tangled mess, I could sense the panic rising in my chest and throat. I remember at that moment that I hated the fact that he thought he knew me, the fact that he was certain I would adore this display and would say yes in a heartbeat. I hated that after what he had put me through the previous year, after he had me cleaning up his mess and putting myself at risk, that he believed I wanted to commit myself to him for the rest of our lives. I hated so much about him at that moment, but I didn't hate him. No, I loved him. I loved him with all my heart.

Lawrie had always put me at ease and made me feel calm, but I was truly frightened of turning him down. I had seen flashes of his anger, I'd witnessed how his hurt translated directly to rage, how in moments of anger he seemed almost to lose himself and everything that was human about him.

I reached down through the panic and took Lawrie's hand. My eyes were glassy with tears, although they weren't the tears of joy I always expected to weep in this moment. Each tear was excruciatingly painful like a needle pricking in and extracting blood. There I was in front of Lawrie, the person I believed I had always wanted, bleeding out.

"Lawrie." I said softly, my shaking voice barely an audible whisper.

"Lawrie." I repeated over and over like a damaged stuck record, it was the only thing I could push myself to say in that god-awful moment. It was the only damn word I knew.

Suddenly, it registered all over Lawrie's face. His beam turned downcast, and he loomed up above me, intimidating me.

"You don't want to marry me, do you Lyla? You don't even love me, you never did." He all but spat at me. Lawrie's face contorted as the muscles of his jaw tensed. He dropped my hand and turned his face away. I could see his glass heart shattering right there in the living room of my dad's house. My hands were the culprit, I had broken him.

"I'm sorry Lawrie, I can't right now, I just can't. If you give me more time, then maybe in the future I can..." I stopped attempting to fight back the tears, they cascaded all down my cheeks blurring my vision. Although he was facing away from me, I felt the hurt displayed all over Lawrie's face. He was hurting so badly; I know because it felt as if somebody had just ripped my heart straight from my chest and left it out to die.

The worst part of it all was that I couldn't even give a reason. I was unable to give him a single reason why I couldn't marry him- he was all that I thought I ever wanted, he was the only person I could think about, the only person who understood my pain and I felt that I was about thirty seconds from losing him forever.

"You could've told me Lyla. You could've warned me that you didn't love me, rather than using me. YOU COULD'VE TOLD ME BEFORE LETTING ME LOOK LIKE A COMPLETE AND UTTER IDIOT BEARING MY HEART TO YOU JUST FOR YOU TO SHIT ALL OVER IT." Lawrie shouted over at me, his tone was terrifying and growing in volume. I should have known better than to have pushed it and aggravated him anymore because I knew how petrifying he was when angry, but clearly, at that moment I didn't know better. I was naïve and careless.

"Lawrie, I still want you." I quivered, then – "I love you Lawrie, you know that I love you. I just can't marry you; I can't be a part of your family. I don't want..." I knew straight away that I'd said the wrong thing. I'd said the worst thing I could've done. Within a split second he whirled on me, sending the China bowl on the table next to him down to the floor with an ear-splitting crack.

"YOU LITTLE BITCH, HOW DARE YOU TALK ABOUT MY FAMILY LIKE THAT. YOU DON'T KNOW ANYTHING ABOUT US. WHAT GIVES YOU THE RIGHT TO ACT LIKE YOU'RE BETTER THAN US?" He was face to face with me now, his face was only inches away from me. His breathing was ragged, and his beautiful, beautiful eyes were illuminated with rage. It was like I'd just awoken the monster which had been dormant inside of him for so long.

"YOU DON'T KNOW ANYTHING." He spat at me again as he picked up and hurled the smooth Champagne bottle against the wall. A ginormous crack rumbled through the house at the point of impact and the room was a haze of glass shards and thick foamy golden liquid. A shard landed and stuck into my thigh; blood began to snake its way out of the wound. I was too petrified to remove it, my feeble frame was frozen in fear.

It all happened very fast after that. His fingers grabbed my throat and shoved me against the yellow-wash walls of the living room, just next to where he had hurled the champagne bottle. I couldn't breathe; I couldn't escape; I couldn't think.

"YOU DON'T KNOW ANYTHING, BITCH." He repeated, staring right down at my terrified face which had likely turned white due to lack of oxygen. Then, his other fist connected against my cheek. I heard the sick crack of it before I really felt it. The pain flooded in like a shockwave, I was completely disorientated, my vision falling in and out of focus. I remember praying he would let me go, praying that I could turn back time and take back what I'd said so that the ordeal never happened.

I caught a glimpse of the real Lawrie that day, what was underneath. The man in front of me was completely unrecognisable to me. I was aware he had a short temper, and he had snapped at me before, but never in a million years did I believe he would have been capable of hurting me.

As quickly as it had happened, Lawrie transformed back into his normal self. His eyes flickered with total horror at what he had done, at how helpless I was. He dropped his hand from my throat and stepped away from the wall. I fell in a crumpled heap to the floor, too shaken up and fragile to be able to stand- it was as if my limbs didn't work.

"I'm so sorry Lyla." He quivered as he ran a hand through his hair. "Not you too, I can't hurt you too." Before I could respond he backed out of the room and ran to the front door which slammed shut behind him.

The silence was suffocating to me. In that moment, I was completely alone. Throughout all my suffering, Lawrie had been there to help me through. Lawrie was the only person who understood, he was the only person who could make me feel safe. And yet that evening, I sat there wondering why the person I loved was also the person who could hurt me beyond all others. I hated that the person I wanted to be here to comfort me was the person who had caused the suffering.

I didn't sleep that night; I just lay awake staring at the ceiling wondering if how I felt was how drowning felt.

****

When I heard a sharp rap on the door the next morning, I expected it to be Lawrie coming back to me the way that he always did when we fought with an apology in hand. Instead, I opened the door and stared in shock at the person across from me. He looked old and weather beaten, but he had those remarkable deep blue eyes which could only belong to one genetic line. Even though I'd never seen him before, I didn't need to take a guess about who he was. Lawrie's father stood on the other side of the door; a frown plastered onto his face. I'd heard so many stories about the monster that he was, I'd seen firsthand what he could do to the ones he loved. My pulse began to fluctuate, and my breathing dropped to such a shallow level that I thought I might have just died.

With no avail, I attempted to concoct a sentence or at the very least a word to say to him. Luckily for me, he spoke first. His voice was sharp and booming, the type of voice that could silence a whole room with no effort.

"So, I heard that my boy asked you to marry him."

Oh no.

I gulped back the sting of tears. I was terrified Lawrie's father would chastise me for turning his son down and offending their family name. I didn't dare imagine what he would say or do. Instead, he said something which still rings around in my mind to this day. He gave me a simple piece of advice that I wish I'd followed.

 "It's good that you turned him down, you shouldn't get involved with the Carson men. We're dangerous, the scum of the Earth people say. I don't know you Lyla, but I know my son and he's no good. You're better off without him."

Carson men? I had no idea what he was talking about but the stench of stale alcohol which surrounded him like a cloud of death suggested to me that he probably didn't have any idea about what he was talking about either.

I was about to ask him what the hell he was talking about, when he turned on his heels and walked back down the gravel path leading to my driveway. It was a strange yet powerful encounter. I understood fully in that moment why Lawrie felt such contempt for his father. He had made me feel like the smallest thing in the world, like a microscopic ant that he was about to crush on the sole of his shoe, and I hadn't even said a word to him. I stood there for a few minutes and watched him wordlessly retreat down the path and open the door of his car which he was visibly way too intoxicated to drive.

****

Later that day, I still hadn't heard from Lawrie, so I plucked up the courage to drive over to his tall, Victorian style home. The encounter with his father earlier in the day still had me on edge; I was terrified that I would run into him, but it was a Monday and Lawrie's dad did have a job. God knows who actually employed him, but still. Someone clearly had employed him, as when I pulled up to the house, his big black monster of a car that I'd seen earlier was nowhere in sight.

I had only been to Lawrie's house a handful of times, he never seemed to want me anywhere near there, but I was never quite sure of why. Physically, his house was a lot nicer than mine, and it was at least three times the size of my dad's house.

Despite its grand stature, up close the house looked in need of some good maintenance. The paint from the door had started to peel away. Green paint flecks covered the porch area amongst sprigs of tatty weeds. The wood of the porch was rotting away and there was a great crack running up the left side of the house. I guessed Lawrie's dad wasn't one for decorating or fixing.

Tentatively, I knocked on the door. I had no idea of what I was going to say to Lawrie. I was still reeling from the day before and the way that he hit me like I was of no importance to him, as if I were just some worthless whore. I shouldn't have been there. I should have blocked his number and never spoken to him again after what he did to me, but I just couldn't. I was drawn to his door; I think the issue was his familiarity. It's hard to let something so familiar and integral to your existence go. When I had lost my mother, someone so important to my very being, I gained Lawrie, and I don't believe I could face letting another person go especially with Jade Town in the state that it was.

It wasn't Lawrie who opened the door though, and it wasn't his father either. It was Rory, his younger brother who I had only met a few times, but I knew that he was still in school. A place where he should have been at midday on a Monday.

"Is Lawrie home?" I asked him. He was a few years younger than Lawrie and me, but he looked very tall for his age. Unlike Lawrie, he had unkempt brown hair which fell slightly down into his eyes. It was clear to see that he was a Hartwell though because his eyes were the same enchanting shade of blue as his elder brother's and father's. The

Hartwell's eyes really were spectacular, I used to call it their calling card.

"No, he's not here. He came around last night, but I haven't seen him since then." He held the door open for me and retreated into the house.

"But you're welcome to come in and wait if you want." I took him up on his offer and followed him into their vintage looking kitchen. The whole house looked like a snapshot into the past as if when I entered, I was transported back into the time it was first made. I half expected to see a flurry of maids fluttering around dressed in black and white robes.

"Why aren't you in school?" I asked Rory as I perched up on the marble counter (the only modern thing in this kitchen and perhaps the whole house). He was silent for a minute, probably attempting to concoct some kind of elaborate excuse before he gave up and just told me the truth.

"I didn't want to go. I'm completely behind everyone in my year because I haven't really been able to focus on school lately. Now that Lawrie isn't here most of the time, I have to do everything around the house and well then there's..." He paused but I knew exactly what he was talking about. I probably shouldn't have pushed but I was still trying to make sense of my encounter with Mr Hartwell this morning and any information I could gather, I believed to be beneficial on the subject.

"You mean your dad? Has he been violent again?" Rory looked at me visibly shocked for a moment. He was clearly completely unaware that Lawrie had told me anything. It wasn't my place to interfere and for a moment I thought that Rory was going to tell me exactly that but instead he sighed, and his poor face looked so hurt like I was the one who had physically struck him.

"My dad's been violent my whole life." Is all he said.

I couldn't imagine it, the fact that someone could grow up with a parent who they fear who makes them feel like they're worthless. I was beyond lucky that I had grown up with two parents who loved me and my brother more than anything.

I didn't know how to respond to Rory so I said the only thing that I could think of the thing that had been rattling around inside my brain all day.

"He came to visit me earlier, your dad I mean."

Rory, who was pouring himself a glass of water, stopped mid action, and turned around to face me.

"Why did he come to see you?". Water from the tap was still audibly dripping down the sink and into the drain.

"I don't know exactly. Well, no, that's a lie. Lawrie proposed to me yesterday and I just couldn't say yes, maybe it's not the right time. Anyway, it didn't go well and Lawrie kind of stormed out which is why I'm here looking for him, but your dad came round and told me that I was right to say no because apparently your family are dangerous. Of course I don't believe that." It felt good to get the weight off my chest. I had been lugging around this secret all day and I suddenly felt a massive wave of relief. I hated secrets more than anything.

Rory finished pouring the glass and turned off the tap. He set it down on the marble counter and looked around the room as if trying to see if anyone was secretly listening.

"I heard about the proposal, my dad told Lawrie he was insane for proposing, and they had another massive fight last night. After that, Lawrie left, and I haven't seen him since. You see, my family's dangerous, Lyla. Well, my dad at least he's dangerous." I was fully aware that Lawrie and Rory believed their dad to be a monster, but I knew that Lawrie wasn't anything like his dad. It was clear that I was making excuses at the time, blaming myself for Lawrie's anger, anger that was unfortunately directed towards me.

"I know about your dad, Rory. I know that he gets violent and frankly you shouldn't be living with him. Social services should have intervened a long time ago, but Lawrie is nothing like that. I know that he would never hurt me." *Wasn't I just lying through my teeth to Rory? Why was I protecting Lawrie?* As after all Lawrie did hurt me.

"Your dad didn't say the Hartwell family though, he said the Carson family, but I mean he seemed completely intoxicated so I doubt he even knew his left from his right." I thought back to the way that he drove away from my home like a maniac, and I really hoped that he got pulled over by the police for drunk driving. If not, he was an accident waiting to happen.

"No, my dad's not lying about the whole Carson thing and he's more dangerous than you think." My pulse began to quicken in the same way that it did a couple of hours earlier when Mr Hartwell had come to visit me.

 "What do you mean, Rory?" I said in utter confusion. It felt as though I was starring in a movie, one where the dumb protagonist finally manages to put the pieces together with the help of her smart side character. Rory glanced up at the clock on the wall and cursed.

"I can't say a lot now because my dad gets off from work earlier on Mondays, so he'll be home soon, and he'll kill me if he sees that I'm not at school." From Rory's expression I gaged that there was something a lot bigger going on than his father's anger filled booze sessions and violent temper. Something I desperately needed him to tell me, so I plucked my car keys from my pocket and turned towards the door.

"Do you want me to drive you?" I asked. I should have been getting ready to go to my afternoon class, but I wanted to hear what Rory had to say.

"Sure, thanks Lyla."

A couple of minutes later, we had settled into my car and were on our way towards the Three Point School, named because it was directly on the border of the three villages: Jade Town, Greenstone, and Knox Village, which was inconveniently on the other side of the village to the Hartwell's home. The only way to it was via winding roads which you could only drive down at the speed of a snail.

"So, what were you saying about your dad and the name 'Carson' earlier?" I asked Rory who was tapping his fingers on the dashboard of the passenger side.

"Well, I'm sure that Lawrie has told you about our mother, but I doubt he's told you the whole story seeing as you had no idea what my dad was talking about. Carson is our real last name I guess- it's my father's last name and Hartwell was our mother's. Carson used to be our last name before everything happened with my dad and my mum's death but then we changed it and moved away to get away from the press."

I was completely baffled, what did he mean press? The story seemed viable on the surface, but I felt as if there was something that he wasn't telling me. I was about to ask when he continued-

"My mum's death isn't as concrete as it sounds or as concrete as we have been forced to tell everyone. My mum and dad used to argue like maniacs. I don't believe that they ever had a happy marriage and then one day my mum met someone else who actually made her happy and she told my dad that she was leaving him. He wasn't happy about that, he was always extremely controlling towards her, so he did something completely awful..." Rory's bottom lip began to quiver, and I knew that whatever he was trying to tell me was truly awful.

"What did he do, Rory?" I asked as I glanced over to him in the passenger seat, his eyes were clouded with tears which had started to trickle their way down his cheeks.

"He killed her." Rory spluttered. A stale silence hung in the car for a moment, only broken by Rory's silent sobs.

He killed her.

He. Killed. Her.

The words were alien to me, my heart left the vicinity of my chest and jumped into the centre of the road. *It couldn't be, could it?* Lawrie's father couldn't be a murderer. My first thought was that Rory must have been messing around, that it was his idea of some kind of sick joke. There was no way people just said things like that, there was no way something like that could have been true, could it?

"What?" I muttered inaudibly; my eyes fixed on the road ahead of me.

"She did die in her car like the news claimed; he was driving with her one day. He had convinced her that he was fine with her leaving him. He had doused the car in petrol, and I think he pulled over and got out and before my mum knew what was happening, he set the car alight."

I sat there in silence completely stunned. I had no reason to not believe Rory's story, but I had no reason to believe him either.

"Well then, why isn't he in prison? Does Lawrie know about this?". My hands had started to sweat, gripping firmly against the steering wheel.

"My dad was a lawyer before everything that happened, so he managed to get himself out of jail time. He knew a lot of powerful people who supported his case, somehow evidence that would convict him seemed to get lost. Somehow the jury unanimously decided there was insufficient evidence to convict him. A report was released claiming the car hadn't been tampered with and that some electric fault caused the fire, so he managed to get away with just a year of community service for driving a faulty vehicle. I don't understand how he got away with it or how he managed to convince so many people to cover up the truth. He moved us away to the smallest town he could find and changed our names to mum's last name as an act of 'honouring her memory' or so he claimed. He didn't want us to ever find out the truth, but we did. You can find it on the internet. Just search up Robert Carson, almost anyone can work out he was guilty. Lawrie knows all about it, he found out one night three years ago. It was the night that he ran off with you. We both found out and that's why my dad was in such a violent mood. Lawrie and he had a massive fight, he was trying to stand up to our dad."

I lost complete focus so I was grateful that at that moment I pulled up in front of the large blue gates of the Three Point School otherwise I'm sure that I would have crashed the car. People shouldn't reveal things to you like the fact that their dad is a murderer whilst you are driving, it's a serious health hazard.

"But how did Lawrie suddenly find out if it had always been on the internet?" I quizzed, it seemed rather strange to me that Lawrie and Rory wouldn't be aware of something that was out there for the whole entire world to see.

"We didn't know much at all about the case at the time, we were both pretty young, and so we never really thought about searching our dad up in the news because why would you? We knew that our mum had been killed in an awful accident, how were we to know that our own father was involved? Lawrie came home one night saying Roman Huxley had told him he overheard his dad talking about it, and we searched it up straight away not expecting to find anything but unfortunately, we did."

Rory obviously noticed that I was sceptical as before he opened the car door and left, he added- "Look Lyla I have no reason to lie to you. Just search it up and ask Lawrie about it. I hope you find him. Thanks for the ride."

That was the first thing that I did as soon as I got home. I pulled open my computer and searched up 'Robert Carson'. It was late by the time that I actually got home, I had been circling the streets trying to process the bomb of information that Lawrie's little brother had dropped right into my lap.

Sure enough, my search was met with hundreds of results which all contained headlines along the lines of - *'Wife killer Robert Carson escapes from jail time.'* or *'Former lawyer in court on suspicion of the murder of his wife.'* I clicked on the top article which was dated four years ago and began to read, my eyes widened with shock as I took in every word.

Former lawyer who planned his wife's murder gets charges dropped.

Robert Carson (52) had the charges dropped against him for the murder of his wife Stephanie Hartwell last summer. Stephanie and Robert were reported to have a 'rocky' relationship which was worsened by Carson's continuous alcohol abuse. Claims of domestic assault had previously been reported by Hartwell, but they had never been followed up.

Stephanie Hartwell was killed after her car burst into flames on a junction leading into Greenstone Village, Lyntonshire, last July. After investigation, the police found that the car itself had no faults, the interior of the car had been doused in petrol and set alight. CCTV showed a man later identified to be Carson exiting the car and pulling out a lighter just before the car burst into flames.

However as of today a report has come to light claiming the car had not in fact been tampered with. With Carson's lawyer claiming the police were 'trying to profile him as a criminal to improve their poor record of catching real criminals.'

In addition to the dropping of charges, Carson also won a custody battle against Adeline Hartwell, the elder sister of Stephanie Hartwell for the custody of his two sons Lawrence and Arthur who will remain in his care.

It was unfathomable. How could Robert Carson have got away with his wife's murder? Every news article was just as vague, each stated that the charges had been dropped and previous evidence had been wrong.

I recoiled in horror at the proximity of the crime, the fact that Lawrie's mother was killed close to Jade Town's neighbouring village,

Greenstone, shocked me to the core. I was at odds to understand why I'd never heard of the incident before Rory had told me of it. I was equally suddenly aware of a pressing feeling of Deja-vu. I couldn't explain why, but it was as if I knew something about the event, some connection I had to it, I just couldn't extract the missing link from the depths of my mind.

I can't even describe to you how I felt- a trio of anger and shock and fear ricocheted around inside me, each vying to be the strongest emotion. A few hours prior, I had been face to face with a murderer and I hadn't even known it. My boyfriend's father was a murderer, I felt as though I had been transported into a crime drama. Cold blooded murders and vicious crimes didn't happen in the idyllic, mind numbingly boring Jade Town- except for the fact that they did....

My phone pinged with a notification- this could only mean one thing. Since Clara disappeared, I had set up alerts on my phone for news about the infamous Jade Town Monster. My heart dropped as I read the headline displayed on the screen of my phone.

'Jade Town Monster strikes again? Another young woman is reported missing.'

I clicked on the article, wondering who the latest missing woman could be:

20-year-old Alessia Chang was last seen thirty-six hours ago leaving her home in the quiet village of Jade Town at around 10 PM. She is believed to be another victim of a serial abductor who residents have dubbed the Jade Town Monster.'

The thing about living in a tiny town is that everybody knows everybody. Alessia Chang was a year ahead of me at school, her parents ran Topaz Café which was the favourite (and probably only) hang out haunt for all the village kids. Growing up, we would always hang out there, drinking milkshakes and chatting about everything and anything.

Alessia had a certain allure about her, she could light up any room by just walking into it. Everybody could tell that she really was going to be something special; she was destined to succeed.

I remembered suddenly how Lawrie worked with Alessia at Topaz Café; they had become quite close friends over the past few years. I figured this news must've been a shock to his system like it was to mine. Alessia was the epitome of nice, I couldn't imagine why anyone in their right mind would want to hurt her. That's the thing though, the

Jade Town Monster whoever he was, clearly wasn't in their right mind, he was dangerous, and the fear which had been bubbling inside of me ever since Clara disappeared two years ago burst through the surface. No one knew who or where the Jade Town Monster would strike next.

The awful argument that had occurred between Lawrie and I earlier rang out through my head. I felt as though what was going on was bigger than that, I needed to be there for him in the wake of the terrible news about Alessia and his dad.

It suddenly occurred to me how strange the timings of the disappearances were. Robert Carson, who had killed his wife in a fit of jealous rage had brought his family to our peaceful town and then a little while later people started to disappear. It had been a couple of years after they had arrived though, so I hoped that there was no connection between Lawrie's father and the abductions. If that was to be the case though, it meant that statistically another resident of Jade Town was to blame. Which meant that somebody I had known my entire life was taking girls of around my age from our town.

Without thinking it over, I leapt from my perch on the sofa and stalked out the front door- I didn't quite know where I was going because I had no idea where Lawrie was, but I just began walking and wouldn't stop.

Jade Town was rather chaotic as the news had clearly spread all around town about Alessia's disappearance. I ran into an old couple named the Edens who warned me for my safety and assured me that I shouldn't ever leave my house for the rest of my waking life; Reverend Jacobs who informed me that he would be praying for me and the rest of Jade Town each night and Daphne Scott who appeared to be having a rather heated debate with a man who looked strikingly like Roman Huxley. I was too wrapped up in my own mind to take notice of any of those things, even the strangeness behind Daphne arguing avidly with Roman when I was sure that the pair had never crossed paths before.

After what seemed like hours and my thirty-third lap around Jade Town, I returned home feeling dispirited and unsure of what I should do - I had lost two important things to me in those past few days. With hindsight, you may wonder why in waking hell I ever wanted to see Lawrie again, but as I said earlier, I believed that he was the only person in the world who could make me feel even remotely safe. It was more of a desire for protection and comfort than anything else.

I was just about to pick up the phone and dial his number for the eightieth time that day when the doorbell rang...

On opening the door, the familiar sight of Lawrie, his tousled blonde hair and piercing blue eyes made my insides well up. I hadn't even realised how much I had missed him; how sorry I was even though I had nothing to feel sorry for. He was carrying a bunch of pink lilies which sparkled in the early evening glow.

"I got these for you Lyla." Lawrie said cool as the night air.

"What are you doing here, Lawrie?" I said defensively. I couldn't let him back into my life that easily, I couldn't let myself be back with the brute who had hurt me. I crossed my arms across my chest and refused to take a step towards him.

"I'm so sorry Lyla, I can't even begin to think about what I did to you. I was angry, you'd offended my entire family Lyla, you made me feel like they were poison, and I was too. I don't understand why you won't marry me, and I didn't think I could ever forgive you for turning me down. But I've thought about it, and I think I can. I need you Lyla, and I know you need me."

So, what did I do? I smiled and I took him back, believing that his anger had been my fault like he said. I believed that I was to blame for the bruises and the scars he caused me.

I launched myself into his arms and let the tears that I had been keeping in cascade down my cheeks. He smelled familiar and safe. I clung to him for what seemed like forever on the threshold to my house- halfway in and halfway out. I didn't want him to ever let me go.

A while later, we were up in my bedroom talking through everything that had happened and our future when I finally plucked up the courage to ask him about what Rory had told me earlier. I told him everything that had happened that day from the impromptu visit by his father to Rory's revelation that his aforementioned father was in fact a murderer.

"Is it true?" I asked him after I had finished explaining. There was an edge in my voice, and I wasn't sure of why. Perhaps I was mad that I had known him for five years and he'd never told me the truth about his dad. Lawrie startled and from his expression, which looked like I had just caught him robbing a bank, I knew that it was true.

"Lyla..." he paused. His mouth moved but no words came out.

An uncomfortable silence hung between us.

"Well, yes… it's true." Lawrie finally admitted. I jolted away from him feeling betrayed, feeling a contempt for everything he'd been keeping from me. All these secrets made me wonder how much about him I really knew. Maybe the mystery surrounding Lawrie's life had been enticing at first, but five years later it just hurt. I wanted to know him fully, I wanted to know his thoughts and what made him the way he was. I couldn't shake the feeling that I loved him, but I'd never really know him.

 "Why didn't you tell me? I would've at least tried to understand Lawrie. I don't know why I had to find out from your little brother. I feel like I don't know you at all sometimes." I didn't know how I could ever readily trust him again after he'd kept such a massive secret from me.

"How was I supposed to tell you? I didn't want you to think that I was like my dad. I didn't want you to think that I was some kind of monster. I have no idea if anyone in Jade Town knows the whole truth, but imagine what they would say or do to me and my family if they knew?" Lawrie said explosively.

The last thing I wanted to do was to have another fight with him. It was clear to see that it was a touchy subject for him. I don't know how a teenager could process the fact that his dad was responsible for the death of his mum and then be forced to live under the same roof as the monster that took her away from him, I don't think that Lawrie ever did truly deal with it.

However, something that Lawrie had said resonated within me. Lawrie and Rory always described their father as a monster and from the small encounter that I had with Robert Carson earlier that day I could confirm that he had the demeanour of someone deserving of that label. Without a shred of thought I blurted out:

"Do you think that your dad could be the Jade Town Monster?".

Lawrie looked at me like I was deranged like I had just suggested his dad was the leader of some ruthless cult.

"My dad, really? Sure, he's dangerous but most of the time he's drunk off his face. You'd have to be pretty smart to murder a couple of girls and not get caught. I don't think my dad has that in him. My father isn't calculating, he's violent and impulsive, he would've been caught straight away."

Strangely, he wasn't horrified by the fact that I had just straight up asked him if his father was a serial abductor. Instead, he had actually laughed out loud when I asked him, his insensitivity was frightening to me. I chalked it down to the fact that Lawrie and Rory clearly had no love for their abusive father.

"We still don't know if they're dead, Lawrie, don't talk like that." I scolded him. I wanted to believe with everything I had that the girls would just turn up alive, but I knew that the hope of that was dwindling with every day that passed.

"Can we not talk about this now please?" Lawrie said in retort as he lay flat down on my bed. I watched him from my perch at the end of the bed. I should've let it go but I just didn't want to, and I certainly didn't appreciate him shutting me down like he did. He never wanted to talk about what was going on in our village even though I needed him to comfort me and to tell me that he would protect me no matter what.

"What about Rory? How is he allowed to live with your father if he's such a monster? Why are you still living there? You're an adult, you aren't legally required to live there anymore".

"Hey, quit it with the questions Sherlock Holmes." Lawrie swatted his hand in my face as if trying to physically deflect all the questions I had thrown his way.

"My dad's secretly been seeing our social worker for the past couple of years so she kind of hasn't interfered with us and I'm not living there anymore. That is what I came over to tell you." He sat up and reached into the pocket of his dark blue jeans and pulled out a gold key, attached to a black leather chain, the number 36A clearly emblazoned on the front.

"I got a place on the outskirts of Jade Town, it only has one bedroom, and it's kind of a mess but it's all I can afford with my wages from my job."

"Anyway…" He continued, his eyes firmly on the floor, "It's a mess but it's mine." He beamed at me and threw the key in my direction so I could take a closer look at it. I turned the key over in my hand and marvelled at the fact that I suddenly felt like Lawrie and I were finally growing up. For so long, we'd been stuck in the same place we'd been when we had first met when we were only kids. Finally, things were starting to change.

"That isn't the best part either." He seemed back to his old self again. As if the ghost of his actions the previous day had been vanquished. He was back to the Lawrie that I thought I knew, the Lawrie that I loved with every part of me.

"I want you to move in with me Lyla."

20 YEARS OLD

Grey. The morning was dismal and pale. It wasn't the kind of morning that I expected to get life changing news. To be honest though, every day is a turning point. Your world can completely transform in the blink of an eye. This was one of those days for me...

Lawrie and I had been living together in a tiny one-bedroom apartment on the outskirts of Jade Town for close to a year, it was quaint but perfect. I'd taken the leap to move in with him and everything seemed back to the way it was before. We didn't mention that day last year or the proposal, it was as if it had never happened.

The police were no closer to solving the case of the Jade Town Monster, although they had an idea of the kind of person they were looking for based on Daphne's description. Nobody however, had come forward to say they'd seen Alessia the night she disappeared, and all the other girls had disappeared without a trace. Whoever was behind the abductions was skilled and careful enough not to leave any kind of a trace behind him. The happenings in Jade Town had become national attention, the unexplained disappearances had swept the nation, and it was now common to see reporters and camera crews littered through the small winding streets of Jade Town. Just that day, I had only taken a trip to the pharmacy on the north-eastern edge of Jade Town, and I'd been approached by three separate reporters asking me to give my view on the disappearances. I responded with something that I don't deem appropriate to relate to you.

A few hours later, there I was sitting in the cramped little bathroom in apartment 36A panicking like hell as I awaited my fate. Three minutes really seems like a long time when you are waiting for potentially life changing news. I watched the timer that I had set on my phone count down- Five.... Four.... Three.... Two ...One.

I paused for a moment before I leaned over and picked up the plastic stick and stared at the front. Two red lines stared back up at me.

Shit.

This wasn't at all like how I'd imagined my life to pan out. I had no idea how Lawrie would react or even if I wanted to tell him. Things had been so good between us and suddenly our lives had been irrevocably altered.

There was only one person I wanted to talk to, the only person that I couldn't talk to. Times like those, truly made me miss my mum even more, and whatever God-Sent advice she would have blessed me with had she been there to see that day. She would have known what to do,

I'm sure of that. I however, had no idea of what I should do. I knew someone who had been through it, falling pregnant at a young age- Tiffany's cousin Daphne Scott, she'd made it work so maybe I could too. I sighed and tossed the test into the bin knowing there was no way life would ever revert to what it was beforehand.

****

A few days later, I was still mulling over what I should do in my mind. I hadn't brought myself to tell anyone about it. Luckily, an opportunity presented itself to me in the form of Lawrie's younger brother Rory.

Rory had been spending a lot of time at our apartment so that he could get away from living under the same roof as his dad who seemed to be as vile as ever. Rory was nearly eighteen years old but until his birthday arrived, by law he had to stay under the care of his father. Although, I'm not sure care is the correct term to use, it was far from care and without Lawrie there Rory was destined to get the entire brunt of his father's rage.

The most ludicrous thing was that I always felt more comfortable talking to Rory about his mum and dad than I ever did when asking Lawrie. Rory always seemed more of an open book, after all it had been he who had informed me the truth about his mother's death whereas Lawrie seemed perfectly content for me to never discover the truth.

On that particular afternoon, I was sitting in the tiny living room surrounded by a pile of books that I was attempting to absorb information from, with no avail. After I had discovered my pregnancy, nothing else seemed to be able to enter my mind; it was like a large stone padlock had been placed upon it.

Rory, who was sitting by the window flicking aimlessly through a textbook, had clearly noticed my anxious disposition, because he put the book down on the sofa and looked over in my direction.

"Lyla, is everything okay? You don't seem at all like yourself recently." If only Lawrie had asked me something like that the past few days, if only he had noticed, then I would've opened up and poured my heart out to him. But Lawrie hadn't noticed, he'd been too preoccupied with work and had been staying out until early light each morning.

"I'm fine, just stressed about these exams I have coming up is all." I said in a voice which I hoped was mildly convincing, I didn't really want to be discussing my situation with Lawrie's younger brother of all people.

I clearly wasn't convincing enough though, because predictably, a moment later- "There's no way it's all about your exams. Didn't you get top grades in all your exams at school and likely every other exam you've ever taken?"

"Yeah... but this is different, I don't feel prepared at all." I attempted to build on the excuse, even though it was a lousy one.

"I don't think you've ever not been prepared for something in your whole life. If anyone should be worrying about exams, then it's me, but do you see me spaced out like a zombie? No. So, now you can tell me what's really going on."

Stubbornness was clearly a common trait in the Hartwell lineage, I could tell Rory was just as unwilling to let things go as his older brother.

"Rory, Look I'm fine. I'm just..." I broke off, my mind attempting to find an end to that sentence which was proving to be as difficult as searching for a needle in a rather large haystack.

"I just keep wondering about your mum and everything that happened, and how your dad just got away with it all, he frightens me, and Lawric will never talk to me about it." I eventually decided upon.

"He frightens everyone." Rory said from his perch on the sofa.

"Unfortunately, I'm not the best person to ask, I barely know a thing about my parents because I was pretty young when my mum died. My aunt knows everything, she's my mum's older sister and they were always really close. She tried to battle my dad for custody of Lawrie and me but ultimately my dad won. I don't even think he wanted us, he just wanted to beat Addy at something, they've always despised each other." I remembered at that moment how Lawrie and Rory had lived with an aunt of theirs after initially moving to Jade Town and wondered if it could have been this aunt, Addy, that Rory was talking about.

"Is that the aunt you lived with after moving to Jade Town initially?"

"Yeah, maybe you should go and see her. She'll answer all the questions you need. I would say I'd go with you, but dad forbid us from going to see her years ago and I just can't risk it. I don't want to think of what he would do if he found out. I can give you her address though, It's about a three-hour drive from here." Rory moved from the sofa over to the coffee table I was perched behind and scrawled some details onto a piece of scrap paper on the table. He passed it to me, and I stared down at the note:

Adeline Hartwell

21 Saffron Close,

Axel Gardens,

West Sussex

"She lives in a tiny house, but you can't miss it, I think you could see it from space. I hope you get the answers you need, Lyla." I thanked Rory for her address and mulled the idea over in my mind. Sure, I had initially said it as a way of covering up what I was really worrying about but truthfully, I still had so many questions about Lawrie's mother and father. I began to think that maybe it would help me to understand Lawrie better and the God-awful day of the proposal which still haunted my every waking minute. It was also a good distraction from everything that was going on.

That is how a week later I found myself driving from Jade Town up to Axel Gardens. I had barely left Jade Town over the course of my life, the only road trips I had taken had been to Knox or Greenstone or one summer when I drove up to London with Lawrie so he could visit different medical schools. Everything seemed to be changing around me though, the trees were shedding their autumn leaves which left a kaleidoscope of oranges and browns dotted everywhere you looked; I'd gotten life changing news which I couldn't ignore; and Jade Town had turned from a sleepy village to a centre of crime, so I felt like a road trip out of Jade Town was just the change I needed.

I hadn't told Lawrie where I was going, which I knew was likely to come back to bite me later, but I honestly didn't feel able to tell him, there were a lot of things I didn't seem to be able to tell him in those days.

My car was wheezing and hissing the whole journey, it had never quite recovered since the night of the jewellery store theft two years ago, and I don't think it was the only one. My dad had noticed and had urged me to get it fixed but every time I thought about the car, I associated it with that night, so I had been very reluctant to even journey in it let alone get it fixed.

I felt truly liberated being out on the road with just my tiny stereo unit for company, playing *Bob Dylan* songs that I fondly remembered dancing around the kitchen to with my mum and Nate. In that moment, I felt the most wistful for my childhood than I have ever been, because everything had somehow spiralled out of control since then. I wished for the simpler times before the events of the past few years. It's funny how I always wanted to grow up and then when I was finally on the verge of doing so, all I wanted to do was go back.

After what felt like an eternity out on the winding roads speckled with Topaz leaves, I drove into a rather odd-looking town. By proximity, it was vastly larger than Jade Town but had all the character of a tiny quaint village. Each house was largely different in size and structure as if each resident had designed their own home in the dark. There was a large array of colours- pink, grey, sky blue, and even one striking banana yellow bungalow on the corner of one street. Rory had informed me that Adeline's house would be easy to spot, that you could see it from space even, but with the expanse of bright bold colours surrounding me I was at a complete loss as to how I was ever supposed to find it.

I stared down at the crumpled piece of paper Rory had written Adeline's address on:

21 Saffron Close.

The trouble with growing up in a box-like village was that I didn't have much experience with finding places, I had simply always known where everything was, and Axel Gardens was a spider's web of winding roads. I passed countless roads and drove around in circles squinting at each of the unnaturally small road signs- *Mariposa Way, Heron Avenue, Copper Grove, Sunset Lane.*

After having driven down a street which was literally named *'The Street'* which proved to be yet another dead end, my patience was wearing thin, and I started to consider slamming on reverse and heading back to Jade Town. The solidity of my plan, or lack thereof, began to break apart in front of my eyes- *I should have called her at least first, I can't just turn up on this stranger's doorstep and demand for her to tell me about her dead sister.* I remember thinking.

In truth I had been reckless, I hadn't considered how hard it might be for Adeline to dredge up details about her sister or if she would even want to talk to me. I knew from my own experience that talking about my mum wasn't a conversation I much desired to have with anyone, let alone a relative stranger.

Then, as I passed down *Heron Avenue* for what seemed like the fiftieth time, I spotted another turning which I had somehow carelessly ignored previously. Sure enough, as I turned, I spotted a street sign displayed next to a large Willow tree- *Saffron Close*.

As Rory's guidance had suggested, I spotted Adeline's house as soon as I started down the street. Around halfway down stood a house more irregular than the rest, it was a soft mauve colour with a bright red door and windowpanes, and a dilapidated climbing rose shrouding much of the left side of the house. I slowed my car to a halt and got out carrying a suddenly weighty suitcase of anxiety in my stomach.

The fence surrounding *21 Saffron Close* was aquamarine blue and had clearly seen better days. In fact, the entire property looked as though it was desperately in need of a renovation. As I walked the meandering path towards the ruby red front door avoiding sprigs of weeds, the suitcase of anxiety grew to such an extent I thought it would burst open and consume me whole. However, a small voice in the back of my mind willed me onwards – *You have to know the truth, you have to know if Lawrie is like his dad.*

Excruciatingly tentatively, I bashed the golden duck shaped brass knocker and waited. No sound came from the house initially, but after a few moments I heard a large clash and what was unmistakably a woman's voice cursing in pain.

Seconds later, the door flung open, and I was standing face to face, eye to eye, with a petite fair-haired woman who had thick candy-striped glasses perched on her nose and was dressed in such a miss-mash clash of coloured clothes that I was sure she must've gotten dressed in the dark.

"Sorry to keep you, I fell over the bloody cat again and crashed into the bookcase- sent the books flying everywhere." She said, as if falling over your cat was a common daily inconvenience for everybody. I had to bite my lip extremely hard in order to suppress the laughter that was rippling through me.

"Sorry, do I know you?" She asked me whilst her eyes travelled across me, clearly taking me in, my long mousy hair, faded blue jeans and old *Nirvana* t-shirt, and I thought for the hundredth time since I left Jade Town that I should've made more of an effort.

"No, you don't know me. You're Adeline Hartwell, aren't you? I was just wondering if I could talk to you about your sister Stephanie and her husband Robert." Adeline's already pale face turned as white as a sheet, as if by uttering Stephanie's name I had conjured her ghost up on the porch of Adeline's house.

Adeline shook her head ferociously and muttered something under her breath. It took me a moment to understand what she was saying.

"Not another one, I don't want to talk about it okay. Why can't everyone just leave me alone?" She made to shut the door, but I stuck my foot out to stop her. I had come that far and dedicated my whole day to finding her, so I knew that I wasn't going to leave without the answers I craved.

"Please, I really need to talk to you. I need to know the truth about it all. I'm pregnant with Lawrie's child." I blurted before really thinking it through. Admitting it felt like a weight off my chest, it felt like I could finally breathe again.

Adeline's ghostly white face contorted with surprise and then sadness.

"Stephanie's boy, my nephew Lawrie?" She spluttered and held the door open to me.

"Of course, come in, come in dear, make yourself at home."

I obliged and followed her through the house, past a lime green hallway with pictures lining every inch of the walls- many of the pictures contained a clearly juvenile version of Adeline and an even younger woman with a naturally pretty, angular face whose golden hair shone like a beacon of light, a woman who I recognised instantly as Lawrie's mother.

Adeline led me into what appeared to be her living room, but it was so cluttered with junk that you could hardly determine the purpose for the room. Items which looked like oriental artefacts, the kind you would find at some expensive museum, were scattered throughout the room.

Upon noticing my quizzical expression, Adeline explained-

"They're fakes, I collect a bunch of artefact replicas. I always have, Stephanie used to think I was crazy for it, but I always liked the idea of owning an artefact- even if it's just a fake." Adeline looked once again overcome by sorrow for a moment after mentioning her sister, just as quickly though, she cast her features into a smile and set it upon me.

"Anyway, enough about that. I want to know about you and my nephew." She sat down upon a cream-coloured chair which had tiny carved flowers climbing up the side, much like upon the side of her house. I once again followed her lead and sat down upon a rather rickety wooden chair which had clearly once been red, but the paint had practically all peeled away leaving the dirt splattered wood underneath exposed.

"Sorry, I didn't quite catch your name earlier." Adeline surveyed me with her pale eyes behind her gawdy candy striped glasses.

"Lyla, well really, it's Delilah, Delilah Kingsley. Lyla is just a nickname everyone calls me."

"I have one of those." Adeline said without any kind of elaboration. Silence fell around us for a moment before she shifted in her chair and spoke again, her tone inquisitive but with an undeniable edge-

"So, you can't be very old Lyla. Twenty or twenty-one perhaps? Unless time has completely passed me by and that does happen…" She waved her hand as if demonstrating the passing of time.

 "Yes, unless time has passed me by, I'm pretty sure my nephew has only recently turned twenty-one."

She was of course correct; it was late November and Lawrie had celebrated his twenty-first birthday only a mere two weeks previously. Practically the entirety of Jade Town had turned up to a party I had held for him, a party which he had grinned and bared, plastering on his most convincing smile. After he had cornered me and was full of anger, asking me why I would ever think of throwing him such a distasteful party seeing as he didn't want anything to do with the rest of Jade Town. This was a vast change from the teenage Lawrie who used to be at the centre of every crowd, always surrounded by people and rarely ever alone.

"I had wanted to send him something obviously, it kills me to miss his and Rory's birthdays, but their father forbade me from having any contact with them and after what happened to my sister, I knew that I couldn't risk angering him at all. You know, I never trusted him, there was always something off with him from the very start, he was quite a lot older than her. I mean she had scarcely turned eighteen when they started dating and he was closer in age to thirty than he was to her." Adeline suddenly revealed. I had an idea that she was a talker, something that I desperately needed.

"How did they meet?" I asked without answering any of the questions she had directed at me.

"Stephanie used to work in a little record store in Axel Gardens town centre whilst in school. It was a dimly lit rather edgy kind of place that attracted an interesting crowd of people. Stephanie often told me about this one guy who often came into the shop and how handsome he was with those bright blue eyes. Yes, she used to go on and on about his eyes, you probably understand exactly how she felt, I bet? I know both of my nephews inherited them."

I nodded, I could picture exactly how Stephanie had been reeled in by Robert because the exact same thing had happened with Lawrie, there was something ethereal about those eyes.

"Stephanie always liked him, and he seemed to like her, he was always in the shop and always asking for her when she wasn't there. One time he strode in and invited her out to dinner; she was overjoyed and wouldn't stop talking about it for days on end. That was until she discovered that he had a fiancée of course."

"He had a fiancée?" I asked incredulously, shocked by this new information, something that even Rory hadn't told me.

"Yes, her name was Christina Beaumont. They had met at university and seemed like the perfect poster-child couple, she was Swiss and truly beautiful in a kind of effortless way. I remember seeing them out together one time, she was tall and as elegant and majestic as a swan. It seemed like Christina and Robert were perfect together, but he broke off their engagement suddenly, it was only around two months before the wedding as well."

"Did he break it off because of Stephanie?"

"He never admitted it, but I suppose that's probably why. Soon after, he took Stephanie out for the dinner he had promised her, and their relationship started from there."

I startled as I felt something furry brush past my bare legs. I peeked a soft auburn cat prowl away from me across the room towards Adeline with its tail haughty and swishing in its wake.

"Don't be alarmed dear, that's just *Charles Darwin*." She said motioning to the orange cat. No, this isn't a fabrication, Adeline honestly had a cat named *Charles Darwin* which was probably one of the more conventional things about her.

"Is he...?" I started remembering how she had told me about falling over her cat when I arrived.

"The blasted cat I fell over in the hallway. Yes, that's him, always in the way. I have another but she's rarely here, a lot more independent than this lap-cat." Adeline leaned down and picked up Cat *Charles Darwin*, placing him on her lap as if to prove the point. Yet he quickly jumped from her lap and stalked out of the room.

"I'm sorry I've been so rude! Can I get you a drink or anything, Lyla?" She suddenly burst out.

I shook my head hoping that she would proceed with her story although I had to admit I was rather dehydrated, the sitting room was so stuffy that I felt as though my head may explode.

"Okay then. Anyway, where was I? Ah yes, Stephanie and Robert started dating each other soon after he broke off his engagement from Christina and they suddenly became almost inseparable. Wherever Robert went, Stephanie followed. Our parents weren't thrilled by the prospect, and neither was I. I could never trust Robert and I told Stephanie that many times, but of course, she was young and in love, so she didn't listen. They married after a year of dating- she was just nineteen at the time."

"Why didn't you trust him?" I inquired, although I had an idea of why. The only brief encounter I had had with Robert Carson had been a tense and terrifying moment, I had literally been rooted to the spot in fear. There was something about him that was just so unnerving, but what was more unnerving was how I remembered seeing that side of Lawrie too.

"He has always used his physical presence to belittle and frighten others, he truly frightened me when I met him, but what seemed more dangerous was how enchanting he clearly was. Almost the whole of Axel Gardens seemed under his mercy, which is a dangerous power to have."

Adeline's description of Robert seemed awfully like Lawrie, he had after all, turned up in Jade Town and almost immediately had everyone at his mercy. I was beginning to detest the information I was hearing; I didn't want to hear any more potential links between Lawrie and his dad, I didn't want to dwell upon the fact that he could possibly turn out like him.

Adeline drawled on, oblivious to the panic that was rising inside of me.

"Stephanie moved in with Robert and became detached from her old life. I didn't see her at all until after Lawrie was born around two years later. She was flighty and panicking and nursing a black eye. In fact, she had bruises over a lot of her body, but she refused to show me most of them. She assured me everything was fine; Robert somehow twisted her mind into thinking that she deserved it all. I begged her to leave him, but she wouldn't, she said she couldn't get away from him. I think she feared what he'd do if she walked away." Adeline's glasses fogged up and by her ragged breaths I could tell she was on the verge of tears.

I was about to ask what happened when she continued-

"I remember she said to me though, if anything was to ever happen to her, she wanted me to look after Lawrie. She said she didn't want him left with Robert; she thought Robert would turn him into a monster.

Of course, I never expected anything to happen to her, but she did. Then, when she finally was ready to leave him..."

Adeline broke off as tears came pouring down her pale cheeks. I left my chair and crossed the room to comfort her, feeling guilty that I had brought her to sadness.

"That night... when he ... he .... in Greenstone..." She spluttered.

Again, I was overcome with a strange emotion like I had been when I first discovered Stephanie Hartwell had been murdered in Greenstone. It wasn't just recognition that Greenstone was so close in proximity to Jade Town, it was something else. I knew there was something else locked tightly in the void of my mind about Greenstone and a car that caught on fire, but I couldn't break that thought free no matter how hard I tried.

"I tried... I t-tried to s-save them... Lawrie and R-Rory ... but I f-f-failed." Adeline was sobbing uncontrollably.

I pulled her into a hug and was overcome by the powerful aroma of tulips and what smelt like thyme. A pair of yellow eyes which I could only assume belonged to Adeline's cat Charles Darwin were watching us from behind my recently vacated chair.

"There's nothing you could've done, you tried to fight for them, didn't you?"

I reassured the inconsolable Adeline who it was hard to believe had been a complete stranger a mere couple of hours ago. Though unable to speak through the tears, she nodded her head frantically. I decided that it was best to change tact or there was no way I was going to receive any more information from her, or, based on the firm grip she had on me, no way I was going to be able to escape anytime soon.

"We met when he moved to Jade Town, before he left to come and stay with you." I revealed more to stop her crying than because I actually wanted to reveal mine and Lawrie's backstory to her.

Almost immediately, her violent sobs subsided, and she looked up at me with her candy-striped glasses askew from the force of her crying.

"Wait, you're the girl." She said as a wave of recognition passed over her face.

"When Lawrie came here, he was reading *The Great Gatsby* which I had been trying to get him to read for years, it had been Stephanie's favourite. He had actually told me he was reading it that summer that Stephanie…"

She broke off again tears once again lining her glassy eyes. The tears didn't fall however, she drew a deep breath and continued as if talking and reminiscing about her nephew gave her an invisible strength.

"After the accident though, he refused to ever pick it up again. He hadn't finished it and I thought it was a lost cause, he never seemed to like anything that reminded him of his mother. But then, when he came here, he was suddenly desperate to read it and he told me about you. He said he liked how you weren't afraid to be yourself or to put him in his place, not a lot of people did that. Lawrie always used to run circles around almost everyone, I think he got that from his father." Adeline's face turned sour at the mention of Lawrie's father, and I understood just how much hatred she must have felt for him.

"Do you see any other similarities between them? Lawrie, Rory and their dad I mean." I blurted out. Adeline broke away from me and began pacing around the cluttered room, looking rather flustered.

"I mean of course there are similarities between them, I think there are similarities between every parent and child." She directed at what looked like a replica of a brightly coloured totem pole in the left corner of the room.

"I would say Lawrie slightly more so. Rory was always so sweet just like his mother, he has the biggest heart around. Lawrie always used to idolise his father growing up and he always seemed to know how to use the power he had for his gain. I can't imagine what finding out the truth about his father would've done to him, I couldn't bring myself to tell them because they were both so young and I believed that the truth would shatter them. How in hell could a child process the fact that their mum is dead because of their dad?"

"Lawrie found out when he was sixteen, but he never told me the truth about it, Rory did." I informed Adeline who stopped pacing and looked physically pained.

"Gosh, only sixteen years old! That must have destroyed the poor boy and then he and Rory still had to live with that monster, they don't still live there, do they?" Adeline asked, her face contorted with worry.

"No, Lawrie and I live in a little apartment in Jade Town and well, Rory's still under eighteen, so he has to live with their dad, but he stays around at our place a lot. I hate the fact of him being there all alone with Robert. I know he's older now, but I hate the fact that Lawrie is no longer there to protect him."

Adeline nodded in agreement, her face ridding itself of some lines of worry.

"Now, let me guess..." She drew her finger in the air like she was physically connecting the dots, the coral shawl that was draped over her fluttered as she did so.

"You find out that you're pregnant and have heard all about Robert, perhaps even seen a striking similarity between Lawrie and Robert. Perhaps young Rory gave you my address and you wanted to come and discover the truth about Stephanie, so you didn't land yourself in a similar situation." It was as if she were speaking directly into my soul, she could see straight through me because that was the exact reason why I had driven to Axel Gardens and tracked her down.

Without waiting for a response, she answered the question which had been rattling around in the cage of my mind ever since the test came back positive.

"I can't say I have much experience with men, Stephanie was my little sister and look what happened to her. So, I'm rather reluctant to open myself up to anyone, but I've made a nice little life here for myself, at least it's safe and I get by just fine. What I will say is that although by blood there are bound to be similarities, Lawrie is not just the product of his father. He is also the child of one of the most altruistic, caring and forgiving people to have ever walked the Earth. I like to think Stephanie is watching over her boys and looking out for them."

This time, it was my turn for my eyes to sparkle with tears. Not purely because of Adeline's ode to her sister but also as a reminder of my own mum. I had always hoped that she was there watching over me and guiding me along my own winding path.

It was armed with that thought, that I thanked Adeline for everything and made my exit, finally sure in my mind of what I had to do. Before I left, Adeline pulled me into a crushing hug and told me repeatedly to keep in touch whilst reassuring me that children most certainly are not destined to be their parents which is the greatest piece of knowledge I can give to you Lacey.

As I drove away from Axel Gardens and back towards the familiar streets of Jade Town, the sun dipped in the sky casting orange shadows all around. The drive back seemed infinitely quicker, perhaps it was because my mood had been lifted. Despite the horror tale of Robert and Stephanie that I had heard from Adeline, I finally understood what I had been questioning for quite some time. Lawrie wasn't his father, he may've shown flickers of the monster inside, but I began to believe that if my mum was watching over me then maybe I was exactly where

I was supposed to be and I had to allow my life to follow its designated course.

Just before reaching Jade Town, I turned a sharp left and headed up towards the steep road towards Jade Town church which was somewhere I hadn't been for years. Ever since my mum's death, my relationship with God had been shaky, in a juvenile manner I had blamed it all on God, but I knew there was no substance behind the blame. A larger reason why I hadn't been back in years was because my mother had been laid to rest in the grounds there and I could never bring myself to go back to the place that had caused me so much hurt.

That day however, with the late November sun warming my back I walked up purposefully to the grave in the fourth row which was shrouded by two broad and obstinate looking oak trees. The state of the withered pink peonies which hung limply at the grave informed me that my dad hadn't been up there in a long time either, he used to visit frequently but had rarely been seen outside of his house for the past few months. I believe that the weight of grief that was weighing on Jade Town caused by the Jade Town Monster had hit my father hard. When you're surrounded by grief, it always makes you think about what and who you've lost.

"Hey Mum." I called as I approached the grassy plot.

"I know I haven't been up here in so long, but I have news. It's really big news and I really wish you were here to help guide me."

I stood there talking into the open air until the orange shadows fell to reveal the inky black night sky. It felt as if she were truly there beside me, listening raptly to everything I had to say about my life over the last four years.

Upon leaving that night, I had no doubt in my mind that no matter Lawrie's reaction to the news I was going to keep the baby. Afterall, my mother had been barely older than me when she had Nate and me. She always told us that she had no doubt in her mind about whether she made the right decision, and I felt the exact same way.

That night, I got home to find Lawrie waiting for me and I told him my news. To my relief, he looked the happiest I had seen him to be in years. In that moment, I felt like despite all the horror occurring in Jade Town, Lawrie, me, and our baby would be able to be a happy family. I hate to quash this beautiful image but as you well know Lacey, Lawrie is not with us in this room talking about how we became this happy family which means that something went horribly wrong. The thing in question will be revealed soon enough but there is much I must tell you before you can completely understand the truth.

****

You were born in the middle of June the next year; I had completely underestimated just how much my life would change. I was lucky if I managed to get five minutes of sleep, and my mind was constantly racing with thoughts of how to cater to your needs- *What did you need? How could I help you?*

The apartment was constantly punctuated by the sounds of your wailing. Lawrie tried to help as much as I believed he could, but he had taken on even more hours at work in an attempt to earn enough money for us to get by.

Speaking of money, we were rather desperate for it. Although, not desperate enough to accept any of the countless handouts we had been offered from a bunch of people ranging from my dad to Miss Samuels our old biology teacher at school who had always clearly shown her disdain for Lawrie but informed me, as she thrust a wad of notes covertly into my palm that she had always had a soft spot for me. I kindly declined her offer and made sure ever since then, that I took a long route back from the village hall so as to avoid walking past her thatched-roofed house, inside which she always seemed to be waiting by the window ready to come out and corner me if I ever happened to stroll by.

It wasn't that I was too proud to accept any of these handouts, it was common knowledge that the residents of Jade Town were hardly millionaires and I felt guilty accepting help from anyone because if anyone had had enough money to move, I am sure that they would have packed up and left Jade Town a long time ago. Jade Town was no longer the idyllic dormant village that people desired to lead a quiet life in, it was a constant buzz of camera crews and news reporters and danger. None of the houses had been redecorated for years, paint was peeling away, and wood was rotting in every direction you looked. It was as if when Clara Yale went missing three years before, the Jade Town that I knew and loved growing up had gone missing too. Everywhere you went, the depravity of the Jade Town Monster's actions was clear to see. It was he, the infamous illusive Jade Town Monster, who had single handily set this tiny village on fire and watched it burn to smithereens all around him. Creating a cloud of ash so large that it consumed everything whole.

There was one resident of Jade Town though who was hardly strapped for cash, the man who lived in the large Victorian property right on the west side of Jade Town, the man who had given nothing to the town and had never even attended a town meeting in the six years he had been living there, that man of course was Robert Carson, Lawrie's estranged father who hadn't visited you once, Lacey, since your birth.

Naturally, I still had suspicions about him. I had proof that he was a murderer which made me believe that if anyone in Jade Town was capable of abducting three girls, it was him. Lawrie, however, wouldn't entertain these suspicions. On many occasions I had tried to broach the subject with him in the hope that by talking about his mother's death, he may realise just how dangerous his father was and how he could be behind the abductions of Clara Yale, Faith Baxter and Alessia Chang. But alas, whenever I tried to argue the point with Lawrie, that fiend of anger inside him would come to life and I would be too frightened to push the subject any further. Robert was a monster, but I always remembered Adeline's words about how Lawrie had idolised his father growing up which made me understand exactly why Lawrie was so reluctant to see his dad's faults.

A week or so after your birth Lacey, I saw the police up at Robert Carson's house, undoubtedly, there to question him, the police of course were aware of Robert's narrow escape from jail so just like I, he seemed to be the first person that they questioned. However, the attempt seemed fruitless as what was so calculating and frustrating about the Jade Town Monster was that he had left no kind of trace, his three victims had simply vanished into thin air.

Rory had told me a few days afterwards that he was in the house when the police had questioned Robert and that the questioning had been brief because Robert had constantly reminded them about their lack of evidence and refused to speak without a lawyer present. Even though it was Rory who had told me the truth about his mother's death, he was equally reluctant to consider the prospect that his father might be the Jade Town Monster. I don't believe anybody could imagine that someone close to them could be responsible for such heinous crimes.

The only person who had been able to give any form of evidence so far was Daphne Scott who had seen Faith Baxter walk off with a man on the night she went missing. No one had come forward to say that they had seen Clara or Alessia on the nights that they went missing, it was unbelievable there had been no real break in the case and I started to believe there may never be.

Daphne had been a saint since you were born Lacey, as she already had experience in parenting from her three-year-old daughter Willow. Unlike I, Daphne had raised Willow completely alone and I fully began to appreciate how difficult that would've been for her. Daphne and I had been meeting up regularly sharing tips and talking through motherhood.

In the middle of July that year, Jade Town begun to buzz with fear once again. A year since Alessia Chang had disappeared was quickly approaching, and the Jade Town Monster hadn't been caught which meant that he may've still been out there searching for his next victim. In response, people began locking themselves in their houses and only journeying out for essentials. Jade Town had become a ghost town, as nobody wanted to take the chance of being the next unfortunate victim...

As a new mother my worries were heightened to the extreme, so I cancelled on meeting with Daphne around five days before my birthday. Lacey, I don't often believe in holding regrets, I believe that you shouldn't dwell too much on the past but rather look into the future. But, cancelling on Daphne that day is one thing that I do sincerely regret, and I believe I always will. Maybe you can predict what I'm about to reveal to you. The fact that Daphne reported her sighting to the police had quickly spread around Jade Town which I think unfortunately placed a red-hot target on her back. Daphne was the only person who had glimpsed the Jade Town Monster, the only person who could potentially lead to his capture and he couldn't let her get away with that.

I remember clearly, it was the twenty-fourth of July, two days before my twenty-first birthday. I had been struggling for hours to get you to sleep Lacey, you had been so restless, but finally after an hour and a half of trying I had succeeded. Leaving you to sleep in our bedroom, I headed towards the kitchen and opened my laptop attempting to get some of my schoolwork done which had been piling up upon me ever since your birth. I was sure it was only a matter of days before I buckled under the immense weight of it all.

However, as I powered up my laptop I was met with a notification. My stomach lurched as I recognised it to be the alerts I had set up for if there was any new information about the Jade Town Monster, these same alerts had informed me about Alessia Chang's disappearance only a year previously. Sure enough, as I clicked on the article attached, I peeked at the bold heading.

'Is the Jade Town Monster at work again? Another Young Woman Disappears from the Idyllic village.'

My body tensed as I searched the article for the name, wondering who the latest victim could've been. On the fifth line of the article, I found it:

The victim is twenty-four-year-old Jade Town resident Daphne Scott who was reported missing by her cousin Tiffany Scott, who discovered Daphne's daughter Willow (3) alone in Daphne's apartment. Tiffany Scott (21) Informed the police that this behaviour was extremely out of character for Daphne who typically would never let her daughter out of her sight. The police investigation for the Jade Town Monster continues. They are urging anyone who may have any information which could lead to the capture of the Jade Town Monster to come forward.

With a thud, I slipped out of my chair and fell to the floor. On hearing the news, I had completely lost control of my body. The other girls going missing had been awful for me because I had known each of them, but Daphne had almost become like a sister to me. It was as harrowing as if the victim had been Tiffany or Quinn or Marina, Daphne had grown up with all of us and she had been the greatest help to me during my whole pregnancy and in the first month of your life, Lacey. I wanted to believe that she would simply just turn up again, but the odds weren't looking likely seeing as Clara Yale had been missing for three years, Faith Baxter for two, and Alessia Chang had been missing for close to a year.

Lawrie came through the door a few minutes later and found me crumpled in a disbelieving heap on the linoleum floor.

"Oh my god Lyla, what's wrong?" He came sprinting to my side in an instant, his brow furrowed, and a worried expression cast over his smooth features.

"She...Sh...She's...g...g... gone." I spluttered, shaking uncontrollably unable to fight back the tears which were dropping all around.

"Who? Who's gone? Is it Lacey?"

Lawrie asked in a nervous tone, his entire body rigid and tense against me. I shook my head violently and he seemed to relax completely. We sat there on the kitchen floor together with me sobbing violently and him holding me for hours, as the necklace he had given me two years before, which I hadn't taken off since that day, glistened around my neck. He didn't once ask me why I was so upset; I wasn't sure if he had seen the news report himself, but he just seemed to know. In that moment, as the sun fell below the clouds and the twilight gathered all around us, we just seemed to fully understand each other in a way that I didn't think anybody else ever could.

21 YEARS OLD

Just like I had always known deep down, Daphne Scott didn't simply return. Just like Clara, Faith, and Alessia, Daphne Scott seemed to have vanished into thin air. Her daughter Willow had since been under the care of Tiffany's parents, Daphne's aunt and uncle, as Daphne's parents had left Jade Town just after Daphne had fallen pregnant.

I visited Willow as often as I could. She was the splitting image of Daphne, with the same olive smooth complexion and wide dark brown eyes. That was the unbearable thing about Daphne's disappearance, the village hadn't only just lost an incredibly bright and friendly woman, but Willow had lost her mother too. As a mother myself, I couldn't bear to imagine being parted from you Lacey, the very idea of it tore me apart inside.

I had been struggling immensely with the increasing workload from medical school, raising you, and dealing with the disappearance of Daphne. Quinn and Marina had finished university and had moved back to Jade Town temporarily both taking up jobs that I knew that they didn't want so that they could be around to support me and Tiffany too. Daphne being Tiffany's cousin meant that she had been hit the hardest out of us all. Tiffany was an only-child with parents who were constantly working whilst she was growing up, so Daphne was the closest thing she had to family.

Since Daphne's disappearance, Tiffany had been scouring the entirety of Jade Town and getting anyone she could talk to involved in the search which wasn't a difficult feat, as Daphne was so loved in Jade Town. Frustratingly, once again we found nothing, not a shred of evidence of where she could have disappeared to. Months passed and we began to lose our last shreds of hope. One by one people stopped turning up to searches of the neighbouring villages, organised by Tiffany until only a few people remained.

One Thursday in late June, I had just returned from another lengthy search of Jade Town hoping to find some kind of trace of Daphne when I saw a familiar face standing by my front door. Weighed down by fatigue, I thought at first, I was imagining her standing there amongst the overgrown grass and weeds. As I drew closer, and she turned around to face me, I knew I wasn't imagining anything. Throughout all the chaos and the unrecognisable state of my life, there stood a reminder of my past and the sheltered blissful childhood I had once had in Jade Town.

Ava Aurelia's tanned face burst into a grin as she saw me lurking behind her, thousands of memories came flooding back through my mind like her presence on my doorstep had just burst a dam in my mind containing all the memories of my childhood. Ava Aurelia, alongside Clara, had been my greatest childhood friend who had moved away from Jade Town many years ago. I had no idea just how much I'd been craving to see a familiar face until that moment.

"Delilah Kingsley." She said incredulously with a faint Australian tinge to her voice, she'd moved to Australia from Jade Town when I was nine which was something I was always incredibly envious about.

 "You know, you haven't changed a bit!" Ava crossed the path and pulled me into a hug which I gladly reciprocated.

"Ava, it's so good to see you! What are you doing here?" I asked, still unable to believe that she was back in Jade Town and there on my doorstep.

"Well, my grandparents live over in Knox village and they told me all about what's been going on here. I couldn't believe my ears, especially about Clara. I sure hope that she's safe and okay."

Ava of course had left Jade Town before Clara and I had stopped being friends. A long time ago Ava, Clara and I were inseparable, we went everywhere together and did almost everything together so I understood how the news of Clara's disappearance would've shocked Ava to the core.

"Yes, a lot has been going on here. Jade Town isn't what it once was when we were kids. Speaking of kids, though…"

"Yes, you have one of your own, don't you? A daughter I believe." Ava said knowingly, I was oblivious to how she knew this information or how she knew where to find me, as we'd unfortunately lost contact years ago.

"Yes, I do, but how did you know?"

"Do you remember my older brother Charlie? He's the one who didn't move with us to Australia." I ran through the extensive list of Ava's siblings in my mind, Ava was the youngest of seven children so remembering each of her siblings was quite a challenge after all this time.

"Yes." I said remembering the eldest of her brothers who had thick dark hair and always slightly had the distinct appearance that he'd been dragged face first through a garden hedge.

"Well, he works out in Greenstone now. He's a manager in a medical technology supplier company there, and he told me about one of his colleagues from Jade Town, called Lawrence Hartwell, I think? Apparently, he constantly talks about his girlfriend Delilah or Lyla as he calls you and his daughter, and I thought to myself how many Delilah's do I know in Jade Town? So naturally, I had to come and check it out for myself. I didn't realise you were going by Lyla now, but I love it."

I thought about the piles and piles of work I desperately had to complete and hesitated for a moment before asking-

"Ava, do you want to go and get coffee or something? I've got so much to tell you."

Ava smiled.

"Yes, definitely. I want to hear all about this Lawrence Hartwell, Charlie tells me that he's rather handsome."

Ava and I drove out to a café in Greenstone as I had avoided Topaz Café ever since Alessia Chang had disappeared. Topaz Café seemed so depressing in the light of Alessia's disappearance, the place simply held too many memories as the place was synonymous with Alessia. Every time I passed the large windows of Topaz Café, I expected to see her in there, waiting tables with a broad smile on her face. It seems that almost all of Jade Town felt the same way as Topaz Café was pretty much deserted all the time.

Upon reaching Greenstone, before I had even located a parking space, Ava asked me a question from the passenger seat. It was a question I'd known she was bound to ask, and I had been dreading it.

"So, did you and Clara remain friends all that time? It must have been so hard for you, her going missing, I don't know why anyone could do such a thing. She was always such a sweet girl."

Ava had clearly not known the person Clara grew into being, a person who enjoyed making my life a living hell some days. Nevertheless, being around Ava made me reflect over the young Clara Yale- my best friend. I agreed wholeheartedly with Ava, even though Clara and I never got along much after I became friends with Quinn, I couldn't imagine how twistedly, purely evil somebody could be to do whatever the Jade Town Monster had done. What I found to be the most horrifying thing was how normal the whole ordeal had become; Jade Town had become so used to the horror and grief that victims like Clara or Faith were no longer in the forefront of their minds. People were too preoccupied with themselves; I believe selfishness to be the greatest vice and the residents of Jade Town had become selfish creatures who only looked out for themselves and not the four girls who were nowhere to be seen.

"Clara... yeah, we were still friends." I lied as I found it easier than revealing the truth that I had been complaining about her and had actually ruefully remarked that I never wanted to see her again. Of course, there was no weight behind that, and yet it came true, for I never saw Clara again.

"So, are you staying long? Where are you staying Ava?" I asked changing the subject swiftly to not have to answer any more questions about Clara or my relationship to the other missing girls. We clambered out of my car which shuddered under the movement and headed towards a mint green banner which displayed *'Greenstone Patisserie'* in screaming pink letters.

"A little while I think. As soon as I came back here, I remembered how much I missed it. Is that crazy, you know because of everything that's been going on, to want to stay around Jade Town?"

"No, that's not crazy at all." I remember responding. I wish I had never said that. For her own good Ava should've packed up and left Jade Town the minute she set foot back there, but of course it is easy to judge situations with hindsight. At the time, I believed that Ava Aurelia being back in Jade Town was one of the best things that had ever happened to me.

We sat in the tiny blue walled, Greenstone Patisserie, for a few hours, the sun gradually dipping below the clouds as we talked about everything that had happened in the years since we had seen each other of which I had to admit a lot more seemed to have happened to me and in Jade Town and it was in that moment that I realised just how irregular the goings on were. Sure, of course I know that what was happening in Jade Town was evil in its purest and greatest form, but I almost grew up with the lingering threat of the Jade Town Monster so hearing about how someone could live a somewhat normal life- without a parent ending up in a coma, a serial abductor stalking their town or having a child with someone who had a twisted upbringing, seemed unfathomable.

Quickly, I will relate to you what happened in Ava's life in the years after she left Jade Town. Ava you may remember I told you previously, was a rather talented performer and I always believed that was what she was destined to become. In Australia, she had further pursued her love of performing and seemed to have done quite well for herself as she was constantly in work flitting about from project to project. However, as often happens in life, Ava changed her mind and she gradually developed a contempt for performing, this of course angered her parents who had given up everything for her so that she could pursue her dream. In response, she leapt at Charlie's revelation about Lawrie and I and jumped on the first plane out here.

"So, what's your plan? Are you going to go back to Australia?" I remember asking as I downed the last of my third cup of inky black coffee.

"Honestly, I don't know." She replied picking at the last of her almost entirely destroyed slice of cheesecake with the edge of her fork.

"I'm tired of my life being on such a tight schedule, you know, moving from project to project and training for a show and then performing it every single day. It just became rather tiring, and I realised that I don't love it in the same way I once did. So, I think I'm just going to hang around in Greenstone and Jade Town for a bit, live with Charlie, and get a job somewhere. Hopefully, then I'll be able to figure out what I actually want to be doing with my life." Ava sighed.

I had an idea of a job for her if she were rather desperate. Lawrie and I were in great need of a babysitter as previously we had just relied on the availability of Quinn, my dad, Marina, or Nate who would often travel down to spend most weekends with us in Jade Town. Nate had set up home just outside Knox village and was closer to us than he'd been in years, and as a family we were once again united. The tragedy within Jade Town seemed to bring everyone closer, because everyone was fighting against the same common evil- the Jade Town Monster.

"You don't happen to need a babysitter, do you?" Ava asked as if reading my mind.

"I don't have that much experience, but I'm sure I would be fine for the job."

"Yes." I nodded.

"I think you'd be great."

****

An hour or so later, Ava and I were driving back through the streets of Jade Town so that I could release Quinn and Nate from their babysitting duties. Quinn of course, had jumped at the chance of spending more time with Nate, she was still just as blatantly in love with him as ever before.

The orange-glowing, near deserted streets of Greenstone completely contrasted to the scene we witnessed when we approached Jade Town. As far as I could initially see, a great coloured wall seemed to stand between the entrance and the centre of Jade Town. Driving nearer however, I remarqued that the wall was rippling and moving, and I noticed in fact it wasn't a wall at all- it was a large sea of people. A group too large to purely be the residents of Jade Town, it seemed as if the residents of Greenstone and Knox Village had flocked to Jade Town.

But why? I struggled for thought. *What were all those people crowded around?*

I had to park the car on a dingy street far from Jade Town as the nearer streets were already littered with people and cars. Upon exiting the car, a large sound emanated from the hub of people, like a mainstream festival had just opened in Jade Town. However, Jade Town wasn't a place for carefree jubilant celebrations of music, and I couldn't help the feeling of dread that washed over me as we approached the crowd. The faces of Clara, Faith, Alessia and Daphne began to swim their way through my mind. There would be only one reason why people were crowded around and perhaps it was a positive reason. My spirits began to lift as I dwelled over the concept- *Maybe they've been found.*

Growing closer and closer, more and more things became clear to me about the scene. The first was the harsh blue glare emitted by police cars which took me horrifyingly back to three years before and the awful night I had to wait for Lawrie as he stole the necklace from Opal Jewellers. Immediately, the presence of the screamingly bright lights had such an effect on me that if it were not for Ava behind me willing me through the crowd, I was sure that I would have fainted or been frozen to the spot.

The second thing I noted on walking closer into the epicentre of the crowd, was that I was right in the fact that the whole of Jade Town and the neighbouring villages had gathered together. At the very back of the crowd I even alarmingly spotted the unmistakable figure of Robert Carson, who I'd never seen outside of his house aside from the one time he visited me two years earlier.

The third thing I noted was that the action seemed to be taking place outside a large stone-built thatched house with a gleaming white painted door which I knew belonged to the Huxley family.

Finally, the fourth thing I noticed once Ava and I had penetrated straight through the throng of people, was that two rather burly police officers had a hold of a tall and athletic looking young man who was screaming his head off. I immediately recognised the man in question as none other than Roman Huxley...

Shock washed all over me, I couldn't understand why the police were detaining Roman Huxley and why everyone had turned up to see.

Unless...

"SHE'S MY CHILD TOO!" Roman's voice screeched through the suffocating noise all around.

"I HAVE THE RIGHT TO SEE HER. I HAVEN'T DONE ANYTHING WRONG, PLEASE BELIEVE ME." He was being dragged from the Huxley's pristine front garden which was Jeanie's pride and joy and towards the nearest of three police cars. Dean Huxley was standing at the foot of the path, his face drained of all colours, he seemed unable to speak or move a muscle. Jeanie Huxley was at his side crying her eyes out and cursing rather loudly as she watched her only son being dragged away by the police.

At the front of the crowd, I spotted Tiffany hurling abuse towards Roman and the Huxley's. Tiffany had been so cut up by Daphne's disappearance, but Roman's arrest couldn't have had anything to do with Daphne's disappearance, or the Jade Town Monster, could it?

A bright mass of auburn hair alerted me to Marina's presence further back in the crowd, she spotted Ava and I and immediately bustled her way through to where we stood rooted to the spot.

"It's insane, isn't it?" Marina asked as she approached us.

"I was just going for a run around the lake when it was found and then I followed the police here and they arrested Roman, I couldn't believe it."

"Found what?" I asked, ridiculously confused.

"What's going on?"

"Oh, you must've just got here!" She exclaimed and then with a hushed tone-

"Well, as I said, I was out for a run by the lake, and I saw the police there. It turns out, someone had found Daphne's car there and upon examining it they found traces of blood which they believe to be hers and DNA, I think it was a few hairs, which incriminate Roman. Her phone was also in the car, and he was the last person who she called. They found something else too in the boot of the car, which is where they found most of the blood- it was a silver ring with the letter 'H' on it I think, which has got to stand for Huxley, right?"

I didn't really absorb most of Marina's words because one singular thought kept ricocheting through me: *they found blood. They found her blood. They found her blood.* The likelihood of Daphne being safe and alive was dwindling right in front of my eyes and the police believed Roman to be responsible. I had grown up with Roman Huxley, I had been in countless classes with him at school and yet he could be responsible for something so depraved, the thought sickened me to the core.

"I don't know what he keeps going on about though." Marina noted as Roman once again screamed out "SHE'S, MY CHILD. I HAVE A RIGHT TO SEE HER," just before his head disappeared below the flashing sirens and into the police car.

Marina may not have had an idea, but suddenly I believed that I did. Do you remember how I told you what Daphne related to me about Willow's father?

"He's younger, I don't think his family would at all approve of me or our child, so I refused to let him have a part in her life."

I knew, as I told you, that the Huxley's were a rather eminent family within Jade Town, a family who looked down upon the other residents. Something that the mayor of Jade Town Dean Huxley definitely wouldn't want to spread around the community would be that his only son at barely eighteen had an illegitimate child with an older university drop out. Dean Huxley was someone who would do anything to maintain his stellar reputation and Roman Huxley barely seemed like someone who was willing to raise a child. Everything lined up perfectly.

"Do the police think he could be the Jade Town Monster?" Ava asked, cutting me from my thoughts and bringing me back to reality.

"They don't know yet, but I think it's possible. There have been four disappearances in the last four years, they must be connected in some way." Marina sighed and tossed her auburn curls from their resting place on her shoulder and squinted towards where the police car Roman was in as it began to move.

"I just can't believe that the Jade Town Monster could be Roman Huxley though, I never would've even guessed, not in a million years."

I couldn't believe it either, something seemed off about the whole thing. Hearing about how Daphne's car was found out in broad daylight, in the open, by Jade Town Lake with blatant incriminating evidence against Roman Huxley vastly contrasted to the clever calculating work of the Jade Town Monster who had previously ensured to never leave any kind of trace behind.

In unison, the entire crowd turned as Roman Huxley was driven away from Jade Town, an entourage of two other police cars following in its wake. Cheers and shouts of jubilation came from members of the crowd as they believed that the Jade Town Monster had just been driven away from them. People couldn't contain their glee at the idea that the terrible ordeal was coming to an end, the idea that they could once again feel safe within their own community.

Even Robert Carson was smirking with his soulless blue eyes fixed on Dean Huxley who was attempting to formulate a word, but no sound left his lips.

Beside Robert, mimicking his expression exactly, stood a slightly shorter, scrawnier version of Robert with bright golden hair. That was the first time since they'd arrived in Jade Town that I had seen Robert and Lawrie in each other's company. Both stood there with their arms crossed, jaws set and almost identical glaring eyes watching Dean Huxley squirm, and it terrified me to see just how similar they appeared to be.

****

For some reason, I couldn't shake the feeling that Roman didn't have a hand in the other girls' disappearances. For the next two weeks it was all I thought about, I needed to know whether my suspicions about Daphne and Roman were true.

The rest of Jade Town didn't feel the same way however, as far as they were concerned, they had locked up the Jade Town Monster and the fear that had been weighing on our little village for the past four years had vanished. Countless tales of how Roman Huxley had become the elusive Jade Town Monster spread all throughout Jade Town. Even Lawrie who typically hated discussing the Jade Town Monster, seemed keen to share how he had suspected Roman all along.

The only person who seemed willing to discuss the idea that Roman Huxley wasn't the Jade Town Monster was once again Lawrie's younger brother Rory, who had turned eighteen on the day Roman Huxley was arrested, the entire event had of course overshadowed any form of celebration for his birthday.

Rory and I had discussed Roman a few times and we seemed to be on the same page. Neither of us could understand why the Jade Town Monster after years of getting away with the abductions would leave incriminating evidence in a place for all the world to see. Everything about it seemed like a set-up. Someone wanted to frame Roman, and I needed to know why.

****

On a sunny afternoon three weeks after Roman Huxley's arrest, I was sitting in apartment 36A's tiny front garden soaking up what was left of the sun when Rory walked up the path towards me. He strolled up to my perch on the unusually cold stone step and sat beside me.

"Hey, what are you doing here?" I asked surprised but glad to see his familiar face. Rory hadn't only become a great friend to me, someone who I could voice my suspicions to as he was a lot easier to talk to than his brother, but he'd become a younger brother too.

"I'm leaving." Is all he said.

"What do you mean, you're leaving?" Rory had never spoken about any future plans of his, I had no idea what he wanted to do with his life after he became free from his father's clutches. I had no idea he'd been thinking about his future beyond Jade Town.

"Well, I turned eighteen three weeks ago so I'm officially free of my dad. I just wanted to get away and start anew from everyone because it follows you. Even here, it followed me, everyone seemed to know what my father did, and I just don't want any connection to it or to him." It wasn't that what he was saying surprised me, I understood exactly why Rory would want to get away from his dad and his past, but I had no idea that the residents of Jade Town knew that Robert Carson had murdered Stephanie Hartwell. Perhaps I assumed so because I had never heard anyone explicitly discuss it, but it's possible that all the hushed whispers about the Hartwell's around town were in fact about Robert and Stephanie.

"So, what are you going to do? Where are you going to go? To your aunt?" I asked, thinking of Adeline Hartwell, her candy-striped glasses, and eccentric clothing style. I had kept my promise to Adeline and had been informing her about the goings on in Jade Town and her two nephews. It always upset me thinking of her all alone in Axel Gardens with only her cat *Charles Darwin* for company and her fear of letting anyone into her heart after seeing what happened to her little sister.

"No, I mean I'd love to visit Aunt Addy, but I think I'm going to go into the army. Because of my dad, I feel like I have to pursue something to help and almost rectify his actions. Do you know what I mean? I really like the idea of serving my country and I really like the idea of being miles and miles away from here."

I nodded. I now know exactly how it feels to feel as though you must rectify the evil work of someone else.

"That's great!" I exclaimed.

"When do you leave?" I asked, expecting to have a few more months with Rory in Jade Town, to have enough time to properly say goodbye as I very much doubted that I would ever see him again after he left. Everything he said sounded so final, everything felt like a goodbye.

"That's the thing. I already joined the army, so officially I leave tomorrow morning."

"Tomorrow morning? Have you told Lawrie or your dad?" If Rory had spoken to Lawrie about leaving Jade Town, it was the first time I was hearing about it.

"Not yet, I wanted to tell you first. Lyla, I think at some point you should leave Jade Town too. Go wherever, it doesn't matter, you aren't safe here."

"It hasn't been safe here for four years Rory, but it's my home." I couldn't imagine leaving Jade Town as it was all I knew; everyone I had ever met lived there and I think most vitally, the reason why I hadn't been able to leave Jade Town was because everywhere I went, I was reminded of my mum when she was full of life. I thought that it would kill me to leave that all behind.

"Lawrie and I can't just up and leave, our whole lives are here."

A conflicted expression I couldn't quite interpret spread across Rory's face, he looked as if he were about to reveal something to me- something immense and shocking, but at the last moment backed out.

"I don't mean you and Lawrie, I mean you, Lyla, and Lacey, you should go. You should leave everything behind here and start afresh."

I was at a complete loss to understand what he meant and why he was insinuating that I should leave Jade Town and Lawrie behind. I never got an answer though, because Rory got up and headed back up the winding streets.

"I'll miss you, Lyla." He said before disappearing amongst the stone houses of our village.

"I'll miss you too." I said into the breeze, and whilst I understood why Rory had to leave, I also knew that I was losing yet another friend.

****

Rory left Jade Town the next morning, Lawrie and I went to see him off as he drove into the rising sunlight. It was a weird feeling watching him leave, I wasn't sure when I would see him again, if ever. The whole thing just seemed like the closing credits of a movie. It also made Jade Town seem a little darker, Rory Hartwell was one of the kindest people in Jade Town and I'd lost so much, that losing him made my chest feel like it was full of lead.

Rory's departure also stoked a fire within me. I felt as though I had to visit Roman in the prison he was being held at about fifteen miles outside of Jade Town and get the answers that I was craving. So, I ensured that Ava could babysit, and drove out to the prison whilst Lawrie was at work. One thing I knew was that I had no hope in sharing my suspicions with Lawrie, I knew he wouldn't possibly contemplate the fact that Roman Huxley could potentially be innocent. Lawrie had been convinced Roman was to blame and kept reassuring me that the ordeal was finally over.

Lyntonshire prison was a large, dilapidated, grey building with sky high fences topped with ferocious barbed wire. It seemed to loom over me, blocking out all light and intimidating me, just thinking about the people housed inside made my pulse quicken and made me realise just how alone I was, standing there with my arms crossed over my chest.

It took me a few long minutes to work up the courage to walk inside but a motivation in the back of my mind kept me going- I had to know where Daphne was, and I believed only Roman could give me the answer.

Evidently, Roman Huxley had never expected me to visit him in prison or to spend any time in his presence at all, because he was startled when he saw me sitting in one of the pearly white chairs in the visitor's room.

"Lyla Kingsley, to what do I owe this pleasure?" He asked, sitting down in the chair directly across from me. He looked incredibly worn out, large dark circles clung beneath his bloodshot green eyes and his hair was sheared dangerously close to his scalp. It was hard to believe that this same man had once been Jade Town's heartthrob.

"I've got a few questions to ask you." I delved straight in, desperately not wanting to engage in any ridiculously awkward small talk when we both knew that I hadn't simply driven to visit him for a coffee and a catch-up.

"Well, what the hell. No one's believing a thing I say right now, so ask me whatever you want. You probably won't believe me anyway."

Roman leant back in his chair and signalled for me to go ahead, so I did.

"Just tell me, are you Willow Scott's father? Are you the guy that Daphne wouldn't let have a part in her life?" Roman looked shocked that I'd made the connection between the pair and paused, before finally admitting it.

"Yes, I am." His voice was weak and very un-Roman-like.

"At first I was fine with it; it wasn't like I was looking to raise a child and my father wouldn't let me anyway, he practically disowned me when he found out." Roman continued in that same feeble voice.

"I saw Willow around though, and one day I just had enough, I wanted to be a part of her life. After all, it should be my right as her dad."

"So, what did you do? Daphne seemed pretty adamant on you not having any part in Willow's life."

"I kept asking, I kept trying and she wouldn't budge but neither would I, and eventually she agreed to meet up and discuss it and that's why I was with her that night… the night she… went missing."

So, Roman had been with Daphne on the night she had gone missing, which made it entirely possible that he in fact had a hand in her disappearance, the thought made me shiver. Was I really sitting face to face with the Jade Town Monster? Was it possible that Roman had been under our noses the entire time?

"I didn't hurt her; I didn't do anything to her, I promise." He assured me, raking a hand over his face.

"When did you last see her Roman? Where did she go after you saw her?"

"It was late, I was out going for a walk to clear my head when I saw Daphne in her car, so I thought I'd take the chance and try to persuade her again." Roman looked pained at having to recount this memory, or perhaps because of his stint in jail for something that he claimed to be innocent of.

"So, what happened?" I pressed. I was completely over letting things go by this stage. In the past, I had let too many things slide and I wouldn't do it anymore.

"Well, we talked, and argued again because she refused to change her mind. She said I hadn't made any kind of effort in the first three years of Willow's life even though she knew that she wouldn't let me within a mile of her." Roman huffed and it was clear that this was a very touchy subject for him.

"My parents have controlled my whole entire life you know. I've never been able to think or do anything for myself. Do you know what that's like, Lyla? It's suffocating, my dad is hell-bent that I'm going to follow in his footsteps and become the next mayor of Jade Town. He's never cared about what I might want to do with my life or considered the fact that I might not want to end up like him." I had always despised Roman without thinking how difficult it must have been to have Dean Huxley for a father. Dean Huxley, the man who had repeatedly looked down upon Lawrie and I for having a daughter so young, when all along his son was a father himself. I began to think there were secrets everywhere in Jade Town, I just hadn't been looking hard enough for them.

"What happened when you last saw Daphne? This is really important, Roman." I stressed the point, I knew I only had one opportunity to talk to him, to attempt to find out the truth. This was it, if he shut me down, I had no chance.

"Right, yeah. We argued and then about fifteen minutes later she told me to get out, she said she was going somewhere to see someone."

What?

It was incredibly possible that the person Daphne had gone to see was the Jade Town Monster. I was right in the fact that Roman held a key, a vital key, which could lead to unmasking the identity of the real Jade Town Monster.

"Do you know who this person was? What exactly did Daphne say?" My heart began to pick up pace, frantically awaiting Roman's answer.

"She seemed to know them, she said she believed they were responsible for something, but she wouldn't tell me what. She practically chucked me out of the car and drove off. I didn't think anything of it at the time but then she went missing, and I can't help worrying that it was that Jade Town Monster that she was going to see." Either Roman was an incredible liar or he had genuinely seen Daphne drive off right into the arms of the Jade Town Monster.

"I care about her; I always have, and Lyla please believe me that I'd never do anything to hurt her, I promise you. It's been eating me up inside not knowing what happened to her, or if she's safe."

Deep down, with my whole heart, I absolutely believed Roman. Call it intuition, maybe, but I knew all along that Roman wasn't the person to blame, and that the Jade Town Monster was still at large. Prowling around our winding streets, pleased to have pulled the wool over everyone's eyes.

"I believe you, Roman." I nodded.

****

Driving home that night, I was weighed down by a slight disappointment. Even though I was sure Roman wasn't the culprit, he hadn't really given necessary information that could help to lead to the capture of the Jade Town Monster. The drive back towards Jade Town seemed to stretch on for hours upon hours and I was immensely grateful when I parked up in front of 36A and opened the front door to find Ava sitting on the sagging couch, staring at the static TV.

"I just managed to get Lacey to sleep." Ava yawned as I put my coat on the hanger.

"Thank you, Ava, you should go home now, it's pretty late." I expected Ava to thank me, grab her own coat and head out the door but instead she just sat there staring at the TV which I realised had been muted. Silent pictures danced across the screen; it looked like some kind of late-night medical drama.

"Lyla, I've got to tell you something and you have to promise that you won't be mad at me for snooping."

"What are you going on about?" I asked, completely ignoring the part about being mad at her, my voice raised, likely due to the frustration I was feeling about Roman's lack of information and Rory's departure.

"Well, Lacey wouldn't stop crying no matter what I tried, so I don't know why but I thought I would have a look in the attic to see if you had anything else like any old toys she liked or anything." I had no idea what Ava was talking about because I had no idea that we even had an attic.

"This apartment has an attic?"

"Yes, there's a little latch just above the kitchen, I saw a couple of weeks ago that it had been left ajar so that's how I knew where it was. Anyway, I think I found something in there." Ava was still refusing to look at me, her visage was painted with worry.

"What did you find?" I hadn't moved. I was still standing right by the front door and the thin front wall of 36A, so was likely in earshot of the whole street.

"It was really dark up there, so I wasn't sure."

"What did you find, Ava?" I repeated. The frustration of the day bubbling over to boiling point. All I wanted to do was fall asleep and forget that the events of the day had ever occurred. All I wanted was to fall asleep and wake up in my childhood bedroom as if the saga of the last few years had never happened.

"A box, it's silver and pretty rusted, but it seemed really strange. Inside there was what looked like teeth and locks of hair and something which had been so burnt I couldn't quite tell what it was."

Immediately, I racked my brains for the previous owners of 36A, and I couldn't remember exactly who Lawrie had purchased the apartment from.

Then, I remembered that I never knew. Apartment 36A had been abandoned for practically my entire childhood and teenage years, which was undoubtedly why Lawrie was able to afford it with only a pittance of money, two years before. Was it possible that there was a reason it had been abandoned for so long? Was there something darker lurking within its flimsy four walls?

"Did you see anything else?"

Ava shook her head. "Nothing worth noting, just a lot of old books and a dusty photo album of a family, and some letters from someone labelled 'S' to someone they called 'D'."

It seemed like the secrets of a past life were hiding up in the illusive attic, an attic I had never noticed before. However, if Ava had noticed it ajar, it meant that someone previously had found it. I ran over in my mind the people who had been in our apartment the last few weeks- Marina, Tiffany, Quinn, Nate, my dad, Ava, Rory, and Lawrie. Any one of those people could've discovered the attic and its contents, but why had no one before Ava spoken out about it? Surely the finder must've been enticed by the mysterious box and its intimate contents, or the old letters and photographs.

A movement outside made Ava jump, and even though it was likely just a cat prowling around the moonlit streets, she suddenly straightened up and headed for the door.

"I've got to go Lyla. Anyway, I think you should check out the attic, I wouldn't usually have thought anything of it, but it really unnerved me." With that, she turned on her heel and headed out of the door before I even got the chance to say goodbye or offer to drive her back to Greenstone.

Thoughts of the rusty silver box and its mysterious contents filled my mind that night, and I even found myself dreaming of opening it and finding something grotesque inside like a shrivelled human head. I tossed and turned all night, unable to shake the feeling of uncertain dread that Ava had placed inside my mind.

So, I wasn't awoken by my phone vibrating loudly on the bedside table at 5AM as I had hardly slept a wink all night. Peering over at it, I noticed that it was a number I didn't recognise but all the same I answered it, grasping onto hope that someone had some information for me about Clara, Faith, Alessia or Daphne.

"Hello, is that Lyla?" came a slightly gruff voice, a voice which I remembered somewhere in the deepest depths of my mind.

"Yes, who's this?"

"Sorry to call you so early, it's Charlie." It wasn't until he added, "Ava's brother." That I realised who he was.

"That's okay, I've been up for hours. What can I do for you?" I was grateful that Lawrie was away on a work trip so I didn't have to worry about waking him up because I was becoming increasingly panicked at why Ava's brother Charlie could possibly be calling me at five in the morning after Ava had left 36A late last night, alone...

My worst fears seemed confirmed as Charlie's voice rang hollow through my ears. "I was just wondering if Ava's there. She didn't come back last night and normally I wouldn't be too worried, after all she is an adult, but with everything going on in Jade Town, it's put me on edge."

A dam containing the fear and dread I had been pushing back for so long broke, and it all swept across me with such force that I was glad I was sitting down, or I knew my legs would've given way beneath me. It couldn't be, the Jade Town Monster had taken so much from me and the whole village, he couldn't have taken Ava too, could he?

My world had been crumbling around me for years, but it was only then that I felt the full magnitude of it. I had given Ava a reason to stay in Jade Town, maybe if I hadn't given her the babysitting job, she would've packed up back to Australia where she would've been safe. I had believed having Ava back In Jade Town was one of the best things to have happened in years but suddenly it felt like the worst thing in the entire world.

With my voice shaking uncontrollably, I answered Charlie. "No, she left here last night, I thought she was going home. Oh Charlie, I'm so worried, do you have any idea of where she could be?" It was the stupidest question I had ever asked in my life, of course Charlie had no idea where Ava was, otherwise he wouldn't have been calling me at the crack of dawn wondering if Ava was with me.

"I don't know; I've called my parents and my siblings, but she hasn't told any of them of any plans to go back to Australia. She might just turn up, you never know, thank you Lyla." I had no idea why he was thanking me when I had been of no help at all. If anything, by being so selfish and not offering her a lift home, I had potentially sent her to the Jade Town Monster who was waiting, teeth bared, and claws sharpened.

"I'll keep a lookout. Hopefully, she'll just go back home." I sighed as I put the phone down and stared at it for hours, willing it to flash up with Ava's name telling me that she was okay, and Charlie and I needn't worry about her so much.

That call, of course, never came...

My mind was set on one purpose, I knew that I had to discover what Ava had seen in the attic. So, I crept down in the weak early sunlight and headed towards the entrance of the attic. Sure enough, after groping around the ceiling for a while my hand settled on a cream latch which had been camouflaged into the equally cream-coloured ceiling. Tentatively, I pushed it up and a rusty silver ladder descended down, which led to the pitch-black hole I had just opened in the ceiling. Taking a torch from the kitchen draw, I ascended the ladder which creaked terribly under my weight, punctuating the silent early dawn.

Apartment 36A's attic was a small and dingy rectangular space which emitted a dusty, dank, and intoxicating odour, signalling to me that some kind of animal must've died and was decomposing up there. Sure enough, as I pulled myself up into the attic, I spotted what looked like a pigeon carcass on the left-hand side of the room which was definitely responsible for the stench. I covered my nose and mouth with my dressing gown sleeve attempting to suppress myself from gagging.

In the centre of the room, amongst beams of rotting wood, were a few dusty boxes. I approached these boxes, the light of the torch swimming golden across the room. The first box was a black trunk which was in surprisingly good condition, with ornate carvings on the side of flowers which looked like lilies. To my dismay, the black trunk was sealed shut and no matter what I tried I was unable to prise it open.

Following this, I turned to the second box, which had once been painted an ivory colour, but paint had scratched away over the years to reveal the wet rotten wood underneath. This box was relatively easy to open, and I shone my torch on its contents. Inside tied up with string, was a packet of what looked like letters. Each one was crumpled and written in the same floaty cursive handwriting. I unwound the string, took the first one from the pile and read:

Dearest D,

How I have loved spending time with you these past few weeks, it felt almost too good to be true. Days seem to fly by when I am in your company, and everything seems a lot brighter than it did before. I love Jade Town too; it is such a picturesque place and is now filled with some of my happiest memories.

I can't wait to see you soon.

All my love,

S.

After examining the contents of that letter, I looked at the rest of the pile. Most of the ink had worn away and bled through the pages, making most of the letters appear illegible but right at the bottom of the pile, one letter stared back at me clear and bold:

D,

I finally told him. I have been thinking about it for so long and finally you gave me the courage that I needed. You gave me the courage to be free. Finally, D, we can be together without fear like we always wanted. You just must take a chance on me like I did on you. He was not as mad as I thought he would be, I think he wants to meet you actually.

I will eagerly await your reply.

Until then, I will dream of what may be.

S.

I had no idea of the meaning behind these letters or who 'D' and 'S' were, but whoever they were, they seemed to be deeply in love. A kind of love which breaks through all barriers, and as I sat there pouring over the pieces of parchment, I desperately hoped that they got their happy ending because Jade Town wasn't a place of happy endings, rather of nightmares in their purest form.

Glinting amongst the other boxes, I spotted it. The rusty silver box that Ava had told me about. It was small and perhaps had once been a jewellery or makeup box. I picked it up and examined it, it looked as though there had been markings on it at some point in time, but the box had rusted over almost completely.

With a great amount of force, I managed to wrench it open. Just as I was about to shine the torch on its contents, it cut out leaving me in the pitch-black darkness and the unmistakable wail of a one-year-old child met my ears, so I was forced to abandon the box and head back into the apartment.

That whole day, I was exhausted yet incredibly alert. Every person I saw, I glanced back at hoping to see the familiar form of Ava Aurelia. Meanwhile, my mind was buzzing with the information Ava had given me the previous night about the attic and I wondered if the contents were as she described.

I had decided to journey back into the attic once I got home, to discover the rest of its secrets. Upon getting home however, it quickly became clear to me that finding out the truth was going to be almost impossible.

As I crossed the apartment towards the hatch of the attic, I spotted a familiar blond-haired figure piling something into bin bags. The something in question looked strikingly like the miniature silver box I had been examining earlier in the day.

 Above Lawrie, the hatch to the attic lay open and I remembered with horror how I had suddenly left in a rush that morning and had forgotten to check if I closed the hatch.

"Lawrie, what are you doing?" Lawrie startled at the sound of my voice; alarm spread across his face for a minute before he fixed me with a bright smile.

"Hi, it's good to see you again. I missed you." As he pulled me into a hug, I glanced over his shoulder at the mass of old boxes and bin bags which had amounted on our linoleum floor.

"What are you doing?" I asked again, breaking away from him. Lawrie returned to packing the boxes from the attic into bin bags.

"Just getting rid of rubbish, it's all worthless stuff, not even worth looking at. You should go and lie down; it looks like you've had a hard day. I'm fine to finish this all by myself." He waved an airy hand attempting to ward me off from looking at the contents of the attic.

"No, that stuff isn't worthless. I was looking at it earlier and there were letters and that little silver box there. They seemed kind of interesting."

I motioned to the box which he was holding in his left hand.

"There's something in there. Ava saw it, she said it contained locks of hair or teeth or something and I was about to look at it this morning, but I didn't get a chance." Lawrie's eyes flashed almost black for a moment, but he didn't falter.

"It's all just junk Lyla, I'm going to get rid of it." He said in a tone considerably more forceful than was necessary, but I wasn't in a mood to let him win. Mentioning Ava again tore my already delicate heart into thousands of bloody red pieces.

She could be out there in danger right now, she could be fearing for her life, she could be...

What if I was the last person to see her? What if I let her walk right into the Jade Town Monster's waiting arms?

"I want to look at it, don't throw it away." I lunged towards the box, but Lawrie grabbed my arm before I could get there, his forceful grip searing through my skin to the bone.

"I told you already, it's just junk, now let it go Lyla." He snapped.

"NO." I snapped back. "LET ME SEE IT." My voice echoed through the room. I was suddenly tired of all the times I let him win, in fear of his temper.

"NO." He roared.

Then, he pushed me backwards, making me lose balance, and fall with a thud to the floor.

"WHY CAN'T YOU JUST LEAVE THINGS ALONE FOR ONCE IN YOUR GOD-DAMN LIFE? NOT EVERYTHING'S ABOUT YOU LYLA."

Before I could get back up, he had picked up the bin bags and left out the back door with them. However, not before I had the chance to peek at one of the bags where I spotted a photo album open to a photo of a tall and broad brown-haired man, with bright blue eyes sitting next to a young pregnant woman with soft blonde hair, a silver ring glistening on her index finger, and in the middle sat a blond boy of about three-years-old with blue eyes so bright that they leapt out of the page. Just next to the boy on the grass, was a miniature silver box exactly like the one Lawrie and I had just fought over but in much better condition.

Unless I was mistaken, I believed that I knew the people in the photo. Unless my eyes had deceived me, I had just watched Lawrie walk off with a bin bag containing a photo album and mementos of the Carson/Hartwell family which had been contained within the attic.

But why? Why were Lawrie's family photos in the attic and why was he trying to hide them from me?

Lawrie came back a few moments later, with tears in his eyes, telling me how sorry he was. He told me he would never push me or shout at me again, that he was stressed and was taking it all out on me. Once again, I nodded and forgave him like I'd become so conditioned to do so. I told myself that next time I would be stronger; next time I would stand up to him and wouldn't let him hurt me.

Every day from then on, I ardently searched for any sign of Ava or the contents of the attic throughout Jade Town. Unfortunately, neither search proved fruitful. I began to believe I'd never find out the truth, that Jade Town would forever be haunted by these disappearances.

Little did I know, we were about to discover the truth very soon...

****

A few weeks later, the police discharged Roman Huxley after CCTV imaging was discovered of Daphne outside a convenience store in Greenstone thirty minutes after she had left Roman. After that, no one knew of Daphne's movements, she was shown leaving the store and getting back into her car, heading west back towards Jade Town. This seemed to convince the police that Roman, who had left Jade Town after his argument with Daphne, and had been spotted in Lynton which was miles and miles from Jade Town where he remained for several days, had no part in Daphne's disappearance. I believe that there was more to it, the fact that Ava went missing whilst Roman was incarcerated meant that the police didn't believe him to be the Jade Town Monster and ultimately believed that the Jade Town Monster was to blame for Daphne's disappearance as well as Clara's, Faith's, Alessia's and then Ava's. The Jade Town Monster may have been clever and calculating but abducting Ava was surely his biggest mistake, it threw the police from Roman's tail and back to looking for him.

Before I tell you the events of my twenty-second year, events which will shock you to the core, I will recap everything that we knew about the Jade Town Monster at that time, for these clues will prove to be vital.

First, from Daphne's sighting of Faith before she disappeared, we believed the Jade Town Monster to be a man whom Faith appeared to know. Secondly, Roman had informed me that Daphne had said she was going to visit someone that she knew who she believed to be responsible for something on the night she disappeared. Daphne's car had been found abandoned by Jade Town Lake with evidence that seemed to incriminate Roman Huxley as his DNA was found there. There were also traces of Daphne's blood and a silver ring emblazoned with the letter 'H'.

Cryptic as these clues may be, they all lead to the same person...the Jade Town Monster.

22 YEARS OLD

It had been close to a year after Ava Aurelia had disappeared before Jade Town started getting answers about the Jade Town Monster. It was the beginning of a scorching hot July, the kind that Jade Town hadn't seen since the 1980s. Everyone was once again becoming apprehensive as the days shot past. We knew by then that the Jade Town Monster had a specific pattern, a girl would go missing every year around the same time in July. Our already tiny population had been depleted by the wicked work of the Jade Town Monster, and the most frightening part of all was that at that point we had no answers. The only leads the Lyntonshire police had followed had been in vain, the only sighting of the Jade Town Monster was an account by Daphne Scott, and she wasn't there to ask anymore. If anyone knew anything, nobody wanted to speak out because there was the ultimate feeling of dread that speaking out was what had made Daphne a victim of the Jade Town Monster.

Daphne's daughter Willow had become a firm friend of yours, Lacey, she always treated you like a little sister of hers. Without being sure of why, I always felt guilty when I saw Willow. She was only a child and yet her life had already been thrown off course- her mother was nowhere to be seen, but at least she had been reunited with her father, as Roman had revealed the truth about Willow and much to his father's contempt had become a small part of her life. Willow was still predominantly under the care of Tiffany's parents, and they too were rather reluctant to let Roman, who had previously been imprisoned, albeit falsely, have a part in her life.

Willow was a clear symbol of the fact that the Jade Town Monster hadn't only destroyed those girls' lives, whatever had happened to them, but that the Monster's wreckage had blown apart so many others' lives too. Clara's mother always looked thin and fragile, she was constantly putting up missing persons posters and she always looked exhausted. Her marriage to Clara's father had broken apart since Clara's disappearance, she always said that Clara was the only thing that had made their family complete. Without her, Mrs. Yale had nothing.

Faith's grandparents who she lived with because her parents had abandoned her as a baby, were constantly asking anyone they came across if they had seen her.

Alessia's parents and younger sisters tried in vain to keep Topaz Café going to bring joy to the village, but you could see how much they were all struggling.

Ava's brother Charlie never left the house anymore. I had tried visiting him in Greenstone a few times, but every time I knocked on the door, I never got a response despite seeing shadows moving inside of the house. I didn't know if Charlie blamed me because Ava had been on her way back from my apartment when she disappeared, even if he didn't, I certainly felt like he did. I felt like every single relative of the missing girls blamed me in some way.

As for me, I had been struggling trying to raise a child and work towards a medical degree. I had a lot of help from my dad, Tiffany, Quinn, Marina, and Nate. However, Ironically, the person who was supposed to help me raise you had become more distant than ever. Since the fight about the contents of the attic, something invisible seemed to have broken between us. Lawrie was often out until late at night without explanation, claiming to be working late which was a feeble excuse. However, it was one that I didn't question for a long time, I was stressed but most of all, under the surface I was frightened of him and what he might've done if I had spoken out against him. The ghost of the day he proposed to me and our countless fights over the years, stuck in my mind as a constant reminder not to cross him. Something was different between us now, however, after every other fight, things had seemed to return to a form of normal but after Ava's disappearance and our fight about the attic, it was anything but normal.

I was aware that something was affecting Lawrie as over the year since Ava's disappearance, he had become a shell of his usual self. Perhaps this transformation had been occurring long before that, but it was only then that I really noticed how Lawrie had turned from an ambitious teenager who desired to be a surgeon, to a man who worked a dead-end job and drank twice his body weight in alcohol every night. Lawrie had transformed to be more and more like his father as time passed, even though he hadn't spent time with his dad in years. I didn't know whether he was intrinsically destined to mirror his father, or whether life had made him that way. All I knew was that I barely recognised him, and everything that I had been so deeply in love with seemed to slip right before my eyes.

Lawrie and I had barely crossed paths for months, which is why the evening of the 23rd of July was so important. If I hadn't discovered what I did that night, things may have been entirely different for myself and the residents of Jade Town.

It was just after 11PM when Lawrie came home that night, and I was ready, waiting. Finally, I was ready to ask him.

I was ready to confront him.

I had been watching his car snake up the road towards our apartment from the tiny window in the singular bedroom, and as I heard his key in the lock, I rushed downstairs into the cramped kitchen.

A few moments later, he entered the kitchen looking exhausted, and a strong stench of alcohol clung to the air surrounding him. I sometimes wondered if he was trying to drown something inside of himself. I had no idea what had caused this shift in person from the one I had met and become almost obsessed with all those years ago.

Lawrie had always had such potential, everyone believed that he was really going to be someone, it made me mad to see the person he had become. Of course, I couldn't help thinking that I had failed him, as somehow under my watch he had thrown away his bright future and I never saw him happy anymore.

Truthfully, I couldn't remember the last time that we had laughed together or spent time enjoying each other's company. We were two people who were stuck together by situation rather than bound by endless love. I apologise for painting this pessimistic picture in your mind, I know you probably wish for me to remember your father with nothing but positivity but when I finish my story, I will let you decide if he deserves to be remembered in a positive light. There is still much more to recount to you, so cast your mind back to the kitchen in apartment 36A where Lawrie had just walked in on the 23rd of July.

"Hey Lawrie, how was work?" I made an attempt at pleasant small talk, blatantly ignoring the cloud of alcohol which had just polluted our kitchen.

Lawrie nodded his fair head, "Fine." Was all he said in response.

"I'm going to go sit down."

With that, he took about three steps from the kitchen and ended up in our living room, leaving me alone. My heart had begun to pulsate more rapidly as I thought about what I was about to do. I had been thinking about it for months, ever since that first meeting I had attended where a man with the last name Wilern had told me that I had to overcome my fears to get the truth.

With my mind murky as a muddy lake, I reached into the cabinet above our sink and pulled out our nicest crystal glass- It had been a present from my cousin Tristan at your christening a few months before. An event which I thought back to with horror because Lawrie had turned up drunk to his own daughter's christening.

My father had intervened and saved the day, he never spoke to me about that day, but I knew he was thinking the exact same thing that I had been pondering for such a long time- What had gone so wrong with Lawrie? Where had the boy who had an appetite for literature and desired so ardently to move to London and become a surgeon gone? I now believe that it was the guilt, the guilt was eating him up inside and making him into a shell of himself and his only escape from it was his choice of poison- alcohol. What was he so consumed by guilt about? That's what I was just about to discover that night...

I filled the glass half-full of whisky, the only alcohol in the apartment that Lawrie hadn't fully consumed. I glanced around to check that the coast was clear, and then on determining that it was, I pulled out a tiny glass bottle containing a white crystalline powder from the pocket of my jacket. The label emblazoned on the front informed me that it was 'AMOBARBITAL.'

I remember how difficult it had been to extract from the hospital, drugs were kept under such high security, and I had almost failed to obtain it, almost but not quite. For reference, I had been working at the hospital on a placement as part of my training for the past year. Despite the criminal nature of my actions, I find it important to communicate to you that I didn't break into the hospital.

I shook the bottle into the glass, my mind fixed on the answers I craved more than anything else- the answers which I was about to receive.

The words of a conversation earlier that day with a short woman with dark stress-lined features echoed through my head as I approached Lawrie, the glass of whisky hanging limply in my hand.

"Just add a tiny amount." She had instructed me.

"He'll be okay. Upon waking up the next day, he'll have no memory of telling you anything."

****

"Thanks." Lawrie muttered nonchalantly a few minutes later as he took a swig from the crystal whisky glass I had placed on the table for him, it was the first I'd given him but based on his erratic body language I had an idea that he'd previously had a lot more to drink that night. For a man who claimed that he wanted to be nothing like his father, he had surely become a carbon copy of Robert Carson and I was petrified beyond belief that your childhood Lacey, would become like that of Lawrie and Rory's.

He appeared to be completely intoxicated, his movements were sluggish and snail-like. His gaze was always slightly off focus, he was in the kind of state where people were prone to reveal the deepest things at the slip of their tongue. I knew I had to try; it was my only opportunity to get the truth. I desperately needed to know why Lawrie had been so out of sorts recently. He hadn't even noticed that you, Lacey, had been staying with my dad for the past few days. I had to have you out of the house because I had to protect you at all costs and I felt you were much safer with my father than with anyone else in this world, especially Lawrie.

I needed to know why Lawrie had been pushing me away for such a long time, why he'd become increasingly distant from me both physically and metaphorically. Most of all though, I had to know what he was hiding in the attic, I had to know why he'd been so mad to find that I'd been up there, and why he had so quickly disposed of whatever had been contained up there.

"Lawrie." I called soothingly. He looked up in recognition, but his gaze was lingering around my left ear rather than on my face.

"Lyla." His words came out slurred and I began to wonder if he was too drunk. After all, drunk ramblings wouldn't be taken seriously, but then I remembered what that woman had told me...

"It begins with symptoms of drowsiness and fatigue. You'll have to wait a moment, but it works incredibly quickly."

Relief swept over me. *It's working, I just need to give it time* I thought. Time, however, wasn't an unlimited resource and I was clearly running out of it.

"Can I ask you something?" I was tiptoeing around the issue. I was frightened that he wouldn't tell me anything and everything would've gone to waste. After all, Lawrie had never been one to share his thoughts with anyone, it was something that I used to admire about him- the fact that what he was feeling wasn't always etched on his face for the whole world to see like mine was. I found it enticing, the fact that he had these hidden depths under the surface that I desperately wanted to break through, like his whole life was an ancient code that I needed to crack. From the beginning of this story, I always stated that I found the mystery around Lawrie to be rather enticing, but I ask myself now- why did I find mystery to be such a good thing? Wouldn't life be simpler if we knew exactly what we were getting ourselves into?

"If you must." He replied gruffly. His glass was almost empty, and he bashed it back down on the tiny wooden table in the centre of our living room which shook in protest. I took a deep breath and attempted to clear the chaotic state of my mind which was whirring at such a speed it was beginning to give me a migraine. Throughout the web of thoughts snaking across my mind, one thought shone through brighter and more aggressive than the others- *I won't let him get away with being so evasive, not this time.*

"I have to ask. What was in the attic, Lawrie? Why did you ditch the stuff so quickly when you learnt I'd been up there?"

A long pause followed and the hope and fire that had built up inside of me started to dwindle, I was sure that he was going to shut me down like he had countless times before. All those times, I had let things that I should have pushed, slide. Everything had been building for far too long and I knew that there was no way I would be leaving that room without the answers I needed.

Luckily, after a few more excruciatingly painful seconds, he began to speak...

"Lyla, you're so obsessed with asking me all these fucking questions, all the fucking time. Don't you know how annoying it is that you're constantly asking things I know you don't want to hear? Did it ever occur to you that I'm not telling you for your own good? I've been trying to protect you for years Lyla, I said I'd do anything for you, and I meant it. God Lyla, I meant it. The truth will be hard for you to hear but you've asked so many fucking times I'm tired of it. So, here it is..." His voice rose in volume as he spoke, I don't remember exactly how I was feeling at that moment or what I was thinking but nothing in the whole entire world could prepare me for what he was about to tell me. His words from that night still rattle around in my brain clear as day, even sixteen years later...

"The reason I didn't want you going in the attic is because... well, first there's stuff about my family up there. You see this apartment has been connected to my family for a long time and that box, in particular, is something I know you don't want to see. Because they're in there... well, not them exactly but parts of them...like tokens I collected along the way."

I was completely baffled for a minute. *What did he mean 'they' were up there? What could he possibly be referring to? I knew that his family minus his mother were safe and accounted for so, what could possibly be in that box?*

I didn't have long to think about it though, as he spoke again seconds afterwards with his gaze suddenly and rather terrifyingly fixed on mine. His eyes looked sunken out and the deepest blue I had ever seen them. No, not blue but black, shining deep black.

"The funny thing is..." and he actually laughed out loud then, the sound was almost deranged and nothing like I'd ever heard before. I was sure that the serum was taking effect, that he was only mere moments from revealing what had been plaguing him for so long.

"Everyone's out there freaking out and searching for those missing girls but it's no use because they aren't missing exactly... actually, they're not far away at all."

My body temperature dropped so rapidly that I was surprised I actually survived hearing what Lawrie was saying. My heart battered my rib cage, sending my pulse soaring.

It couldn't be true... It just couldn't be.

I couldn't have missed it....

I couldn't have been so fucking blind...

I wanted to speak out. I wanted to scream but my mouth was slack with a thick film of saliva, I'd lost all control over it. Internally I was yelling, fighting with myself because I didn't want it to be real, I didn't want to have been so astronomically naive.

And suddenly, harrowingly, it all started to make sense to me. It all slotted into place, all the clues I hadn't managed to put together, everything I couldn't work out led back to one person…Lawrie.

He had known Clara well; Clara would never have met up with a stranger, she would only have agreed to meet up with someone that she had known well and possibly someone who manipulated her into thinking she had a chance with him. I'd complained to Lawrie about Clara and how I never wanted to see her again, and then days later she was reported missing.

Lawrie had retaken a year at school where he was in a few classes with Faith Baxter, who Daphne had last seen walking off with a young man who she appeared to know. Lawrie had heard that Daphne had potentially spotted the Jade Town Monster when she told the group of us at Topaz Café, and Roman had said that Daphne was going to confront someone she knew well. After all, Lawrie had spent large sums of time with Daphne over the years he'd been in Jade Town.

Of course, the silver ring in the boot of her car was a mistake; it wasn't staged, and the 'H' didn't symbolise Huxley but rather Hartwell, a silver ring which had once been owned by Stephanie Hartwell, present in the photo I had seen from the attic.

Then, Ava Aurelia informed me about the attic and went missing straight after, we'd heard movement outside I remembered. Perhaps it was Lawrie outside listening to our conversation, ready to offer her a lift home.

Every one of those girls had known Lawrie, had trusted Lawrie even. The clues had been there all along, but I didn't want to connect them. I couldn't bear to think about the prospect that the Jade Town Monster could be....my Lawrie.

As everything slotted into place in my mind, I regained control over my body.

"Lawrie, are you...?" I asked slowly, my eyes firmly downcast on the floor. I couldn't bring myself to look at him, I had no idea who the man sat across from me was. A stranger had entered the room and replaced the one person I believed that I knew, the one person I believed I understood and who understood me. Nevertheless, this stranger had always been there underneath the surface and the mask, but I simply never allowed myself to peel back the lies and bravado to find him.

"The Jade Town Monster?" He asked, his voice completely devoid of any emotion. However, out of the corner of my eye I could see a smirk painted across his pale face. It was the worst sight I had ever seen in my entire life.

"Congratulations Lyla, you know you've always been an intelligent one. I'm mightily surprised it took you so long to figure it out. I didn't think I would get away with Clara but somehow, I did. Of course, I had a couple of scares, Daphne very nearly had the police on my tail, and she put the pieces together in the end, it was just a shame for her that it was too late. I already knew I had to get her out of the way, but I couldn't have done it straight away or it would've looked suspicious. Then of course, there's poor Ava. You see I was outside, back from the work trip early and ready to surprise you when I heard her annoying pitchy voice telling you about the attic. There was no way I could let her get away, so I offered her a lift home, but she never made it there. It's rather easy in this village to get away with it, everyone seems to trust everyone which is what I think is ultimately your downfall Lyla, you're too trustworthy and you always believe the best in everyone even when there's no good in them."

I remained staring at the grubby carpet of the living room of apartment 36A for the longest time as his words washed over me, each of them splintering into my side. I kept coming back to what he had just said- *"you always believe the best in everyone even when there is no good in them."* I had always believed Lawrie to be a good man, I had no idea how I let myself become so trapped within his spider web of lies. He had always been so superficially charming, I had been drawn in by him on that very first day we met, everyone had been, and he had been playing and twisting everyone all along, like we were simply puppets in his depraved show.

The memory of Lawrie out with the rest of Jade Town searching pointlessly for Clara, five years before, was painful to think about. He had scaled those woods with the rest of the village, each of us pleading for a sign of Clara's whereabouts, when all along he knew exactly where she was and what had happened to her.

What had happened to them? Where were they, were they still alive? The thoughts came rushing through me as powerful as a tsunami wave washing over and drowning an entire civilization.

"Where are they, Lawrie? Tell me where they are." I stuttered, tears had begun prickling in my eyes and they scratched their way down my cheeks. My hysterical state completely contrasted to Lawrie, who, I noticed as I finally dragged my eyes up to him, was sat with his jaw clenched and his soulless void eyes twinkled with malevolence.

He was the picture of serenity. I was falling apart.

"That's the question on everybody's lips, isn't it? Do you remember our special place on top of the hill, the one we visited countless times? The spot that you told me only I had discovered when I showed you all those years ago. Somewhere around there, I don't remember exactly, you see it's been such a long time that everything kind of blurs into one haze of memory. It was always dark, and I was barely able to see what I was doing. I can show you if you'd like." His voice was haunting and unchanged.

Silence filled the room again, only broken by the hammering of a torrent of rain that had spiked up outside from a soft drizzle. I remember my body shaking uncontrollably as I listened, and I threw up all over the floor, but I couldn't even bring myself to care. Lawrie made no effort to move either, he seemed transfixed in memory and unable to stop revealing the truth to me.

All I could think was as he had said, we'd been up to the spot on the hill countless times. The day he gave me the golden necklace which still hung around my neck for example, and the missing girls had been up there all that time. I had been so close to them, and yet I had no idea.

It was another few excruciating moments before I brought myself to speak again, and my words were barely a whisper.

"Did you...did you kill them?" I couldn't believe I was asking; I had no idea how I had let myself get into the situation I was in. How didn't I see what was going on? How had Lawrie managed to fool me for so long?

His hollow haunting voice echoed again through the room.

"I didn't mean to harm Clara, not really, I just wanted to teach her a lesson after what she'd done to you. I was so mad Lyla, so I told her to meet me, and I hadn't thought about what I was going to do until I was standing over her. I was so overcome with rage that I leapt for her, and I honestly meant to stop but then, it just felt so liberating. After Clara, it stoked an inextinguishable fire within me. I felt it my duty to rid us of those who did us wrong. I did this all for us, I care about you so much Lyla, and I couldn't stand the idea of you leaving me like everyone else. You're all I have Lyla; you're all I've ever had. So, I had to make sure you'd stay. I couldn't let anyone take you away from me. I won't lose you, not ever."

"They were just innocent fucking girls Lawrie. You hurt innocent people." I suddenly exploded with rage, unable to contain it any longer. His blatant excuses, the fact that he was trying to present himself as a martyr within the situation was diabolical. Nobody deserved what happened to those girls, there's not an excuse in the entire universe which could justify it. I had no idea what had driven him to commit such callous acts, but I did know how I felt - a noxious combination of disgust, heartbreak, and self-loathing.

"It was never supposed to end up this way, Lyla. I've been driving myself mad the past few years. Everything seemed to spiral out of control, I would do anything for our lives to go back to the way they were before."

The trouble I found was that I could no longer distinguish between sincerity and lies. How was I supposed to know if he was manipulating me or telling the truth?

One thing that stuck in my mind was the pattern of the disappearances. How after Clara, each girl went missing in July always around the same time and always around my birthday. People had been speculating over the connection, wondering whether an annual curse was to blame or if the Jade Town Monster had a particular reason to want to take revenge in late July.

"Why the pattern though, Lawrie? That's what I don't understand. Why did all the disappearances occur in July?" I said in the calmest tone I could muster.

"Because that day in July, more specifically your fourteenth birthday wasn't only the day that your world fell apart, it was also the day mine fell apart too."

At this revelation, a ghost of a memory swam through my mind. I remembered something my mum had said before she left the house in search of birthday cake candles, it was the memory that I had been searching for since I was nineteen years old, when Rory had told me the truth about his mother's death.

"I'm just heading into Greenstone, all the shops in Jade Town are closed now but I think the corner store is still open in Greenstone." She'd said before I watched her stalk her way effortlessly down our drive and hop into her car.

I had found out when I was nineteen that Lawrie's mother had been killed in her car by Lawrie's dad just outside Greenstone, something which I had always felt subconsciously connected to… perhaps because I was connected to it.

Paramedics had told me that they only found my mum because they had been tending to an accident where a woman had been trapped in a burning car. My mum had been at the scene of Lawrie's mum's murder that day and somehow, she had ended up in a coma. There was no doubt in my mind that the two things were connected. That Lawrie and I had always been connected.

"Have you worked it out yet?" Lawrie asked in his drawling voice, which I was beginning to despise with every fibre of my being. His voice symbolised everything malevolent in the world- famine, war, and disease amongst other things.

Without waiting for me to respond, he continued-

"You see my dad told me about your mum, when I confronted him with what he'd done to my mum, when I was about sixteen. He never knew that she was your mum, but he told us that a woman's car had broken down and she'd seen what my father had done and had tried to intervene and save my mum, so he attacked her. He couldn't have any eyewitnesses to convict him. I guess she ended up in the state she did because of that. I knew of course that it was your mum from that story you had told me about her back in the hospital."

I was seething with anger. I was appalled at how nonchalant Lawrie was when talking about the whole ordeal. Pulsing hatred filled me, Lawrie's father was the reason that I had grown up without a mother and I had never wanted to hurt anyone more in my entire life.

"That doesn't explain why you decided to kill innocent people, you monster." I exploded as white-hot rage shot through my veins. The rage was a drug, altering me entirely, closing off my mind to every other purpose except that of hurting Lawrie and his diabolical father. He was right when he had told me that the Carson's were dangerous, they were the worst scum of the earth.

"Don't you see?" Lawrie asked as if it was obvious, as if I was struggling with a particularly simple mathematics equation.

"My father destroyed both of our lives that day. So, I knew I had to use that day to get revenge on those who did us wrong. I was doing us a favour Lyla, because without anyone in our way we can live happily together as a family- you, me, and Lacey. Maybe we should get away from here and start afresh somewhere new, people are starting to get too suspicious." He made to get up from his chair as if he were planning on going to pack a bag upstairs and leave Jade Town that night, which was something that I couldn't let happen.

"Why Lawrie? Why didn't you kill your father, if you had to kill someone, why did you target innocent people?" I pressed without wanting to hear the answer, I didn't want to know why he did it, I didn't want to know the details and I couldn't comprehend the fact that I was even asking. But, if asking questions was the only way I was going to stop him from leaving Jade Town, then I had to try. I had to stall him, I had to sit face to face with the man who'd destroyed our village, who had caused so much hurt and who had had everyone fearing for their safety for years.

"I couldn't kill my father, he's my dad, Lyla." Lawrie said and what looked like the first flicker of emotion I had seen all night spread across his face.

"You said it yourself. He was the one who destroyed our lives. Not any of those girls, a lot of them were my friends, how could you possibly think you were helping me by hurting them? You are just like your dad; do you know that? In fact, you're worse than him." I was beyond the point of caring about angering him, the fact that the Jade Town Monster had been under my nose for all those years made me detest myself to the highest degree. I had introduced Lawrie to all those people, I was the reason that Lawrie had stayed in Jade Town, and perhaps it was my fault that Clara, Faith, Alessia, Daphne and Ava were all gone. I was crawling in my skin, I desired to burn all of it off, to permanently scar myself as a constant reminder of how foolish I had been.

"I'm not anything like him." The monster of anger was clearly rising inside of Lawrie, I could see the fire burning behind his eyes. His jaw clenched and I knew the nonchalant façade he paraded around behind was about to slip. The monster within was about to be released.

"My father's a drunk waste of space who's never cared about anyone but himself. I on the other hand am protecting you, I do everything for you Lyla. You are all I have ever had, and these girls had the power to take you away from me, they knew things that I couldn't let you find out. I couldn't lose you Lyla, I don't think I could bear it because I would have no one left without you. You are all I have in this world, and I need you Lyla, God do I need you."

Despite insisting that he was nothing like his father, Lawrie sounded exactly like Robert Carson who went to extreme lengths to ensure that Stephanie Hartwell would never leave him.

"So, you attempted to frame Roman Huxley for it all? Why did you target him, Lawrie, what had Roman ever done to you? He was nearly going to rot in prison for crimes he didn't commit." Lawrie's face contorted into a mirror of disgust upon the mention of Roman Huxley's name.

"I despise Huxley's existence not because of who he is but because of his awful father. Remember that my mother met another man, a man who was having an affair with the same man who she decided to leave my father for. A man who lived in a little village called Jade Town, Dean Huxley. Dean Huxley is the reason that my father went after my mother, and he's the reason that my dad killed her. Dean Huxley completely manipulated my mother because he was never planning on leaving his wife and son for her. As soon as she died, he just carried on with life as if he'd never laid eyes on her. I knew that the only way I could get revenge on the man who led to my mum's death was by framing his dear son Roman and after discovering that Roman was Willow's father, it seemed so easy to do, and my plan nearly worked."

This revelation knocked me senseless. I always wondered why Lawrie used to hang out with Roman even though he seemed to despise him, but it all made sense. Lawrie didn't despise Roman, he hated his father, and then Robert Carson of course had chosen to move his family to Jade Town to keep an eye on Dean Huxley, the only man who knew the extent to which he had abused his wife.

The love letters from 'S' addressed to 'D' were written by Stephanie Hartwell for Dean Huxley. Their secret rendezvous took place out of sight of the rest of Jade Town, in the long-time abandoned apartment 36A. Of course, after Stephanie's death, the almost invisible attic was the easiest place to hide any evidence that Dean had ever known Stephanie. Undoubtedly, it had been easier for Lawrie to blame a stranger for his mother's death than his own father which was why he had been so fixated on getting revenge on Dean Huxley.

"Why?" I repeated calmy.

"So, Dean is a horrible man, and the worst thing possible happened to your mother at the hands of your own father, but that doesn't excuse what you did Lawrie, what you chose to do. What possible reasons could you have for what you did?"

Lawrie gave me reasons for why he did it, but I won't communicate them to you because I believe that there should be no excuse for his behaviour, there is no explanation- he is evil right through to the core. Besides, my memory of the rest of that fateful night is rather hazy. They say that your brain attempts to block out memories of extreme trauma and I think that my brain has blocked out a lot of what happened that night in apartment 36A.

****

The next thing I remember clearly is being sat in a pale box-like room a day or so later.

It was a sticky, scorching hot July day and the little air conditioning unit in the corner of the room was coughing and spluttering, about to give up the ghost. My palms felt sticky as I laid them down on the wooden desk in front of me. A rather willowy yet broad looking dark-haired man and a short woman with dark features were looking across at me expectantly.

"How was it, Lyla? We understand it must've been very hard for you." The woman spoke with a sympathetic tone. I nodded in response, and she scrawled something onto the notepad in front of her. The clock was ticking extremely audibly. I felt as though it were taunting me.

The man cleared his throat. "Yes, it's a very brave thing you did for us Lyla. Without your continued help, we'd be a lot further away from catching the culprit than we are."

The woman nodded in agreement.

"I take it the Amobarbital serum helped him to open up to you like we suggested it would do?" I glanced down at her name badge which had 'Detective Rosen' labelled across it along with a photo of herself which had clearly been taken a long time ago as the lines which now littered Detective Rosen's face were nowhere to be seen.

"Yes, it worked perfectly. He told me everything, I didn't even have to push him much." True to Detective Rosen's advice, Lawrie had woken up the day after I spiked his drink with Amobarbital, completely unaware that he'd told me anything. He believed that I still had no idea about the twisted monster that he was, but once I knew the truth, I could never understand how I hadn't suspected it all along… or had I?

I reached into the pocket of my trousers and fished around for my phone. I pulled it out in one swoop and placed it upon the table. Beads of sweat were trickling down my forehead, signs of a headache brought on by dehydration began to surge at my temples. I could barely think straight. With great effort because my hands were drenched with sweat, I fumbled around on my phone, searching. I could feel Detective Rosen and Detective Wilern still looking at me. I located what I was looking for and turned the phone screen towards them.

"Here, I have the recording of the whole thing, he had no idea I was recording, I made sure of that."

"Good," Detective Wilern and Detective Rosen chorused together. I pressed play and Lawrie's voice from that night filled the tiny room.

Lawrie's confession had been a long time coming, months of planning had gone into that moment and finally I felt free from his clutches.

That's right, Lawrie wasn't the only one hiding something. His anger and evasive behaviour had me suspicious for a long time, I just had to get the truth out of him somehow. Finally, all the secret meetings with detectives had been worth it. Detective Wilern had said it himself; they couldn't have done it without me. I hadn't wanted my suspicions to be true, but more than anything I wanted Lawrie away from me and you, Lacey. I didn't want that monster anywhere near you. Not for the first time, it occurred to me that everyone in Jade Town seemed to have secrets, some were just simply darker than others...

23 YEARS OLD

I will never forget the morning of my twenty-third birthday for as long as I live.

The sun threw circles on the curtains and a lone bird howled its morning song. Everything appeared to be normal- except for one thing...

In the distance, I could hear a faint buzz. A buzz which grew and grew. Something was approaching.

Karma was approaching....

I got out of bed and peered behind the curtains. The cause of the buzz was right in front of my eyes, they lit up with the harsh blue flair of police lights.

 "Lyla, what's going on?" Lawrie had suddenly startled awake. You know what they say- there's no rest for the wicked and well, Lawrie was the devil in sheep's clothing.

"It looks like police sirens." I said breezily, fixing him an empty smile. I hadn't felt this calm in a long time which was crazy when you think about the depravity of the situation. Lawrie, however, wasn't quite as nonchalant about the situation as I was. He'd gone as white as a sheet; all the blood and colour had drained from his face.

The moment of reckoning had finally come for him.

"What are they doing here?" He panicked, and I remembered how he believed that I had no idea about the cold-blooded mass murderer that he was. In his mind, I still believed him to be the cute, charming teenager with whom I shared an unexplainable bond.

I, however, now knew what that bond really was. Mine and Lawrie's paths had been inexorably entwined through our mothers before we'd even met each other. I used to think that he was the only person in the world who understood my pain, but he didn't understand pain in the same way I did. Our pain, though similar, had moulded us into two entirely separate entities. Lawrie chose darkness, and I hope that I chose light.

"I have no idea." I reassured him.

"Maybe I should open up the door and see what they want? I wonder if they have any information on the Jade Town Monster. It would be great to finally know the truth, wouldn't it?" Lawrie's eyes were full of fear and his body began to shake. I think at that moment he realised just how trapped he was. He wasn't going to be able to charm his way out of this one. Finally, the monster had been cornered, finally he'd messed up and now he was going to pay for everything he destroyed.

At that moment, a sharp rap sounded on the door and a booming voice filled our tiny apartment.

"Police, open up Mr Hartwell, we know that you're in there." Lawrie jumped from the bed, reached over, and grabbed my arm frantically.

"Lyla, you can't let them in, they'll send me to prison. I can't go to prison. Please Lyla, please don't do this to me." He genuinely looked miserable. Someone might have taken pity on him; I probably would have taken pity on him if he weren't a stone-cold sociopath who'd taken the lives of five innocent people. I no longer knew how I felt, everything that I had felt up until that moment seemed like a lie. Everything I had ever known or believed to be true, seemed like lies. Jade Town was a hornet's nest of lies, and there was Lawrie right at the centre, injecting everyone with his poison.

"Surely, you've got nothing to worry about. You don't have anything to do with the Jade Town Monster, do you?"

Lawrie looked as though he was about to tell me that in fact, he had everything to do with the Jade Town Monster, that he was behind the disappearances and that it was he, hiding behind the mask. But he couldn't seem to bring himself to do it. I don't believe he could face what he'd done which made me detest him even more than I already did.

Lawrie's grip on my arm tightened as if he were trying to detain me. I twisted and prized out of his grip and headed for the door.

"WHAT ARE YOU DOING, YOU BITCH? DON'T YOU DARE OPEN THAT DOOR." Lawrie seethed. It was as if a switch had flicked right in front of my eyes. I had only seen him like this twice before, that night when I was nineteen when I turned down his proposal and when I discovered what he was hiding in the attic. It became clear to me that in these moods, he was capable of hurting anyone, even the ones that he loved.

He looked so menacing that I was sure that he was only mere moments from attacking me. I wondered if this was it, the moment I saw the monster in his true form, saw what he was really capable of, just as I was about to be freed from his clutches forever. He was a predator circling his prey, ready to pounce. Lawrie Hartwell was dangerous, and he needed to be behind bars for everyone's safety, we couldn't have a monster like him roaming free on the streets.

I turned and ran as fast as I could to the door which was only a few paces away. Lawrie followed me in pursuit. He was a lot faster than me and reached the door just as I put my hand on the handle.

He loomed over me. "I told you not to open that, when will you learn Lyla to stop being so selfish. When are you going to get it? I did this all for you, for us, for Lacey."

His words struck me physically like a grenade had just detonated inside my body. He did it for me. If it were not for me, would these girls still be alive and free to live their lives? Was I really to blame?

The Police bashed on the door again. "IF YOU DON'T OPEN UP, WE'LL HAVE TO BASH THIS DOOR DOWN. DO YOU HEAR ME?"

I turned to face Lawrie and looked up at his face which was twisted with rage. I took a deep breath which took all of my strength to muster and spoke...

"Lawrie, if you want to do something for me and Lacey then open this door and accept the punishment for what you've done. If you want to do something for me, then stay the hell away from me and Lacey." I didn't want to fight with him, I just wanted this to be over. I wanted him to be out of my life for good.

Lawrie stood there absorbing my words as the police's rap on the door grew more and more aggressive. Previously, I would have averted his gaze, I would have been unable to look into his menacing eyes and unwilling to see the monster lurking there behind them. The only thing that kept me there with my eyes fixed staring back at his was the thought of you Lacey and your safety. The thought of you seemed to bring me great strength, rendering me finally able to face and stand up to the man who had had me living in fear for so long.

Stood there staring into his face that I knew so well, I couldn't remember what I had so earnestly loved about him, and I didn't know the point I had stopped being in love with him either. Was it when I learnt of his depraved crimes? Or was it when he had thrown away his future and become a shell of the person he used to be? Or was it when I turned down his proposal when I was nineteen because even back then I knew that I didn't want to spend the rest of my life with him? For so long, I had stuck with Lawrie out of fear for my safety from the Jade Town Monster, little did I know that the very person I was seeking protection from was the very same person causing all the suffering and horror in Jade Town.

After what seemed like hours, Lawrie was the one to break the gaze and he hung his head in defeat as the monster inside of him retreated solemnly into the depths.

"You're right Lyla, I'm sorry. I'm so sorry for everything." Lawrie broke down, he seemed to return to his normal self, or the Lawrie that I knew. I no longer knew who this man was, and I didn't want to think about the fact that he may've been playing me all along. A twisted game of deception, and I had the losing hand every single time.

"I don't want to hurt you Lyla, I love you and I ended up hurting you. I should face up to what I've done. My dad never did, and I always said I wanted to be a better man than him, but I fear I may've become him." Sometimes I wonder if Lawrie's dad made him that way. The fact is that Lawrie's dad never took responsibility for Stephanie's death, he just let his children and the world believe that Stephanie Hartwell died in a horrific accident. I suppose it was easier to hear than the truth. The truth is never easy to hear.

"Okay." I breathed a sigh of relief, glad that I no longer had to fight him.

"I'm going to open this door in three seconds, okay, and you're going to go willingly and hand yourself into the police." He hesitated for a moment, his eyes faltering and glassing over with the makings of tears. His eyes pleaded with me to protect him. The most heart-shattering thing was that his eyes were the same as they always used to be before the callous crimes. It tore me apart to let him go, because for a moment he looked just like that fifteen-year-old boy who had just lost his mother, who needed to be loved.

He took a deep breath, and he seemed set in his purpose.

"Okay."

"Three…" I began feeling the then familiar signal of oncoming tears well up in my hazel eyes.

"Two…" The tears grew in number and began to snake freely down my cheeks.

"One." My hand shaking, I pressed down on the door handle and felt the sunlight stream in, illuminating apartment 36A with a golden glow.

Quickly, I moved aside as three police officers entered the apartment and walked towards Lawrie who remained rooted to the spot with his eyes fixed straight ahead at the dusty village road.

"Lawrence Oliver Hartwell." The tallest of the three policemen called as he grabbed Lawrie's left hand.

"We're arresting you on suspicion of the murders of Clara Yale, Faith Baxter, Alessia Chang, Daphne Scott and Ava Aurelia. You don't have to say anything, but it may harm your defence if you don't mention, when questioned, something which you later rely on in court."

The second police officer handcuffed Lawrie and together the police officers walked him out of the apartment and towards the mass of police cars waiting outside. The chaos had brought about a crowd, not quite as large as the one that watched Roman Huxley be arrested, but for that early in the morning it was rather astonishing how many people had left their houses and were crowding around the tiny front garden of our apartment. Each of them sporting a dressing gown, patterned pyjamas, or fluffy slippers. Others, I could see with their noses pressed against their windows, fogging up the glass and not even attempting to be incognito.

With the eyes of the residents of Jade Town burning into me, I felt the worst I had ever felt in my entire life. The worst part was that because of our small community, I recognised every single pair of eyes staring at me. And some more so than others- across the street stood Quinn, her eyes glassy with tears being comforted by Nate who looked hurt and full of rage. Just next to them, stood Marina, her brown eyes alight with a concoction of sorrow and disgust and on her left side swaying back and forwards cursing at the top of her lungs was Tiffany who I couldn't even bring myself to look at. Daphne was like Tiffany's sister, and the man I had stuck by for so many years was the reason that Tiffany had been so unbearably damaged and grief-stricken. He was the reason her heart would always have a hole scorched right through the centre.

More so than Tiffany, there was one figure who stood a little way apart from the crowd. I couldn't bear to even glance in his direction. My father who had lost the love of his life to Lawrie's father, who had had that wound of loss burst open every time another girl went missing, stood watching the scene unfurl. I felt as though I'd failed him and had failed my mother and her memory. In fact, I felt as if I'd failed every single person who was standing watching the scene unfold, as well as Rory, Adeline, and everyone I had ever met.

With the sun searing down upon us, the dry earth cracked immeasurably, Lawrie was led out into the closest police car. Before he disappeared beyond view, I caught one last look at the man who I once loved completely but looking at him I just felt completely empty. All the sparks and passion that had once enticed me had well and truly extinguished because I finally saw him for what he truly was, the person who people had been warning me about all along. His brother

Rory and even his own father had warned me about Lawrie, but I had been too blissfully blind to take any notice.

Heckles and cheers emanated from the crowd surrounding us as Lawrie was driven away. Despite this, it was clear to see the mist of sorrow which clung around that morning. Every single person there had known Lawrie for years and had praised him to the highest degree, and yet he had committed the ultimate betrayal. A betrayal which Jade Town could never truly recover from. Although there had been suspicions, no one really believed that one of our own could be the culprit of all the destruction.

I stood there rooted to the very spot, on the threshold of apartment 36A, unable to move in or out even long after the chaos had died down and everyone had returned to the safety of their homes. That's the best depiction of how I felt, teetering on the edge, not belonging to one side or the other: standing on the edge between my past and my future.

The last nine years of my life had driven away from me that bright morning. Everything I had built in those years and all the progress I had made seemed to unravel in front of my very eyes and I detested myself for allowing Lawrie to become such a vital part of my existence when he had been an enemy all along. I can't remember exactly how long I was frozen there but, by the time I shut out the outside world and retreated into the dark depths of apartment 36A, the sun which had just been rising was blaring at full heat.

"Happy birthday to me." I laughed out loud, a hollow laugh which sounded nothing like me. I ran a shower as hot as I could physically stand it, hoping that the pain would bring some retribution for my part in the disappearances. By the time I got out, my skin was red raw and screaming for mercy.

An hour or so later, I had settled in next to you Lacey. I honestly believed that no one would want anything to do with me ever again, that I was destined to live as an outcast forever separated from the rest of the world. Which is why I was so surprised to hear a sharp rap on the door a few moments later.

I'm probably imagining it. I remember thinking. *No one's going to want to see me.* The sharp rap sounded again and upon deciding that it may be the police desiring to search the apartment I headed towards the door.

As I flung the door open, I was met by the sight of seven pairs of eyes each looking rather sympathetically in my direction. Quinn, Marina, Tiffany, Nate, my father and two younger girls who I recognised as Alessia Chang's younger sisters Alaina and Carolina were huddled on the doorstep, and the sight of them all there immediately made my eyes well up and panic rise inside of me.

What could they be doing here? I was petrified of the response.

"Hi there, Lyla." Quinn spoke first. "Can we come in?"

"Oh…of …of course." I mumbled moving aside to let the crowd bundle into the apartment. "So…uhm…what do you all need?" I asked, unable to help myself.

"Well, it's your birthday Lyla, and people typically celebrate birthdays." Nate said smiling.

"But not this year. I can't believe any of you would even want to be in the same room as me right now…. I'm deplorable… the worst excuse for a human being… I'm…" I could've gone on all day listing how much of a waste of space I'd become but I had an idea that they didn't want to hear it.

"You're our friend." Marina piped up.

"You're also a sister and a daughter." She motioned to Nate and my father.

"You aren't …well, you aren't him okay. You're a good person and everyone here, everyone in Jade Town knows it." Marina struggled upon saying Lawrie's name and suddenly it felt taboo, as if mentioning his name would conjure up all kinds of evil.

"We're here because our sister liked you, Lyla. You were always good to her, and we know she would want to celebrate your birthday if she were here." Alaina said whilst Carolina nodded. The resemblance between the three Chang girls was immeasurable, looking into the faces of Alaina and Carolina I could have been peering into Alessia's familiar bright face. Alessia truly was one of the most kind-hearted people I'd ever met in my life. She was an angel parading around in human form perhaps, who returned home a little too soon.

"Why, though?" I couldn't comprehend the fact that these people were here for me in my defence. "He destroyed your lives and took away your sister and I… I should've stopped him."

"How?" Carolina quizzed me. She was considerably younger than everyone else there but seemed very confident for her age.

"No one knew it was him, did they? How were you supposed to know?"

She spoke the truth, Lawrie had hoodwinked the whole of Jade Town, no one had known that he was behind the mask of the Jade Town Monster until I pulled it clean from his face. Even I, who had been working with the police to bring him down always felt like it would lead to a dead-end displaying Lawrie's innocence and my subsequent stupidity for ever suspecting him.

Everyone murmured in agreement, everyone aside from Tiffany who'd been silent the entire time. She stood slightly detached from the group, close to the door as if wishing to run out at any moment. Alaina and Carolina may not have blamed me for their sister's disappearance, but I thought Tiffany must've blamed me for Daphne's. Still though, she'd shown up with the others, hadn't she? So, there was still a flicker of hope for our friendship.

"Lyla, if we all here know one thing it is that you're a good person. You've chosen to dedicate your life to helping others and despite everything, you must know that I'm proud of you. I'm so proud of the woman you've become, and I am always here for you." My father's words warmed my heart and as he hugged me my nose detected his familiar scent. It was the smell of the safe home I once lived in with him, my mother and Nate, just one perfectly ordinary family coated in love.

It became clear to me at that moment that home wasn't simply a place. Home wasn't just the house I grew up in or Jade Town. Home was and always will be a feeling between people, the people who you know will always be there for you and show up no matter what has happened or how much time has passed. Every single person stood there in the cramped living room on my twenty-third birthday despite all the misery, was and will forever be home to me.

"Okay, okay, sappy moment over. Now I believe we're here to celebrate someone's birthday, aren't we? So, let us celebrate then." Tiffany called from the back of the crowd; a slight smirk spread across her olive features.

"Well, what do you want to do Lyla? We didn't get a chance to plan anything, because of everything that has happened recently." Nate said looking rather embarrassed.

"Yeah, I'm sorry, this is probably the worst birthday you've ever had." Quinn caught eyes with Nate and they both grimaced.

"No, it's perfect. Just having you all here is enough, it's all I could ever want." As soon as those words left my lips, I knew that I truly meant them more than I had meant anything in a long time.

Despite the devastation of that day, I remember it fondly as one of my favourite birthdays, possibly even my favourite because that day we sat and talked whilst drinking wine (apple juice for Carolina) and talking about everything under the sun. We all acted as if that morning had never occurred, as if I had never been in a relationship with a serial killer, as if Lawrie Hartwell had never even existed. And just for a moment, I forgot that he ever did.

****

The days following Lawrie's arrest all seemed to collate into a blur. There was a constant police presence in Jade Town, more than I'd ever seen. Every part of Jade Town was upturned and scoured in an attempt to find the whereabouts of the missing girls and the mysterious clues that had once been hidden in plain sight in our attic.

If I could help it, I barely left the house as cruel headlines had already begun surfacing about me and my potential place or allegiance with the Jade Town Monster. Despite my friends, my dad and Nate's constant reassurance that no one in Jade Town placed any kind of blame upon my shoulders, I didn't want to feed the papers anything which they could twist and report about.

I was constantly tuned into the news, unable to break my eyes away from the revelations in the Jade Town Monster case. Honestly though, I felt detached from it all. Watching the news blurt away in front of me, Lawrie Hartwell could have easily been a stranger and not the one person who I put everything into for years of my life. Whenever I saw his photo flash up on the screen, instead of feeling warmth or fear like

I had done for the past few years, all I felt was a dull pulsating hollowness in the pit of my stomach. That man could've been a stranger to me. Some evil man you'd discuss once after seeing the news and then forget about.

The apartment was constantly dark and had acquired such a thick layer of dust that everything appeared grey and ancient. I was in no mood to complete basic house chores, and I barely coped in the days after Lawrie's arrest. The only bright part of my day, the only solace, was you and the frequent drop in visits of my greatest friends and family. They would bring me food and tales of the goings on in Jade Town.

As we had worked our way through a packet of custard creams one cloudless Friday morning two weeks after Lawrie's arrest, Quinn informed me how after the truth about his affair seemed to circulate around Jade Town, Jeanie Huxley left Dean as fast as she possibly could. He'd since stepped down from his position as mayor. It seemed that the whole of Jade Town had suffered a stake to the heart, even those who always seemed above it all.

That night, I was stationed in front of the TV like I constantly had been since the arrest, when the bald thick-set newsreader who'd been drivelling on about a fire somewhere in Exeter, said something which captivated me...

"In Jade Town, Lyntonshire, the police have discovered the remains of five women who've been identified as the missing women: Clara Yale, Faith Baxter, Alessia Chang, Daphne Scott and Ava Aurelia who all disappeared over the course of five years at the hands of a person who'd been known to residents as the Jade Town Monster. A twenty-three-year-old male, Lawrence Hartwell from Jade Town has been arrested on suspicion of the crimes."

Pictures of five people who I recognised very well began to flick across the screen along with their names- Clara Yale, Faith Baxter, Alessia Chang, Daphne Scott and Ava Aurelia. All the hope built up that these girls might turn up alive and unharmed crashed and burned in that moment, I felt as though a nuclear bomb had detonated inside of my heart. Everything was painful because it was all over, and I was never going to see them again. No one was going to see them again.

Seeing the pictures of five young women who used to live alongside me, who had hopes and dreams and fears caused the reality to set in properly for the first time.

Before, I was too wrapped up in my own self-pity and self-loathing to understand the loss and to understand just how fortunate I was to still have my heart beating and blood coursing through my veins. Just how lucky I am to be here breathing, thinking, and feeling because they aren't, and they can't.

Clara never got to leave school, she never got to grow up or travel to every corner of the world like she always told me she dreamed of when we were kids.

Faith never got to reach her goals, never got to become a footballer or a swimming coach or a tennis player, all her training sessions and repeated hard work were for nothing.

Alessia never got to get out of Jade Town like she always wanted, she never got to really start her life in the way she wanted.

Daphne never got to hold Willow again or to see her grow into the person she became.

Ava, oh Ava came back to Jade Town to find her place in the world, to understand where she fit, and she never got the chance to find out.

None of them would get the chance to get married or grow old. They never got to see the sunrise again or were able to feel the chill of dawn upon their faces. In their final moments, each of them would've been scared beyond anything I can imagine.

I don't desire to imagine it much, but I like to talk about them and the amazing things they may've achieved if they'd been given the chance.

As the reporter drawled on, I blacked out with the unshakable burden of grief pressing all around me.

24 YEARS OLD

There aren't many mornings where I've woken up wishing that I were dead- but the morning of the last day of the trial was one of them.

I woke up in a panic, sweat pouring down into every crevice of my body. I hadn't seen him in a year but that day I had to be face to face with him- with the monster who murdered girls in cold blood and then came back to sleep under the same roof as me and my daughter. The trial had been going on for a few days, but I had been putting off going to give my statement for as long as I possibly could. I had to look a man in the eye who had lied to me for years, who had done unspeakable things and had wrecked so many lives.

I had never felt so worthless in my entire life, I couldn't even begin to describe the immense guilt and shame weighing on my weary shoulders to anybody else. I hadn't been able to look at my reflection for weeks as if I were worried to see the monster of him peering out from behind my own eyes. I was worried our souls had been so inexplicably entwined over the years that I no longer could distinguish where I ended, and he began.

Tentatively, I got dressed feeling the weight of the world precariously perched upon my fragile frame.

Everybody will be looking at me, they'll all be blaming me. I remember thinking.

The idea of standing in front of a room of people who were all judging me, and my situation made me feel sick to my stomach. The idea of even stepping outside made me want to peel my skin from my bones piece by piece, until I broke down to nothing. Unfortunately, I had to make sure Lawrie was condemned. I needed to do all in my power to make sure he never had the opportunity to hurt anyone ever again.

My friends had been attending the trials and sending me updates. The last text on my phone that morning was from Marina telling me that Lawrie had switched his story and he finally decided to plead guilty due to the evidence that was mounting against him, and my statement and recording was likely to bash the nail into his coffin of condemnation. It had been a futile thing to do, attempting to plead not guilty when there were mountains of evidence against him. Maybe he believed that because his father got away from the law then he could too? I no longer pretend to understand the inner workings of his mind, something which I used to believe only I held the key to

****

Pulling up to the grand court building, I wrestled with myself for a few moments because all I really wanted to do was turn on my heels and run somewhere, anywhere. Plucking up a slither of courage that I didn't even know I possessed, I set my mind and walked purposefully through the wooden double doors taking no notice of the barrage of press who created a blinding whirl of light and noise. I caught wind of some comments, though:

"Lyla, did you know who your boyfriend was? Did you try and help him cover it up?"

"What's it like to date a serial killer? Give us a statement, love."

"Does your child have the evil gene too? Best look out for her."

I wanted to turn around and hurt every single one of them until they were bruised purple, yellow, and blue. Because to them, everything was just a story, another way to get ahead of the competition. But it was my life, and I couldn't just put the paper down and escape from it if I wanted to, laughing about how stupid the woman on the front page was for staying with such a monster.

"Alright, Lyla?" A voice I recognised called from my left side. Nate was standing there in the same black suit he'd worn for our mother's funeral, I noticed. He appeared both sympathetic and agitated. I only nodded in response, as the entire collection of words from the English language seemed to escape me at that moment.

"I should've come with you here. The reporters are brutal out there, I shouldn't have let you walk through that alone. I'm sorry." He hung his head and sighed deeply. I suddenly felt sorry he was here, I felt so unbelievably wretched that anyone was here at all. If only I'd never spoken to Lawrie that first day at school, if only I'd ignored his text that night when I was sixteen, none of this may ever have happened.

"No, it's okay. I had to drop Lacey off at Dad's and I don't think I wanted company this morning, I wanted to be by myself to do this for myself, you know?" I responded as Nate closed the distance between us and placed his arms around me.

"We all need people, Lyla. You can't just do life all by yourself. Especially at times like these." Times like these indeed, and I understood his point entirely, but I also couldn't help pondering over the fact that letting people in and trusting them was what had gotten me into the mess that I was in.

In the corner of the waiting room, I spotted another familiar sight, one which hurt my heart beyond belief. Adeline Hartwell stood in the corner, her signature candy-striped glasses askew, her disposition sombre. She was all alone. She spotted me then, and I could see her eyes behind her glasses begin to fill with tears. I offered her a weak smile and walked towards where she was standing, Nate following in my wake like my personal bodyguard.

"Lyla." Adeline said softly as I approached.

"Oh, Lyla, I can't understand it. He was such a sweet little boy, he had so much potential. How could we have known?" The tears cascaded down her face, and I felt her pain. I understood her anguish, the idea of believing you knew someone. I think everybody expects evil to be blatantly obvious to the naked eye, and sometimes it is, but other times it is buried below down in people you'd never expect. Another thing I believed to be playing on Adeline's mind, as it had been playing on mine since Lawrie's arrest, if he had lived with her instead of under the abusive clutches of his father, would he have become the killer, the Jade Town Monster?

"Lyla..." Adeline continued when I didn't respond, as I was unsure of how the hell I was supposed to respond to that.

"Is it wrong that I don't know who I'm here to support? What happened was despicable and I hurt for those poor girls and their families, but he's, my nephew. He's Stephanie's little boy and I promised her, I promised I would protect him and Rory. They're all that is left of her, and I let this happen. I let him become his father."

Before I could respond, a booming voice came from a speaker on the left side wall, which I hadn't even noticed was there.

"Delilah Kingsley, the prosecution is calling you as their witness. Please take the stand." My hands shook violently in protest. This was it. I'd never been more nervous for anything in my life. I was about to condemn the love of my life and send him to prison. I was about to put a monster in a steel-iron cage. I was about to free our town from the cloud of darkness that had descended years before when Clara went missing.

I shut my eyes and took a few long deep breaths. I thought of my mum and then my dad and Nate and poor Rory and then finally I thought of you, Lacey, and how I needed to do this for you because I couldn't let a monster like Lawrie be anywhere near you.

As if sensing my distress, Nate turned to me.

"It'll all be over soon Lyla, and then you and Lacey will be finally safe and free. You just need to be brave for a little while, like we all know you can be."

That was all that I wanted. I wanted to be free from Lawrie Hartwell's evil grasp once and for all. I wanted to finally start my life for myself.

Nate squeezed my hand, and I smiled up at him, suddenly channelling the same calmness that I found a year earlier when Lawrie had been arrested under the scrutinising eyes of Jade Town.

After taking another deep breath, I walked up into the courtroom and onto the stand with my eyes firmly fixed on the ground. I couldn't look at him, I couldn't let him see how much he was hurting me, how much this was tearing me apart piece by piece. My heart was bruised and burned. I'd pulled it from my chest and let Lawrie hold it in the palm of his hand as it withered away for years, and finally I felt him drop its corpse right there in the centre of the courtroom.

From what I could tell, the room was packed with many people that I recognised and some that I didn't. Jade Town was too small to have its own court, so we were miles and miles away from home in the city of Lynton. It looked like the whole of Jade Town had turned up though, everybody wanted to see the Jade Town Monster finally get the karma that he deserved.

"Please state your full name and your relation to the accused- Lawrence Oliver Hartwell, born as Lawrence Oliver Carson." The judge's voice boomed across the room. Hearing that one sentence made me realise how I never really knew Lawrie, he'd always been hiding behind a façade even when I first met him, because this man was Lawrence Carson. He wasn't Lawrie Hartwell, and he never really had been.

"My name is Delilah Gabriella Kingsley. My relationship to the accused is…" I paused momentarily unsure of what I should have said. I don't believe that whatever was between Lawrie and me could ever be described as a tangible thing, let alone put into a singular labelled box. Because, truthfully, I never knew what Lawrie and I were to each other especially since everything had gone up in flames between us.

"My relationship to the accused is…" I repeated, suddenly very keen to study each fibre on the courtroom floor rather than look in the direction of the judge or worst of all at Lawrie. I could feel his presence across the room, his eyes blaring through into my soul.

"Ex-partner." I finally decided upon.

"Miss Kingsley, please place your hand over the bible and repeat after me. I do swear, by almighty God, that the evidence I shall give shall be the truth, the whole truth, and nothing but the truth."

What is the truth exactly? I had spent the last few years completely unaware of it and perhaps running from it, that it felt strange to me to be there in that moment swearing to reveal the truth.

Shaking, I placed my hand over the bible and spoke in a voice which didn't sound like my own, the voice was strangely confident and assured.

"I do swear, by almighty God, that the evidence I shall give shall be the truth, the whole truth, and nothing but the truth." I looked up at the judge and she nodded her head in response. I took a deep breath and tried to remember the fact that there were people in that courtroom there to help me, we were working against a common form of evil between us.

An average sized man with a deep lined face and circular spectacles stood up from his chair just in front of me, clutching a piece of paper which had writing scrawled all over it.

"Miss Kingsley I am Barrister Fleet, the prosecution barrister for the court. Please could you talk us through your relationship with the accused and any times he displayed anti-social or out of the ordinary behaviour."

Barrister Fleet looked up at me expectantly. I shut my eyes for a moment attempting to clear my head which was a trick that my mum had taught me when I was about seven years old, how to shut everything behind a sturdy locked door in the back of my mind. I needed to clear my head at that moment more than I've ever needed to in my life. I believe that the moment in the courtroom was the most important moment of my life to date because I had to do something I had never dreamed I would do. I had to detach myself from my emotions, I had to remove all feelings within me and tell the courtroom and the world the truth.

So, I did. I told the courtroom everything, right from beginning to end.

I fixed my eyes on my friends who were sitting in a line at the back of the court, a row of supporters- Marina, Quinn, and Tiffany. Throughout everything they'd been there for me, and they were there for me in that moment too. Each of them smiled sympathetically, their eyes all clouded with tears, and then Nate appeared with them and hooked his arm around Quinn's shoulders. They'd found each other during everything that had happened that year. They finally realised that they were meant for each other, and I had never been so happy for anyone in my life. They had found their happy ending and I had to find mine too, a happy ending without Lawrie.

With great trepidation as I spoke, I kept my eyes firmly fixed on my friends. It wasn't until after I'd finished that my curiosity got the better of me and I glanced over at Lawrie at the counsel table.

He looked very, very young as if he were a naïve child and not a fully grown man. He was dressed in a grey suit jacket and trousers which were evidently too big for him, they looked like they were going to swallow him whole in a matter of minutes. His blonde hair was tatted, and it hung down just above his eyes in a crumpled mess. He didn't look like a monster, he just looked like a lost little kid. My heart stopped as he caught eyes with me for a moment. I couldn't read his expression, he just looked completely empty and sunken out. For a minute, I thought that he might give me a goofy smile like he always did but instead he just stared, his gaze was cold and hard. I couldn't really expect anything else from him though, after all I did just testify against him, but it was abundantly clear to me in that moment that the Lawrie that I knew, and I thought that I loved was gone. The façade that he'd been parading around in for God knows how long had finally broken apart and underneath all that was left was a monster.

Nobody knew exactly what turned Lawrie into the monster that he was. Was it the drunken abuse that his father had constantly inflicted upon him? Was it the fact that his father murdered his mother in cold blood? Was it the fact that social services abandoned him and his brother, so they were forced to live with a monster? More horrifyingly, was he just born like this, with the destiny to be a killer? I believe it was a combination of all these things. Lawrie had been abandoned by everyone and had been shown nothing but abuse his whole childhood, but he still chose that path for himself. He chose to be wicked, and he chose to lie. Sometimes I wonder if I made him into the monster that he was. He always said that he did it for me, and maybe that was true? He needed me so he was prepared to do anything in his power to make sure that I didn't leave him like everybody else. After all his concept of love came from his parents, his idea of what love was had been twisted and manipulated by all the horror and destruction of his childhood.

Lawrie's eyes were still locked with mine from across the courtroom. It had been hell to testify against him. I felt as though they'd drenched me in gasoline and lit me on fire. There I was, dying a slow and excruciatingly painful death in front of everyone that I'd ever known.

I felt stupid for loving such a monster. I felt stupid for lying next to him all those nights after he'd taken away innocent lives one after another. I felt stupid and evil for missing him after he left, for replaying every good memory we had together until I knew them all by heart. I felt stupid for believing that anyone kind and genuine could ever love me. It was hard to resist the urge to scream at him and at everyone else in the courtroom whilst I was engulfed in an invisible flame.

After the prosecution had asked me an abundance of questions about Lawrie and our relationship, I was finally free to go. As much as I wanted to run out of the double doors to the court and rush all the way home, I couldn't leave. I had to see it through, I had to know that he was definitely going to go to prison. After all, his father had dodged jail years before. So, could Lawrie do the same?

Aside from Adeline sitting in the left-hand corner of the room, no one had shown up in support of Lawrie. Not his father, nor Rory who hadn't been heard from ever since I saw him leave for the army just after his eighteenth birthday. I think that I felt sorry for Rory most of all, he'd lost everyone: first his mum, his dad was a lost cause and finally he had lost his brother too.

He'd urged me to leave Jade Town too, and up until that moment in the courtroom I'd never considered it. There was nothing tying me to Jade Town anymore, aside from memories.

Painful yet blissful memories.

I walked to the back of the courtroom avoiding Lawrie's gaze which I could feel following me with every step I took. I reached my friends' perch after what felt like the longest hike in history but was in reality only a few metres and sandwiched in between Nate and Tiffany to watch the rest of the trial.

"You did great up there, Lyla." Tiffany whispered to me as she squeezed my shaking hand.

I smiled back in response. The others also whispered praise to me, but I was completely numb to it. My whole body still burned as if somehow, I was still on fire, and no one could extinguish the flames.

 An inextinguishable fire burning.

The rest of the trial was a blur, I felt as though I was only half there watching it. The other half of me was somewhere else entirely. The other half of me was fourteen, stuck in the school corridor just about to run into the man who would ruin so many lives for the very first time.

Clara's parents sat huddled in front of me. I couldn't bear to imagine how difficult it was for them. They lost their little girl at the hands of someone she knew really well, someone she was practically in love with, and then there was me. I was her childhood best friend, and I couldn't help believing that I was responsible for it all. If I hadn't complained about Clara that day, would she still have been here? Would they all still be here?

I visited Clara's parents a few times after Lawrie was arrested, they assured me that they didn't blame me at all. They said Clara died at the hands of a cruel, vicious, and unforgiving psychopath. There was always an edge to them though, I think they too were aware that if Lawrie and I had never been aligned, then he wouldn't have had a direct reason to crush Clara's life in his hands.

In the courtroom, the audio from the night Lawrie confessed boomed. I hadn't heard the secret recording since I'd played it to DC Wilern and Rosen, and it felt like a bullet to the heart to hear it. Lawrie's voice drawled on about the reasons for each of the murders. Again, I won't disclose them to you- I'll never talk about the reasons to anyone, because I don't think there are any fathomable reasons for what Lawrie did. Most of all, I don't believe Lawrie should get away with blaming the murders on something.

My eyes flicked to where Lawrie was sitting as the audio was being played, his expression and body language were completely unchanged. He just sat there, calm as the surface of Jade Town Lake on a summer's day. I remember being torn about the recording; I'd felt like I'd committed the most ginormous betrayal, one that made the assassination of Julius Caesar look minuscule. I'd been expecting the worst for a while about Lawrie so I worked with the police in the hope that if my worst suspicions were true, I could be free from him once and for all.

Listening to the audio felt as if I were being repeatedly shot in the head. The memory was an intoxicating cloud of acid. As I thought about it and remembered it, it just burned me more and more and the shots in my head embedded themselves further and further in. Another thing contained in that audio was Lawrie's account of how he killed these innocent girls. They were killed in a way that horrified me that I was still alive- I'd been with Lawrie every day for years and somehow no real harm aside from emotional trauma had been inflicted upon me. But he had the power to cause such harm, and my heart aches for those girls and their final moments.

I've been asked countless times over the years how I see Lawrie, after everything that I know now. Do I see him simply as a monster or do I see the man I believed I loved for ten years of my life?

The best way to quantify my feelings is: there is a stark difference between hearing about a fire from somewhere and actually being in the centre of it. Somebody on the outside would have an entirely different perspective than I did, on the inside, my body turning to ash.

What eats me up inside is that I truly believed I was in love with him. I was in love with the façade he presented to the world maybe, but I was in love with something.

Once the audio stopped playing in the court and Lawrie's defence lawyer had made his final appeal, the jury stepped out to discuss their verdict. It was highly ironic to me that Lawrie's father, who was once a hot-shot lawyer, hadn't organised any help for his son. In all honesty, I don't think Robert Carson ever did anything beneficial for his sons or desired to have children in the first place. Of course, something I didn't realise when I was younger was that Lawrie and Rory would have been to Robert a constant reminder of Stephanie and her betrayal.

After what seemed like days but was probably only a couple of hours at most, the moment of truth had arrived. The jury returned and the judge's voice filled the whitewashed courtroom.

"Have you all reached a verdict regarding Lawrence Hartwell?"

The jury nodded in response.

"Okay I shall proceed. On the charge of murdering Clara Yale, how do you find the defendant?"

The speaker for the jury stood up. Everything that had happened in the seven years that had elapsed since Clara disappeared when we were just seventeen, had culminated to that very moment. Everything I'd done, the meetings with the police, the recording, and each night lying by his side wondering if I were lying next to a monster- it all led to that moment.

That was it.

"Guilty." The speaker for the jury stated as the entire room collectively sighed with pure relief.

Finally, Lawrie was about to get his karma for what he did to Clara all those years ago. I couldn't imagine how terrible Clara's last moments on this earth must've been, she must've been frightened out of her mind and in excruciating pain. She must've felt so utterly betrayed that she was dying at the hands of someone that she once almost worshipped, someone who she tried so hard to impress. He lured her away from safety and snatched the light from within her. He took her future and robbed so many people of ever getting the chance to meet her. The thing about Clara Yale was that she was the type of person who everybody knew was really going to *be something*. She had such a bright future ahead of her, all the girls did.

"How do you find the defendant on the murder of Faith Baxter?"

"Guilty."

Faith's grandparents were sitting right at the front of the court, their arms around each other. Her grandmother burst into tears as her grandfather stroked her greying head. Out of all the girls, I knew Faith the least. She was a year below me at school, but I used to see her around in the corridors all the time. She always had a smile painted across her freckled face. She had a flair for sport, she was captain of basically all the teams at our school. I remember seeing her on the field each summer playing football with all the boys who she used to run rings around. I'm sure she would've been one to watch if she'd just been given the chance.

"Okay, and how do you find the defendant on the charge of the murder of Alessia Chang?"

"Guilty." The court once again sighed.

Alessia's parents and two sisters were sitting at the back of the courtroom. They'd shut down 'Topaz Café' shortly after Alessia's body was discovered, they said that they couldn't go on with the business without Alessia. She was practically a part of the furniture at the café. In years gone by, we used to sit in there, drinking different flavoured milkshakes and talking about everything from our exams to our music tastes. Whenever I would drive by the café it was as though the ghost of her past self was still sitting in the window, talking and laughing eternally. That's where she'd always be, a happy memory forever replaying itself in my mind.

"How do you find the defendant on the murder of Daphne Scott?"

"Guilty."

Tiffany collapsed back in her chair, relief washing all over her. She wanted Lawrie to rot in hell for taking away Daphne's life. Daphne was a few years older than us, but I fondly remember hanging out with her, Tiffany, and Clara on the swings all day- swinging until we felt like we might throw up our breakfasts. In the final years of her life, she'd become a great friend. She was the only one who understood my situation as a young mother. My heart bled for Willow, knowing that she'd never get the chance to know just how incredible her mum was.

Tiffany shouted a string of expletives so loud that the court whipped around in her direction. Not Lawrie though, he looked everywhere but at Tiffany. He knew how much he'd hurt her; he knew that she'd never be able to forgive him.

No one would.

"Finally, how do you find the defendant on the murder of Ava Aurelia?"

"We find him to be…" The juror paused and my heart kicked up inside of my chest, Lawrie was so close to being punished for everything. We couldn't let him get away with anything…

"Guilty."

I heaved a gigantic breath that I didn't even know I was holding in until that moment. Ava's entire family had turned up from Australia. Her mother and father sat two rows from the front surrounded by all of Ava's brothers and sisters. I knew they were all thinking the same thing, that Ava should never have returned to Jade Town and should never have gotten involved with Lawrie and me. I think I felt the most responsible for Ava's death out of all of them, because it was I who had convinced her to stay. I'd given her a job and it was me who she was warning about the contents of the attic before she disappeared. Ava's warning to me had provided a vital clue in the Jade Town Monster case as without her informing me, I never would have known about the existence of the attic let alone its contents and I never would have discovered the full story. We owe Ava with helping us to catch the Jade Town Monster, it's just heart-breaking that we couldn't have caught him before he took her as his final victim.

"Based on the jury's verdict, I hereby sentence you, Lawrence Oliver Hartwell, with 5 counts of murder in the first degree. I sentence you to 125 years in prison without the possibility of parole for your crimes. Now, you'll be escorted out of the courtroom and will be transferred to a maximum-security prison."

Just before he was escorted out of the courtroom, he locked eyes with me. His blue eyes that I once loved so dearly looked like a grey pool of sludge. It was as if at that moment that we'd never met, that I'd never locked eyes with him in the cafeteria that first day. His disposition had been irreversibly altered from what it once was, or perhaps it had always been that way and I'd only just broken free from his spell and noticed.

My brain whirred with the possibility of what was about to happen, a hundred lines auditioned themselves in my mind each attempting to predict what Lawrie would do before he was taken away forever.

"I'M SORRY LYLA, I FAILED LACEY, I'M SORRY." I imagined him exclaiming with his eyes still fixed firmly on mine. My eyes would've clouded with hot tears because it was true, he failed you Lacey, he's the reason you don't have a father.

I imagined him breaking down right there in the centre of the room, apologising for everything he'd done, a crumpled heap of regret.

I imagined him pleading with me to stick by his side, like I'd so naively done for years. I imagined him begging for forgiveness, maybe even telling me just how much he loved me.

In reality? Nothing.

Once again, my mind built up something that was never there, that would never happen. Once again, I was victim to my own delusions because in reality, he did none of those things. Lawrie simply looked at me without any expression clouding over his eyes. Then, he looked away. Simple as that, he took his eyes from mine as if I were nothing to him. It was as though I'd never mattered, he put up no fight, he gave me nothing.

I didn't think any of it remained but at that moment he took a sledgehammer to my blood-red crystal heart, which shattered and burned into thousands of pieces.

I watched him walk over the mess as he was escorted from the courtroom and I knew, that even if it could be repaired, the parts would never fit together as perfectly as before.

As I watched Lawrie leave the room, I remember collapsing with the emotion of it all- the relief it was all over, the sorrow for the victims and their families and the ache that I was never going to see him again. It wasn't that I wanted to see him, but he'd been my entire life for the last ten years. It was hard to lose something that had been such a constant for a decade, but I had the wonderful support of my friends, my dad, and most of all I had you Lacey.

That night after returning from the courtroom, I took Rory's advice. I packed my bags and left Jade Town.

I vowed to never return.

28 YEARS OLD

Normality. My life had fallen into a normal pattern- as normal as it could have ever been based on my past that is. He didn't have a hold over me anymore; he couldn't have a hold on me anymore. It had been four years since the trial and since Lawrie had gone to prison for his crimes, and each day became easier as I were healing bit by bit in the time that elapsed.

"Lyla, we need an IV drip in this room." My supervisor shouted over the chaos of the A&E ward. Each person who lay around me had a story, a family, a life. You see that's where we were polar opposites- whilst Lawrie was hell-bent on taking lives, I desired ardently to preserve them. I thought of it as a compensation, a way to fix what Lawrie broke.

"Lyla, can't you see I did it all for you?" Lawrie's words would often repeat over and over in my brain like a stuck record, they were always there taunting me pushing me to work harder. I'd thrown myself into work in the four years since the trial, pushing myself to the brink of exhaustion. I desperately didn't want to give my mind any time to mull over what had happened. I desperately hoped that one morning I'd be

able to wake up with a clean slate, with no memory of Lawrie Hartwell and what he'd done.

"Okay, we need critical attention to this patient; he was the victim of a prison attack."

Prison attack.

Prison.

Attack.

The words were bullets shot into my brain. It seemed like he was still following me, that the universe couldn't let me move on from him. Quickly, I composed myself and told myself that I had no reason to be feeling so anxious because there were over one hundred prisons in the country and thousands of prisoners- there was no logical way it could be him.

"The victim is a 28-year-old male inmate who was the subject of an unprovoked prison attack. We don't know much about it so far aside from the fact that he was attacked by a group of prisoners, he was found in this state and a guard called paramedics. It appears he's sustained a large quantity of internal bleeding, so he needs to be seen to straight away."

I glanced innocently down at the victim. His body was bruised in vile shades, livid hues of purple, yellow and blue like a sadistic kaleidoscope. He'd been hurt beyond recognition; every part of his body was off colour.

He tentatively strained to open his eyes, I could sense the sheer amount of pain he must've been in, and I couldn't imagine what could've provoked any human to do anything so unbelievably evil to him. The victim's eyelids opened to reveal his ocean eyes which stared back at me, deep blue eyes which flickered with shock and recognition…

It felt like time had stood still or ended entirely. Everything around me blurred, my head felt heavy, and the sounds of the chaotic hospital ward became out of focus like I was tripping on a hallucinogenic drug which had altered my mind beyond anything I'd ever experienced.

It was inconceivable.

It was utterly unbelievable…

Lawrie Hartwell was laying on the bed looking up at me, mirroring my state of shock exactly. *He couldn't be here… how was this possible?* I'd moved far away from Jade Town, from everything, and I'd begun to build my life on my own terms and yet here he was. The fates had sent me the one thing I didn't want, the one thing I never wanted to see or hear about ever again.

Lawrie's practically lifeless body was wheeled into an empty bay, and he was lifted onto the bed. He'd been hit hard, practically bruised beyond recognition; the only piece of him that remained pristinely intact was his genetic calling card- those deep blue eyes.

I didn't know how to react. I didn't want to stay; I shouldn't have stayed. I should have told someone who he was to me and left, but I simply couldn't. No matter how hard I wrestled with myself, I couldn't leave him there and I hated myself for it, I hated every single part of me for staying there. The rest of the staff who'd wheeled Lawrie's corpse in, rushed off leaving me alone.

Alone.

Alone, with Lawrie.

"Are you okay, Lyla?" said a voice behind me. I turned around and saw that it belonged to Tom, a junior doctor who had always been there for me since I started working at the hospital. He knew about the case; his uncle was the prosecution lawyer you remember I told you about, Barrister Fleet. Despite this, he'd never judged me for it, and he'd barely even mentioned it in the four years I'd known him. If anybody else at the hospital knew they never let on either.

Tom was Lawrie's polar opposite. He had these striking dark eyes which glowed golden in the sunlight and straight dark hair. He had a warm, friendly, and sweet disposition and was easily one of the kindest people I've ever met in my entire life. You could also read him like a book as everything he felt was always etched upon his face, there were no secrets or hidden personalities- what you saw on the surface is what you got.

I had no idea back then that he would become so important to me, I had no idea that he would become my person. I think the biggest thing that Tom has taught me is that being in love shouldn't be painful, it shouldn't ache or burn or break you down to the core. Being in love with Lawrie was the most exhausting thing, one minute I felt safe and the next I felt trapped and terrified. Mine and Tom's story overlapped with mine and Lawrie's that day as if the three of us had our paths entwined for a reason.

"Yeah, I'm okay thanks." I waved him off and forced a weak smile, but he clearly wasn't convinced by it.

"Lyla, you shouldn't even be in the same room as him. I know who he is- who he was to you. I should let someone know and have you escorted out of this ward, but it isn't my place. This is your story to tell and not mine."

"Really I'm fine, please just let me stay for a bit." I said despite better judgement. Tom was completely right, I shouldn't have even been in the same room as him, I shouldn't have wanted to be in the same room as him, but I did.

Tom nodded.

"Okay, but I'll be just around the corner I promise, and if you need anything at all, shout for me and I'll be here in a second flat I promise." He assured me as he clutched my hand for a moment, casting a dark look in Lawrie's direction before turning around and retreating down the corridor out of sight.

I couldn't quite tell because his face was so bruised, but it looked as if a flicker of anger illuminated Lawrie's face for a minute before it returned to normal. I looked down at him then properly for the first time since he'd arrived in the hospital. He was thinner than I remembered and more weather-beaten but there were still striking similarities. We carried on in silence for a minute both just processing what had just happened before he finally spoke with a voice that was so weak.

"Lyla, what are you doing here?"

"I work here, I have done for four years now. What about you, how did you end up in such a state?"

What looked like the makings of a smirk twitched across Lawrie's face as he winced with the pain it took to move his black and blue spiralled jaw.

"I don't know exactly." He huffed a ragged breath like he'd just run all the way here from Jade Town.

"Those guys, the ones that I stole from years ago, do you remember them? They ended up in the same prison as me and last night they just attacked me, and I honestly thought I was dead. I half wish I was. I don't remember anything until I woke up with you standing over me under that bright light, like an angel." As he strained his feeble voice, images of the night Lawrie had convinced me to sit and keep watch whilst he robbed a jewellery store in Knox village filled my mind. Even back then, he'd manipulated me, and I had been too blinded by what I thought was love to see it.

"Yes, I remember that perfectly." I said sharply.

"How could I forget how you made me get caught up in all of that?" Anger was bubbling inside of me, a thousand-year-old dormant volcano which suddenly began to activate.

"I didn't make you do anything. You did it of your own accord." A hint of an edge was forming in Lawrie's tone. Once again, I'd said something out of line that he didn't like, something which made the monster inside of him claw its way to the surface. However, whilst I may have always cowered away from it or changed the subject to save myself, I was done with it. Afterall, he was the one crumpled purple, yellow and blue on the hospital bed and for once I was the one with the power.

"Don't. Don't you dare try to make me feel like the problem. Like I had any part in your depraved actions, you don't have a hold on me anymore Lawrie, you understand?" I stood over his fragile frame; my eyes alight with the rage I had suppressed for so many years. I could have easily hurt him like he hurt all those innocent people, I could have ended his life in one swift move, a flick of a switch, and Lawrie Hartwell would be no more than a distant memory- a lifeless corpse.

But I'm not a monster. I'm not Lawrie, and no matter how much rage and disgust I was saturated with I wouldn't and couldn't ever harm him.

A few seconds of silence passed between us, and in sync the rage inside of us both seemed to subside.

"How is she, Lyla? Have you got my letters?" I never told Lawrie I moved from Jade Town; I hadn't had any contact with him at all; his letters were probably piled up on the dusty porch of our old place. I felt so protective of you Lacey, I didn't speak about you to anyone. But he was your dad, he was your flesh and blood. I couldn't keep you from him.

"She's good." I said and then as an afterthought without even thinking before I said it-

"She keeps asking me where you are." I added.

Lawrie looked the saddest I'd maybe ever seen him look in the whole time I'd known him. It had been truly gut-wrenchingly heart-breaking, you, the picture of innocence asking me where your dad was and why he left you. You sat up night after night at only eight years old asking me if you were to blame for why he left us.

"What did you tell her?" I had given a range of excuses, that Lawrie was away at war, or that he was on a long holiday at first. But as you got older it became impossible to keep up with the lies. I never understood how Lawrie had such a knack for lying and manipulation I think it just came easily to him. I never quite knew what to tell you because I didn't even want to admit the truth to myself.

"I don't know what to tell her, Lawrie. What can I possibly tell her?"

"Tell her that I left you. I don't want her thinking I'm a good man because I'm not Lyla. I'm not a good man." Lawrie's attempt at being altruistic seemed transparent because I was sure you would look upon your father with greater fondness if he'd just up and left us instead of ending up in prison for such callous crimes.

"She deserves to know the truth at some point." I stated although I had no idea how I would ever actually be able to recount the years passed. I hadn't been able to talk to anyone about the last ten years of my life, I'd tried countless therapists with no success. No one could draw the memories out from the depths of my mind.

Lawrie thought about this for a moment, I could see the cogs in his mind whirring.

"On her eighteenth birthday, tell her then because then she can choose how she feels about everything. She can't grow up thinking that she's going to be like her father or her grandfather. Finding out the truth about my mum almost destroyed me and I wouldn't wish that on another human being, let alone my own daughter."

That's why I kept the truth from you for so long. I was always going to tell you, but I had to fulfil the one thing that Lawrie wanted for you. He didn't want you to grow up thinking you were destined to become some kind of monster because he and his father were. He was worried that if you knew the truth you would grow up to hate yourself because of who you are, and I want you to know that it doesn't matter who your father is or what he has done- you aren't him. You have the power to forge your own path.

"You'll take good care of her Lyla; I know you will." Lawrie looked directly up into my eyes. I nodded in response, but I couldn't believe him truly. I didn't believe I could have raised you well because I was, and I am riddled with imperfections. My track record in life proved that I made terrible decisions. It proved that I didn't know what was right and that I saw the warning signs but ignored them as forcefully as I could.

"It's so horrible in there, Lyla." Every word he uttered was a bullet to my ear. Each syllable conjured up so many memories, memories of a life lived with Lawrie. I used to say I had two lives, my first which died with the end of Lawrie and I's relationship and the second which began thereafter.

"It's a prison, Lawrie. It's not supposed to be nice. It's not a hotel, it's a punishment for everything you've done, everything that you've taken away from me and from my friends and family and the whole of Jade Town."

For years, my dreams had been littered with Clara, Faith, Alessia, Daphne and Ava. Even though I was far away from the crime scenes, my mind was still stuck there unable to move on or let go. Sometimes, I still dream about them now, but I don't fear these dreams like I once did, but rather embrace them. The victims of the Jade Town Monster are kept alive in my head, forever in their prime and I don't wish to ever forget them.

"Can you even say their names?" I pressed, unsure of what I wanted to hear.

"Lyla, I'm sorry." He couldn't, he couldn't even say their names.

358

"I don't want to hear it, Lawrie. I shouldn't even be here right now." The longer I sat by his side, the more I knew that Tom had been right that I shouldn't have even seen him in the first place but something invisible whispered encouragement to stay. Something inside me knew what was happening and what was going to occur.

"But you are." He responded and I thought I saw the makings of a smile tug at the corners of his mouth.

"Yes I am."

We didn't talk after that, we just sat there in the strangely comfortable silence. Both of us communicating without the need for words. The years passing between us, memories haunting the room.

At some point, he reached over and touched my hand with his. As he did so, the past blinked in front of me like a film projector: the first time he caught my eye in the cafeteria; the day I'd seen him in the hospital and told him the darkest secret I possessed; the golden rain night when he kissed me for the first time; the disastrous proposal; Lacey's birth and the end of it all- his arrest, the trial, the last look he'd given me. All of it played out on the big screen. The kind of life I'd led seemed the perfect plot for a novel, maybe I'll write about it one day when I'm ready.

Despite myself, I offered him a weak smile which he returned instantaneously. He clutched onto my hand, and I felt... a large expanse of hollow nothingness. No excitement, no warmth- just cold.

They say that there are two emotions more powerful than man that these emotions can elevate you above anything: Love and Hate. I used to be overcome by love for this man and then my bones glowed with hatred for him. At that moment though, neither. Halfway perhaps, like when I was standing on the boundary between my house and the street on the morning of his arrest, halfway between darkness and light, halfway between life and death.

Halfway between love and hate.

We sat for a while drinking in the silence, the only sound in the room was the slow buzzing of the heart rate monitor, weakening slowly with every second that passed. He'd sustained a great deal of internal bleeding during the attack, we both knew deep down that he wasn't going to make it. There wasn't much the hospital could do for him.

Time truly seemed to stand still that morning, every minute that I spent with Lawrie felt like an eternity.

I don't think that true forgiveness would ever be possible. But, just for a minute, just for a second, it felt just like it always had. Just the two of us together.

Somehow, we were back together for this moment. I'm not sure whether it was meant to be a form of karma that I saw his eyes dim just as he'd seen the eyes of those girls dim to nothingness, or if it was an ethereal way for me to truly let go. Sometimes, I wonder if it was always supposed to end this way, that from the moment we met all those years before as two naïve teenagers we were always supposed to end up here.

"Can I see her? Can I see Lacey? Can I see her one last time?" Lawrie's voice was less than a whisper, the epitome of fragility. He was barely moving anymore.

"Close your eyes, Lawrie." I hesitated, attempting to keep composure.

"Close your eyes and you'll see her again, I promise."

And for once, maybe the only time in his life, Lawrie obeyed. His eyelids fluttered shut and those opalescent eyes were extinguished forever, sunken into the back of his head.

That rather bland and dismal morning in October, I had to lose him all over again. I felt as if my heart had been wrenched right out of my rib cage and it just lay on the bed in front of me- bloody and stone cold. Lawrie left this mortal world that morning, crossed over to whatever awaited him, and everything burned and seared around me. I didn't know how I was supposed to feel, I didn't want to feel anything again because the last few years had drained me of all emotion. Bone-dry but still hurting.

When I look back, I don't believe Lawrie and I were in love. Both of us clung to the idea of each other, I needed protection and he needed someone to care for him. In his case, the monster inside finally took over, dragging him to eternal darkness. He was buried in an unmarked grave; I don't know where and I don't wish to know where. Any trace of the life of Lawrie Hartwell is now only alive in old news articles and in the minds of the residents of Jade Town. We will never forget him, no matter how much we desire to.

I believe our souls were inexplicably entwined; from the fate of our mothers to the first time we met. Our paths kept crossing even until the end, a cruel twist of fate possibly but fate all the same. Besides, our paths will forever be crossed because despite our presence in different worlds we will always share one thing, one rose amongst the thorns, a light amongst the pressing darkness- you.

That was it.

The guilty end.

PRESENT DAY

I finish the story and absorb the silence that hangs between us. Lacey didn't attempt to speak throughout the entire story, so I have no idea how she's feeling or whether she was able to comprehend the tale in its entirety. Or worse, whether she even believes me. That's an easy fix however, as I know Tom is right that there are still articles circulating about Lawrie Hartwell- the Jade Town Monster even years after he was caught for his callous crimes. Maybe I'll have to show her for her to believe me, maybe she doesn't want to see them. I can't be quite sure.

"Okay." She says after a moment.

"Okay." She repeats over and over like that's the only word she knows of, like she can't remember how to speak or function properly.

"Lacey, I..." I begin suddenly, wanting to take back everything I told her, wanting life to return to the way it was before this day, but I can't do that. I can never go back, only forwards.

"I understand." She says only two words, but they carry so much weight within them. The fact that she understands some of my motives and that she hasn't shouted her hatred for me already is undoubtedly a good sign.

"You understand?" I ask.

She nods her blonde head slowly; everything seems slower after I told her the truth, as if my life was on fast forward until this very moment and suddenly everything has been put right again, as right as it can be that is.

"I understand why you waited to tell me. I don't think I'd have been able to accept it earlier, I still don't know if I will be able to. Going from knowing nothing about my dad to knowing about the cruel man he was is difficult to get my head around. I spent so many years thinking maybe he'd come back and find us. I used to wish for it on every birthday when I blew out my candles, but not this year." Her head falls into her hands, and she's silent again for a moment as if struggling to say what's inside of her head. I can't tell what it is.

"I'm glad I didn't know him." She reveals finally and my heart burns, for their lack of relationship, for the loss of what I once considered eternal, for the man he became.

"I'm sorry Lacey." I say, hoping that it will bring some retribution for everything, but I know they are only empty words, I'm not sure words hold any weight anymore.

"For what?" She rounds on me. Her blue eyes suddenly enraged.

"What could you possibly be sorry for? You stayed with my dad even when he hurt you. Despite your feelings, you delivered the man you loved to the police so that everyone in Jade Town could be safe. You saved me from it all, Mum." I can't quite believe what I'm hearing, I never expected this reaction from her.

"I think you're my hero."

Hero? I'm a damaged soul who's just clinging on, fighting against the burden of guilt. Sometimes I think Lawrie had it easy, it would've been a more torturous existence for him if he had to live every day surrounded by the heavy guilt of everything he did, like the second-hand guilt I experience daily through his actions. Then again, was Lawrie hardwired to feel such a raw human emotion like guilt? I don't think I'll ever know.

"I don't think that I'm a hero Lacey, only someone who had to do what was right after she spent so long doing what was wrong." I can find solace in this; I may not be perfect or decent, but I understand what is right and I will pursue the right path despite all the obstacles, until I am blue in the face.

"Call it what you want." She gets up from her chair, her tall figure backlit by the last remnants of the sun. She looks strong and no longer like my little girl who I tried so desperately to protect from the dark corners of the world, from the darkness in her genes. She doesn't need my protection anymore, and thus his hold on me is relinquished, I can finally and completely move on with my life.

"But you're my hero. You always have been, and you always will be."

With that, she stalks away, back out into the garden where Mila is sprinting away from Tom who's following her with the garden hose. Madison is laughing her head off, sat perched high upon his shoulders. This is my life now; my life is stereotypically normal perhaps, living in a small town where every day seems to follow the same pattern, where I know what's going to come next. In the past, the idea of this would have sickened me, I didn't want to lead a humdrum small-town existence like everybody else, where I felt like I would never be remembered, and Lawrie provided me with an escape from all of that. Now, however, I crave normality and structure above all else. I want my life to be simple, not rich in monetary value but rich in blissful moments, just like this one.

There is one thing I must do now, though. To feel truly free of his clutches, there is one thing I still need to do…

I follow Lacey out into the garden and pull Tom aside after he manages to blast Mila right in the face with water from the hose. She screams in delight and skips off to join Madison who's sitting in the corner of the garden now, her nose in a tattered book which I don't expect her to understand for years to come but with which she seems engrossed in, constantly asking Lacey the meaning behind every second word. *The Great Gatsby* is displayed on the dog-eared front page.

"How did it go?" Tom asks me.

"Did you tell her everything? I kept trying to glance over but I didn't want to make the twins suspicious." His warm brown eyes find mine.

"Yes, I did, and I honestly feel..." I wave a hand around trying to find the perfect word to describe the feather-like feeling I'm experiencing.

"Lighter. I feel as if a weight has been lifted from upon me."

"I knew you'd feel better. Well, that's it now, is it? Everything's over?"

Almost. I'm so close but haven't yet crossed the finish line which for the first time I can see glistening in front of me.

"There's just one last thing I have to do, now."

Tom gives me a quizzical look, but he doesn't ask me what it is. Tom has never been invasive the same way that Lawrie was, he understands that there are some things I just can't share and even though I've never been able to reveal everything to him, he still loves me deeply. I can't believe I found someone who's so good to me.

"Don't be long." Is all he says.

"I want you back here with me, always." I know he means it and there is nowhere else I'd rather be. Soon I'll be able to be here without burden or anxiety, I'll be able to live out my days as if I'd never met Lawrie.

Soon.

I rush inside and grab my coat and keys from the table, the quicker this is over the better.

I drive and drive for what seems like hours. The sky is a constellation of illustrious pink, orange, and gold. It tells me that tomorrow will be a good day, I can feel it in the humid air.

Houses and fields fly past as I stare down the road listening to the old *Bob Dylan* CD my mum and I once loved so much. The evening is calm and collected just like her. I believe she's a part of the earth now, that they all are, at one with the earth and the sea and the sky- they are truly at peace.

****

After a while, the sign in the distance tells me that I'm close, very close. I didn't quite know what I expected by coming here. The storybook village that was rocked by horror is once again sleeping. I drive through the winding streets, the memories flooding past like the ocean lapping over me as I pass more and more things that I recognise.

The park where I used to hang out with Clara playing on the swings like we were on top of the world; the derelict café building where I used to drink milkshakes with Alessia Chang; the school field where I used to see Faith running circles around everyone else, truly in her element; the corner shop where Daphne and I used to work on the weekends; the tiny townhall where Ava and I used to take dance lessons together; and looming above me to my right is the tallest point in the village where Lawrie and I shared our first kiss. To my left, is a shadowy plot where the Hartwell's house of horrors (as the locals liked to affectionately name it) used to lie.

A few years after the events of the Jade Town Monster, the council decided to tear the house down because nobody wanted to buy it. After

Lawrie went to prison, Robert Carson disappeared off the face of the earth. The last people heard from him; he was living on the Spanish coast somewhere avoiding the authorities for tax evasion. Rory Hartwell hadn't really been heard from since he left town for the army just before Lawrie's trial. He visited me once a few years ago, he'd left the army and become a detective sergeant. He really didn't deserve the childhood that he was subjected to, he lost so much or maybe he never had it in the first place. Rory's the perfect example that your lineage is not your destiny, despite all the horror, he became a good man.

Nate and Quinn got married around ten years ago and now have two kids and a cute little Jack Russell, I see them as frequently as I can. Marina and Tiffany both moved over to New York city to pursue their respective dreams of being an artist and an actress, we still message each other every day and I know that they're happy. Tiffany officially adopted Willow years ago and she has been the best parent I've ever known, Roman goes over to visit her when he can.

Willow is a woman now, I can't quite believe how fast time has shot past, I remember Daphne cradling a little new-born Willow as if it were yesterday. She looks strikingly like her, and I love to think that Daphne is living through Willow. Willow will always be a reminder of the bravery of her mother who lived her life without the constraint of caring for other's opinions and who confronted the Jade Town Monster in the hope that he'd stop his reign of terror.

Everybody seemed to have moved on from Jade Town, everybody had left. My father even, had moved from Jade Town in the latter years of his life and into Knox Village, I don't believe he desired to be far from where my mother lay. Even though I'd visited him countless times over the years, I could never bring myself to journey into Jade Town, the place which held the entirety of my past in its dilapidated stone walls. Everyone had left Jade Town, I'm not sure I'll recognise anyone who lives there anymore.

Now at this moment, I understand why- the memories here are suffocating. Memories of the life I once had, and the life I believed I would live, just Lawrie and I against the world. If anything, it ended up being just me there, alone, to pick up the pieces left behind, and I only have one piece left now.

 A piece that I must finally leave behind.

I slow the car down to a halt as I approach the glistening lake in front of me, Jade Town Lake was the only real reason why Jade Town could have been considered any kind of tourist destination when I was growing up. Now, people flock there all year round to learn about the

Jade Town Monster (I think they even run tours). The lake glitters in front of me in the light of the summer sunset, a collection of thousands of tiny sparkling diamonds. It truly is beautiful out here. It's hard to believe that something so abhorrent occurred in such a picturesque village.

I suppose you never know how one small encounter in a tiny school cafeteria one Monday in October can change the course of life forever. How one fleeting, innocent glance, sets your life up to be the way that it is. If Lawrie and I had never met that day, would those girls be dead? Was Lawrie always destined to be a killer or was I the missing piece that led him to carry out such brutal crimes? That is something that I will never quite know. What I do know which brings me great joy, is that he doesn't have the power to hurt anyone anymore.

As I exit my car and walk towards the bank, my mind is full of the day when Daphne's car was found here and how Roman Huxley was framed for everything, the thought makes me sick to my stomach.

Then, I think of the summers I spent splashing in the lake with Quinn, Marina, Ava, Tiffany, Daphne, Alessia and Clara and now I think of how four of those people are gone, that their lives were tragically cut short. Finally, I'm thinking about the times I sat by the lake huddled next to Lawrie's familiar golden locked figure and bright eyes scouring the page of some obscure novel which he would then beg me to read, and how I believed nothing in life could be better than sitting there with him forever.

Forever.

Tentatively, I fish my hand into the pocket of my charcoal trench coat which is too large for me as it billows out behind me like grey smoke in the slight wind. My hand closes around the cool metal chain inside which has been sitting dormant in there for such a long time. In one swoop, I pull it out from my pocket. The golden necklace glimmers alongside the lake. The inscription on the back of the heart chain, now slightly rusty, is illuminated in the low sun:

'Lyla, here's to forever, with love always, Lawrie.'

It's funny isn't it, forever is a rather antiquated concept because forever must end at some point. Nothing is truly infinite, and yet we have a word for it. Internally we understand the concept that everything ends because we don't remember the moment we were informed that life comes to an end, and yet we seem to know that we are destined to die one day. It's as if we've always known that there is an end. And yet, we create words and expressions which suggest that things like love never end even between the veil of death. Maybe I have that kind of love with Tom, that eternal easy love and he is my person. But at one stage, before I saw his truth, Lawrie was that person for me, the one who I believed I would love eternally.

Most things do have a given end, and this now is the end for Lawrie and I. Twenty-four years ago we began our journey together, ten years ago he left the living world leaving only minuscule parts of his life behind which I clung onto only until I could tell Lacey the truth and could truly let go. Time has healed the gaping wounds left by it all, but the scars remain there, and they always will. My past has shaped me into the person that I am today and whether I'm a hero like Lacey claims or as I believe, just a broken woman trying to do the right thing I am only where I am today because of everything that happened. I still feel as though every life I save through work is somehow making up for my debts. I hope to help more people in the future, I hope to set a good example for Madison and Mila, and I hope that one day I can forgive myself.

Taking a deep breath, I shut my eyes and hurl the necklace into the bottom of the lake. I open them in just enough time to see the golden emblem snake out of sight under the water. The last ghost of him gone forever to rest at the bottom of the lake. A person who I once loved so much, in a place I once loved above all else.

Purposefully, I turn on my heels and head back up the bank towards my car without looking back once.

Acknowledgements:

A completed book is a result of a multitude of things. This book is the result of a global pandemic, several lockdowns, and many people who've supported me along the way. Never did I think the ramblings of a sixteen-year-old and characters and plot lines that rattled about in my head would lead me here, with a book to show for it!

Nevertheless, I couldn't have gotten here without the unwavering support of a few amazing people. So first, thanks Dad for showing me there's a world out there waiting for you and always encouraging me to go after what I want.

To Emma and Mia, the best older sisters I could ask for, thank you for always believing in me and my dreams no matter their size. I know I'll always have your support and I couldn't be here without you. I'm so proud of everything you've achieved and can't wait to see where we all end up in this life.

And a special mention to Mum, the strongest and most selfless woman I've ever met who taught me all that I know. The person who read my first ever draft and provided me with pages and pages of improvements! Thank you for teaching me kindness, patience, and love. There won't be a day where I don't miss you.

Finally, thank you to everyone who's shown support along the way and followed my journey here. I'm so lucky to be surrounded by so many incredible people, and I can't wait to see what the future holds.

ABOUT THE AUTHOR:

Freya Lyndon was born in 2004 in Portsmouth, England. An avid reader, she's always been fascinated by writing and the idea of one day creating a novel of her own. The idea for Façade came as the result of her passion for true-crime and is her first full length novel. She has a passion for social media and is currently documenting her journey as a self-published 20-something author.

Follow her journey @freyalyndonbooks on Instagram and TikTok.

Printed in Great Britain
by Amazon